Books By Donna Schwartze

Suggested reading order:

Eight Years

The Only Reason

Wild Card

The Runaway Bride of Blitzen Bay

Truth or Tequila

Raine Out

No One Wants That

Leave It On The Field

Pretty Close to Perfect

RAINE OUT

DONNA SCHWARTZE

ISBN: 9798773157915

Published by Donna Schwartze, 2022

donnaschwartzeauthor@gmail.com

❀ Created with Vellum

RAINE OUT

DONNA SCHWARTZE

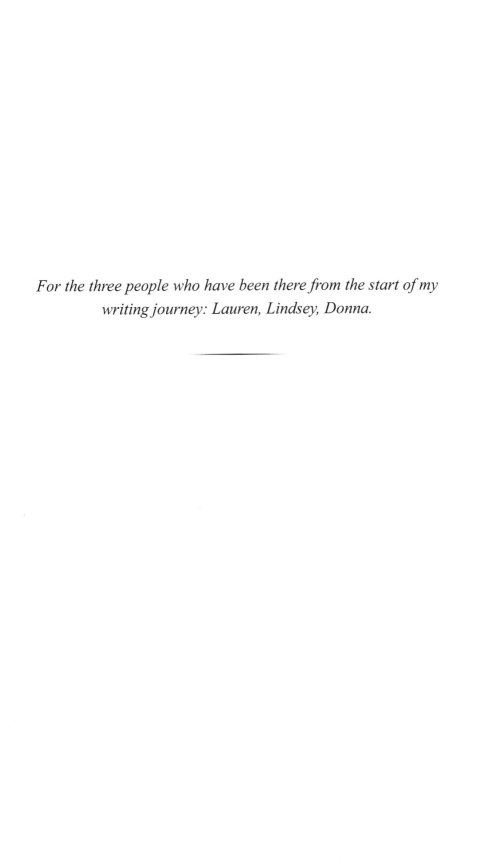

For the three people who have been there from the start of my writing journey: Lauren, Lindsey, Donna.

"The only way to find your true self is by recklessness and freedom."

— Brenda Ueland

Chapter One

RAINE

"Did you get one or two beds in our room?" Butch says as he walks across the patio, stuffing the last of a cheeseburger into his mouth.

"We have separate rooms." I cross my arms firmly over my chest. "You already know that."

"Are you going to give me a key to your room? Or do I have to breach the door?"

Hawk wanders over from where he's manning the barbecue grill. "Butch, depending on the hotel, I think you can probably bust it with a battering ram. I don't think you'll need to bring explosives."

As of today, Butch and Hawk are officially former Navy SEALs. We're at their retirement party. But even in civilian life, I have no doubt they'll use their skills—including kicking in any door that's inconveniencing them.

"Stop it!" I say, reaching up to shove them in their chests.

"He's only coming with me as cover—so my friends won't try to set me up."

I'm barely five foot, four. These guys tower over me, but I learned quickly when I started working with them that they respond much faster to physical feedback.

Hawk looks down at me and shakes his head. "Shoving isn't effective, Raine. I've told you before to go for the balls if you want to immobilize a man—"

"No! Don't say a word." I point at Butch as he swallows his comeback—his face almost bursting as he tries to control his grin.

I've worked with these guys for almost five years as the CIA liaison to the SEAL teams in Virginia Beach. They're like big brothers to me. They're no more interested in dating me than I am in dating them. When I asked Butch to be my plus-one to a friend's wedding, I knew I'd have to endure hours of teasing, but I had no idea it would be this relentless.

"You know," Butch says, pulling a piece of food out of his beard, "you told me you were a lesbian the first day I met you. Maybe tell your friends that."

"I told you that because you very inappropriately asked me to get a drink with you ten seconds after we met." I slap his hand as he puts the leftover crumb of food in his mouth. "Gross. Don't eat food out of your beard. And telling my friends I'm a lesbian won't stop them. They'll just try to set me up with a woman."

"God, I'd be so in favor of that," he says, closing his eyes and letting out a long breath.

I shove him again. "Stop thinking about me with a woman."

"Never. And so we're clear, I asked you to get a drink because you were so quiet. I was trying to help you fit into the team—not trying to sleep with you."

"Are you sure you weren't trying to do both?" I say, crossing my arms over my chest again.

"I guess we'll find out on St. John." He grabs my arm as I try to backhand him and curls up my hand. "Slapping doesn't work as a self-defense move. Ball up that fist to get the most impact. Ask Millie. She knows."

He nods to something over my shoulder. I turn around to see Millie—my best friend since our agency training days—standing a foot away from us. I grab her arm and pull her over. "Will you please tell him to stop torturing me? You're the only one he listens to—"

"Since when does Butch listen to me?" Millie tries to pinch his cheek. He spins her around and puts her in a fake chokehold. This is the way SEALs play. We're used to it.

"Hey! Easy," Millie's husband, Mason, swoops in and pulls her away from Butch. He wraps her protectively in his arms. "She just had a baby."

"You can't tell me what to do. I don't work for you anymore," Butch says, laughing.

Mason was the leader of the SEAL team until he retired about a year ago to be with Millie and their new baby.

"No," Millie says, raising her eyebrows, "now you work for me. I'm going to be a much tougher boss than Mason ever was."

Millie resigned from the CIA, but the director convinced her to run a special projects division out of San Diego—where she and Mason live. I'm on a month's hiatus as I transfer out there to be her agency handler.

"Will you tell me how you're going to discipline me, Mills?" Butch rubs his hands together. "Be as specific as you can. The good stuff's in the details."

Mason whacks Butch on the side of the head and looks at me. "Are you sure you want to take this Neanderthal with you to your friend's wedding?"

"I don't want to take him at all, but the rest of the team are active—except Hawk—and he wouldn't be any better," I whine. "Mills, will you please let Mason have a hall pass for the weekend? I'd much rather take him."

"Why do you have to take anyone?" Millie says as Mason pulls her tighter against him and kisses the top of her head. They're the sweetest couple I've ever known. When I'm around them, I can't help thinking I'm never going to find anything close to what they have.

"You know how my childhood friends are. They're different than us," I say, sighing. "I don't want to spend the entire weekend answering questions about my dating status and/or my sexual orientation. I shouldn't even go. I'm canceling."

"Excuse us," Millie says to the guys as she takes my arm and pulls me across the patio. She grabs my shoulders and gets in my face. "You're going. It will do you good. When's the last time you've had more than a day off? It's only for a long weekend. You know Butch will be a blast. He's just teasing you."

"I know," I say, covering my face. "It's not about him. I haven't been around my old friends for so long. It's not the same anymore. You know how it is when you hang out with people who aren't in the business. I can't even tell them what I do for a living. What do you tell your childhood friends?"

"I don't have any childhood friends. When I left home, I cut all ties. You know that." She takes a step back. "And it wasn't healthy. You've kept in touch with Sophie—"

"She kept in touch with me. No matter how much I ignore her, she keeps coming back."

"Good." Millie wraps me into a hug. "Sophie's cool. I liked her when she spent the weekend with us in D.C."

"She liked you, too. Maybe you should come with me instead of Butch."

"Are you forgetting I have a baby who's literally almost always attached to me?" She squeezes me again before she releases me from the hug. "And if you took me, they would definitely think we're a couple. Didn't Sophie already ask you that?"

"Yeah, I think she roots for us to be a couple."

"She ain't the only one," Butch says as he walks up behind us.

"Are you still trying to live out that fantasy?" Millie slugs his shoulder. "We've told you if we ever hook up, you'll be the first to know."

"And I await that news anxiously," he says as he puts his arm around me. "You know I'm just messing with you. I'll behave like the perfect gentleman when we get there. And I'm the best wingman ever created if you require those services."

"Are you really taking this idiot with you?" Millie's dad, Mack, walks over holding her adorable son, Mo.

"You know I'd take you if Carol would let me." I smile a

little too broadly. I've had a crush on Mack from the second I met him. He's a retired SEAL, too. But unlike all of these other guys, I find him wildly attractive. He's almost dangerously tough, but it's his boundless tender side that makes my heart ache. "You're everyone's first choice, Mack."

"He's definitely mine," Butch says, taking a step away from Mack in case he swings at him. It wouldn't be the first time.

Mack shakes his head at Butch. "You better treat this young woman like the queen she is. If I hear you didn't, I'll kick your ass and enjoy every second of it."

"Yes, sir," Butch says, saluting him. "I think you're the only person who could kick my ass, but only because you fight dirty—"

"Damn straight I do," Mack snarls, "especially when I'm protecting my daughters."

Mack's started calling me his daughter. It's adorable and it's made me crush on him even harder. I know he's not an option. It's the only thing that keeps me from acting like a complete idiot in front of him. As soon as a hot guy starts showing me any attention, I become totally awkward. I've been that way since I was a teenager.

"Whatever you say, chief," Butch says as he walks away. "You know I don't want any part of you."

Mo starts crying and reaching for Millie.

"Mills, he's hungry again," Mack says, handing him to her. "I've already fed him the two bottles you packed in the cooler, so we're going to have to go directly to the source. I swear he eats as much as I do."

Millie starts to reach into her sundress to pull out a breast for Mo.

"No!" I put my hands up to stop her. "Millie! No!"

"Raine, it's just a boob," she says as Mason leaps across a lawn chair and starts pushing her toward the house.

"I know it's natural and nothing's wrong with it," he says as Millie tries to resist, "but there's not a chance in hell you're breastfeeding him in front of these deviants. Hawk said you could use his bedroom."

"Fine. Come with me, Raine." Millie grabs my hand as she kisses the strawberry blond curls starting to form on Mo's head. "We're not finished with this discussion."

I follow her back to the bedroom—head down and dragging my feet—like a kid who's about to be disciplined.

"Raine Nira Laghari," she says, patting the spot next to her on the bed. "Do you want to tell me what's really going on? Why are you resisting this trip so much?"

"Damn, using my full name." I plop down on the bed. "You sound like my mom."

"I love your mom. That's a compliment."

"God, she loves you, too. I shouldn't have brought you home for Christmas that first year we met."

"Did I tell you she sent Mo a Baby Ganesh? It's enormous. It almost takes up half of his room."

I groan. "Ugh, Millie, why did you have a baby? She won't stop talking about him. She legitimately thinks she's his grandma. She keeps texting me that picture you sent her—like I haven't seen him already. She thinks it will encourage me to get married and start popping out kids."

"Ding, ding, ding. We have a winner." Millie smiles. "Finally, we're getting to the real reason you don't want to go on this trip."

Chapter Two

ALEX

"Come on, man," Seb says as he follows me off the field. "It's my wedding. You're my best friend on the team. You have to be there."

Seb and I play for the baseball team in Miami. He's the catcher. I'm the shortstop. We've played together for most of the eight years we've been in the league. Sometimes I think I could catch his throw to second with my eyes closed. Actually, I think I probably have a couple of times.

"The only reason I ever liked you was because you were grumpier and more jaded than me. Somehow, you've always made me look like a nice guy." I throw my glove onto the bench in the dugout. "But since you met Sophie, you're all happy and stuff. It's weird. You're always smiling now. It creeps me out."

Seb met Sophie about a year ago, fell in love probably the second day he knew her, got engaged within six months, and is marrying her next week. They're perfect for each other. I'm happy for them, but I'm also jealous and pissed off that he's found someone he wants to spend the rest of his life with—when I struggle to find someone I want to spend the rest of the night with.

"Speaking of Sophie," he says, trying not to smile as he says her name. He fails. "She'll be sad if you're not there—"

"Don't play the Sophie card with me," I say, pointing at him. "You know I like her way better than I like you."

"As you should," he says as he pours a little water over his head and shakes the excess off.

"Damn, Seb," our equipment manager says as he tries to wipe the water off his shirt. "Give a guy some warning. I don't want your sweat all over me."

"Wear that fucking catcher's mask in ninety-degree heat. Then you get to complain."

"There," I say, shoving Seb as I walk away, "that's the grouchy guy I like."

Seb follows me to the end of the bench. "We're not done, Alex. You're one of my best friends. You have to be at the wedding. I think it's like a law or something."

"Fuck you. You just invited me last week." I look up as Jack swats a single to left field. That means I'll have to bat this inning. Our equipment guy hands me my shin guard. "And didn't you tell me Sophie wanted a small wedding? Why the change?"

"First of all, this was a last-minute thing, so we just invited everyone last week," he says, sitting next to me. "Second, we did want a small wedding, but our friends just bought a resort on St. John. They're getting ready to open and offered the entire resort to us as kind of a test run for their staff. It seemed too good to pass up, so I chartered a few planes to fly everyone down there. Come on, man. It's the Caribbean. Let's wrap up the season tomorrow, head down there, and have some fun."

I take a deep breath and blow it through my teeth. "I'll be there if you promise you won't be all over Sophie the entire week."

"I definitely will not promise that. I don't even think it's possible not to touch her when she's near me."

"Yeah, we know," Manny says as he walks by us. "It makes us all want to throw up with how happy the two of you are. My wife won't shut up about it. She's so jealous. You're making the rest of us look bad, asshole."

Seb shrugs. "Can't stop. Won't stop."

Manny grabs his batting helmet and heads to the on-deck circle. "Alex, you have to go to the wedding to keep me from killing Seb. He's paying for everything, so if for no other reason, let's go down there and spend as much of his money as possible."

I look at Seb. "I'll come down there, but you have to tell Sophie she can't try to set me up again. That last woman she introduced me to is still stalking me."

"I don't get why you didn't like Allie," Seb says. "She's cool—pretty, nice, funny—"

"Boring."

"She's not boring," he says, laughing. "She's usually the life of the party."

"Exactly. All show, no substance. Boring." I grab my bat out of the cubby and point it at him. "If you weren't with Sophie, would you date Allie?"

"If I weren't with Sophie, I'd be walking around grumpy and pissed off, just like you are now."

"Exactly," I say, heading up the steps to the field. "Tell Sophie no setups. Not even the one-night stand kind. Okay?"

Seb sighs. "I'll tell her, but she and Maisie scheme about this stuff behind my back."

I stop and turn around. "Now that little Maisie, that's one I'd be into—she's a firecracker."

"A married firecracker—happily married. That's a non-starter. I like her husband. She's off-limits."

"Well that just sucks," I say, stepping onto the field. "I mean for me. Not really for her, I guess."

As I head to the on-deck circle, I hear Sophie yell, "Let's go, Alex!"

I turn around to the players' family section and nod to her. When she smiles back, I know I'll end up going to their wedding. Despite her persistent and annoying attempts to find me someone to love, she's become like a little sister to me. Seb's one of my best friends—and I'd do anything for him—but I swear I'd walk through fire for Sophie. She might be the sweetest person I've ever met.

As I take a few practice swings, I watch Manny foul one off and then take a called strike. I want to walk to the batter's box and punch him. It's the bottom of the ninth, one out, tie game, Jack's on second. Manny's an amazing bunter, but he thinks it's beneath him. He takes a huge swing on the next pitch and misses by a mile. He walks back to the dugout—his head down.

"Could you not at least get Jack to third for me? You're a pitcher, asshole, not a homerun hitter. The next time you pass up a bunting opportunity in front of me, I'm going to start taking my practice swings at your head."

"I know, I know. His fucking sinker gets me every time. I swear he puts some kind of hex on it."

We didn't make the playoffs this year, so these last two games of the season don't really matter. The only thing that's on my mind as I walk to the plate is getting Jack home, so we don't go into extra innings. I've owned this pitcher all year. Jack's fast, so I know he can score from second if I get a decent hit to right field. I take the first pitch, low and away. The next one comes in about waist high. It's his sinker, but it doesn't sink. I slap it down the right field line and jog to first. I turn around when I touch the base to see Jack sliding safely across home plate for the game winner.

The first base ump, Vince, slaps my back. "Thanks, Alex. I didn't want this one to go into extra innings. You got big plans this off-season?"

"Nothing too much. I'll head back home to see my family for about a month." I hand my batting helmet to the batboy as he runs over to me. "And I guess I'm headed to St. John next week. Seb's getting married down there."

"Is that right? Good for him. I'm glad he's locking her in," Vince says, whistling as he looks over to the stands where Sophie's bent over picking something up off the ground. "Her ass is—"

"Nope. Stop right there, Vince. She's off-limits for any kind of talk. Don't let me hear it, and damn well don't let Seb hear it unless you've figured out a way to ump with two broken arms."

He laughs as he walks away. "Loud and clear, brother."

As I get to the dugout, our general manager's waiting for me—like he has been every game for the last month.

"Nice job, Alex," he says, holding out his fist. "So did you decide about our offer? We want you back, man."

"Drew, I've told you about a million times, I'm not deciding until the season's over. We have a game left, don't we? Back off. And you really need to talk to my agent about it. You shouldn't be talking to me directly."

"Mrs. Morris is very interested in keeping you," he whispers as he follows me down into the tunnel. "It's her first big thing as the new owner of the team. She bugs me about it every second of every day. What's it going to take to sign you? Give me a number."

"Look, I know you're trying to keep your job," I say, accepting a high five from our clubhouse guard, Chick, "but I'm not thinking about it right now. You'll know when I know. Now leave me alone."

"Nice hit, Alex," Chick says, leaning back in his chair. "You've always owned that pitcher. What's your average against him now? It has to be over four hundred."

"Something like that. How's your new car driving?"

"Damn, that thing is nicer than my house." He pauses as he looks up to the ceiling. "I still can't believe Seb bought me a whole goddamn car. Did I tell you it has those seats that heat up?"

"Naw, man," I say, laughing. "Do you need those in Miami, though?"

"The heat feels good on my old bones. I crank the AC to the highest level and turn on the heated seats. I swear if I don't concentrate real hard, I'll fall asleep driving. It's like a massage on wheels."

"Be careful, man," I say as I chuck his shoulder. "You know we can't even play a game if you're not sitting here."

As I walk into the clubhouse, Seb's already coming out of the showers. He used to be the slowest player on the team. But since he met Sophie, he's out of the clubhouse in a tight twenty.

"Thanks for preventing extra innings," he says, nodding at me.

"Yeah, I did it just for you—so you don't have to be away from Sophie one second more than necessary."

"And I appreciate it."

"Hey," I say as he walks by me. "I'm coming to your wedding. You know I'm happy for you. I've just got a lot on my mind."

"I know," he says, slapping my back. "You're the smartest person I know. You'll figure it out. And I'm glad you're coming, man. Wouldn't be the same without you."

Chapter Three

RAINE

"So is Sophie still trying to set you up?" Millie looks at me as she puts a few pillows on her lap and lays Mo on top of them. "Is that why you're resisting this trip so much?"

Mo starts nursing urgently—like he hasn't been fed in days. "Do you feed that child?"

"We feed him constantly. He's always hungry." Millie sighs as she kisses his cheek. "And stop avoiding the question."

I ignore her again. "He's definitely your kid. I'm not sure how you eat as much as you do and never gain weight."

"Please. I gained so much weight with him. You remember how big I was," she says, patting her almost-flat stomach. "Poor Mason lived at the grocery store for my last trimester. I was sure he was going to strike at some point."

"When has Mason ever refused to do anything for you? He lives to serve you. You're the most adorable couple I've ever been around and I hate every second of your cuteness."

She shrugs. "You could have this, too, if you put in any effort. Now answer me. Is Sophie trying to set you up? And who's the target this time?"

"I don't know." I grab a pillow and hug it to my chest. "I swear my mom still calls her to strategize."

"I thought you told Sophie to stop taking her calls—"

"I did!" I hug the pillow tighter. "But you know my mom. She always finds a way to get to her victims."

"Well, it probably doesn't help that Sophie was the one who set you up with Dak. Your mom thought he was the one."

"Everyone thought he was the one," I say, looking up at the ceiling. "Except me."

"You dated him for like seven years, right?"

"Yeah, all of high school and most of college."

She shakes her head—her ponytail flipping back and forth. "How? How did you date him that long if you knew he wasn't the one?"

I sink further down into the bed. "Because that's what everyone wanted. Again, everyone except me."

"So, did you break up with him because your parents wanted you to marry him? Like a rebellion thing?"

"Please. I didn't rebel against my parents for one second of one day growing up. I was always the good girl."

"So what happened?" she says. "Breaking up with him was a huge rebellion."

"It wasn't a rebellion. It was more of an awakening." I let out a deep breath. "When the agency started sniffing around during college—asking me to interview for the training program—that was the first time I realized I could do something different with my life. Something completely separate from my parents' expectations."

"That sounds like rebellion."

"Maybe," I say, sighing, "but it was more like I was starting to see who I really was, you know? Seeing the possibilities to be the person who I knew existed deep in my soul somewhere."

"And Dak didn't fit with that new person?"

"Not at all. He didn't even fit with the old person." I pause for a second. "Don't get me wrong. He's a nice guy, but I was never attracted to him like that."

"Well, it doesn't have to be Dak, but someone—"

"What's the point? I never want to get married."

"I didn't think I wanted to marry Mason at first either." She leans back against the headboard and closes her eyes. "Even after I fell in love with him, I didn't want to get married, but the right guy might change your mind."

"Shut up," I say, reaching for her hand. "Didn't we agree back in training that we'd never get married?"

"We swore on it," she says, squeezing my hand. "But I didn't know there was a Mason-kind-of-person out there. He appeared out of nowhere and relentlessly pursued me. You saw how hard he came after me. I tried to resist, but he wasn't having it. And I'm so lucky he pushed because he's the best thing that's ever happened to me. Maybe if you let a guy in—"

"I let guys in."

"Really?" She raises her eyebrows as she stares down at me. "Since when?"

"I had a date last week," I say, looking away from her.

"Girl, I can tell when you're lying even if you're not looking at me. Your voice goes up at least two octaves."

I spin my head back around to her. "Okay then, a guy asked me out last week. Is my octave level better now?"

"Yes, much better." She smiles and tilts her head. "Who asked? And why did you say no?"

"I didn't say no. I told him I'd think about it—"

"At least two octaves," she says, rolling her eyes. "Maybe three. And your right eye's twitching."

"God, I hate that my best friend's a CIA interrogator. It's really inconvenient."

"Then tell me the truth, weirdo. Who asked you out?"

"A guy at Chipotle," I say, trying not to smile as she starts laughing. "Shut up! He heard me speaking Spanish and told me he liked Mexican women."

"What?" She's laughing so hard now that she shakes Mo off her chest. He looks up at her and grunts. "Oh, I'm sorry, sweetie. I forgot you were dining. Did you tell the guy you weren't Mexican?"

"Why bother? You know that kind of guy. I don't think he knows the difference between someone of Mexican or Indian heritage. His IQ level was not a match."

"I think he was probably lacking a lot more than sufficient IQ numbers," she says as she reattaches Mo. "And anyway, no one's IQ level is a match for yours, Miss Genius Level."

"I'd settle for someone getting close. Maybe even someone who's read a book in the last month so we'd have something to talk about. Honestly, I don't know why I bother. I don't even find any guys attractive right now."

"Except my dad—"

"What?" I roll away from her like she tried to attack me.

"Raine," she says, grabbing my arm to prevent me from falling off the bed. "C'mon. I know you have a crush on him."

"Oh my God. How long have you known?" I groan. "Does anyone else know?"

"I've known since the day you met him," she says. "You talk about him—and to him—like all of my high school friends did. Honestly, I've never had a girlfriend who didn't have a crush on him. And everyone knows—*everyone*."

"Not Mack though, right?" I feel my cheeks starting to burn. "Please tell me he doesn't know."

"Of course he knows. Do you think he doesn't notice the way you look at him? It's not a big deal. Believe me, he's used to it."

I pull the pillow over my face and groan again.

"It's fine, Raine. You know it's impossible to embarrass him. He loves you."

"I always make everything so awkward with men," I mumble into the pillow.

"You do not," she says, trying to pull the pillow off my face. I keep a firm grip on it. "You're completely normal and confident around these guys."

"These guys, yes. Because they're not possibilities." I peek above the pillow. "The minute a hot guy starts hitting on me, I become an idiot. Do you remember Kyle back at the agency? I was fine when we were just hanging out, then he asked me to dinner, and I fell apart."

She pulls the pillow down further. "Oh my God, I forgot about him. You did kind of implode. I thought you just didn't like him like that."

"I really liked him. It's my pattern. I'm the picture of confidence when I'm just buddying up to guys, but when they show any kind of interest, the confidence disappears."

She squints at me. "So are you taking Butch to the wedding as kind of a shield? To protect you from having to interact with real possibilities?"

"Yes, Millie. I'm not like you. I'm not loose around guys. It's not how I was raised."

She whacks my leg. "What do you mean loose?"

"Not like that—not slutty—I mean natural. You're so easy and flirty with guys. Teach me your secret."

"There's no secret. Just put yourself out there. Be vulnerable. Didn't you tell me Sophie's marrying a professional baseball player? Maybe flirt with one of his teammates. That could be hot."

"You think a professional athlete's going to want to date me?" I say, throwing the pillow off my face. "When they have Sophie-types floating all around them."

"Oh, come on. Who's this person?" She scowls down at me. "I've never known you to be unsure about anything. You're the most confident person I know."

"About most things. It's just when I get around Sophie, I revert to the dorky bookworm who never quite fit in with the popular girls."

"Sophie adores you. You told me that you were inseparable until you went to different high schools. I know you've taken different paths, but you're still one of her best friends."

"I know. I love her, but I always feel invisible around her and Maisie. They're like you. Guys fall over when they see them. Men barely look at me."

"Whatever! That's not even close to being true. You're beautiful, and funny, and sweet, and unbelievably smart." She tugs at the collar of my crewneck T-shirt. "And you have a smoking body if you'd ever let anyone see it."

"I have a smoking body?" I say, pushing her hand away. "What are you, twelve years old?"

"I'm just saying, you're going on a beach vacation, maybe show some skin and let those curves breathe a little bit."

"My mom would not approve. You don't even know how sexually repressive she was when I was growing up. You never had to deal with that—"

"Seriously? My grandma thought I was the devil when I wore v-neck T-shirts. You're a grown-ass adult woman now. Get over it. Wear what you want."

"Mmm." I grunt and cover my face with the pillow again.

She whips it off and throws it on the floor. "You need a total attitude adjustment and this trip is the time to do it. You'll be on a Caribbean island. Let loose. Be free. Flirt with hot baseball players. Be whatever person you want to be. You don't have to look for your husband. Just have fun. You're on a month's sabbatical. Have a good time. Maybe even hook up with some beautiful man—"

"Hey," Mack says as he pushes the bedroom door open and peeks in. "Is Mo done eating? Do you want me to burp him?"

"Dad," Millie says as she pulls Mo up, "you know he's never done eating."

"Yeah, he's definitely of our gene pool. Come here, little piglet." Mack puts Mo on his shoulder. "Millie, Butch is looking for you. He wants to play poker. Apparently, he hasn't learned his lesson from the last smackdown you gave him."

"Well, I'll have to teach the lesson with more force this time," Millie says as she pulls me up.

"Nope," Mack says, looking at me as his eyes start to narrow. "Raine stays here with me."

Millie drops my hand. "Damn, what'd you do? That's his disciplinary voice."

"Wait, what?" I try to pull Millie between Mack and me, but she spins out of my hold. Mack's pointing at the chair next to the bed. "No, wait, Millie don't leave me."

"You're on your own," Millie says as she turns toward the door. "I've been on the receiving end of that voice my entire life. If you've adopted him as your dad, you have to deal with this side of him, too."

"But I didn't do anything," I say to Millie's back. I think about running after her, but I know Mack could—and would—stop me, even with a baby on his shoulder.

When I turn around, he's still pointing at the chair, his eyebrows raised. "Sit down, Raine. You and I need to talk."

Chapter Four

ALEX

When I get in the shower, I let the hot water stream over me—trying to melt away my bad attitude. I've been in a foul mood for months. My thirtieth birthday's coming up, and I feel like I haven't accomplished anything I wanted to get done in my twenties. I mean, yeah, I've played in the majors for eight years, been an All-Star, won a few Gold Gloves, but that's baseball stuff. I have so much more I want to do.

Unlike most major-league players, I came into the league after graduating from college. Eventually, I want to go to law school, but I can't seem to pull the cord. I'm scared to quit the league, scared to try something different, scared that I'm going to fail at something. I haven't failed at much in my life, but not because I'm better than anyone. It's because I don't put myself out there. I've only done what comes easily to me.

My contract with Miami expires this season. They're worried that I want to become a free agent to get a more lucrative contract with another team. That's not the issue. I don't want to play for another team. My problem is that I don't know if I want to play at all anymore. Physically, I could play for another decade, but I know down deep I'm ready for something else. Everyone's going to flip out if I retire in my prime —especially my dad.

I'm thinking about all of this as I walk out of the shower. Our beat reporter, Ray Franklin, is sitting by my locker "Getting near a hundred RBIs. That's something else for a leadoff hitter."

"Thanks, Ray. The bottom half of our lineup does a great job of getting on base to give me the chance to hit them in—"

"You never take the credit," he says, shaking his head. "For once, I want you to say, 'Yeah, I make this team work. It would be nothing without me.' Speaking of, when are you going to sign your contract?"

"Nice segue, Ray. Can I at least get dressed before you pepper me with the same damn question you've been asking me for half the season?"

"You can," he says, looking at me over his glasses. "And I'll stop asking when you finally answer it."

Even though I take my time getting dressed, the media's still surrounding my locker when I turn around. I avoid answering questions about my contract for about ten minutes and then wave them away. Manny walks over to me—his hands in the air.

"Are you finally done, princess?" he yells. He's been pacing behind the media scrum for at least five minutes. "You know I have to get home before Caroline sends out a search party."

"Quit talking to those Instagram women and she'll stop

tracking your every move." I grab my bag out of the locker. "You gave her your password. You know she sees every DM you answer."

"You make it sound like I gave her the password voluntarily. She forced me. And I'm just being polite to my fans by answering their questions."

"Yeah, I'm guessing all your fans don't have the response rate that the pro-ho group has."

He gets closer and whispers, "You see them in your DMs. Some of the stuff they say—and the pictures they send—damn, it's hard to resist answering. I'd never take it further, though. Caroline knows that."

"I don't look at my DMs. I barely look at social media at all. And I can't believe Caroline's okay with you talking to those women like you do." I follow him out of the clubhouse. "If she is, she shouldn't be. That's all kinds of disrespectful."

"Worry about your relationship." He stops and turns around. "Oh wait, that's right, you can't get any woman to tolerate you for more than a night."

His phone rings. He holds it up to me. It's Caroline calling on FaceTime.

"Hey, honey," he says, pointing the camera at me. "Princess took his time getting ready again. Sorry. We're leaving now."

Caroline's glaring at the camera. "Do a pan so I can see that you're still at the stadium."

Manny spins the phone around—stopping when he gets to our teammate Dane. "Tell Caroline I'm still at the stadium."

Dane blows her a kiss. "Caroline, I've told you before,

you're the only one who's attracted to him. There's no need to be jealous."

She snorts. "Turn the camera back to Alex. Did you make up your mind about Seb's wedding?"

"I'm going," I say, frowning into the camera.

"Good. Manny's always more fun when you're around." Manny rolls his eyes behind the camera. "Do you need a date? My sister wants to go."

"No, I don't need a date and I don't want one." I grab the phone from Manny and growl at Caroline. "If she shows up again, I won't let her on the plane. It was so awkward when you ambushed me with her on the New York trip. I'm serious, Caroline. She's not invited."

"Come on, Alex. She's not into you like that. She just wants a free trip to St. John."

"I don't care," I say, handing the phone back to Manny. "I'm serious. If she's there, I'll feel like I need to take care of her. Don't bring her."

Manny holds the phone up to me again so I can see her pouty face. "She's going to be really upset. She's already packed."

"That's on you, Caroline." I point at Manny. "Talk to your wife. I swear, if her sister shows up again, I'm not boarding the plane."

"Caroline," Manny says, looking at the phone. "You don't need a travel buddy. Tell her she's out."

"Fine," Caroline snarls. "Are you coming straight home?"

"Yeah, I need to drop off Alex, but I'll be home after that."

"All right. I'm timing you." I hear the phone hang up as Manny slips it back into his pocket.

"Man, you have the most dysfunctional relationship. It makes me uncomfortable."

"It works for us," he says, shrugging as he clicks the doors open on his car. "Not every couple can be as perfect as Seb and Sophie. Hopefully, they'll be out of that whole honeymoon phase before long."

"That's never going to happen. They'll still be pawing at each other when they're senior citizens."

I stop to high-five a food vendor who works the box seats. She always slips me chicken fingers in the dugout. I pull a couple hundred out of my wallet.

"Is this enough for the past month?" I say, handing it to her.

"Two-hundred? Seriously, Alex, how much do you think chicken fingers cost?"

"Well, I mean," I say, trying to shove the bills into her hand, "I know stuff costs more in the stadium."

"Yeah, more, but not that much." She plucks one of the bills out of my hand and gets into her money pouch to give me change. I stuff both bills into the pouch.

"Just take it, Marcie. It can be a downpayment for next season."

"Really?" She smiles as her eyes widen. "Then you're coming back next year?"

"God, not you, too. No comment."

She laughs and turns around. "If I don't see you tomorrow, have a good off-season. Be safe."

As we drive out of the stadium, the fans swarm our car. Manny waves as he maneuvers around them. I sink down in my seat.

"Do you want to stop to sign a few?" He looks over at me.

"Not at all. And isn't Caroline timing you? I don't think she allows for autograph time."

"Probably not, but you always want to stop. What's up with you? You've been way crabbier than usual lately."

I pull my T-shirt over my face as some fans peer in the windshield.

"Is it the contract? Jeff's been texting me non-stop trying to get me to talk to you about it."

"Well that pisses me off even more," I say from under my T-shirt. "Just because we share an agent doesn't mean he can ask you to work me."

"Come on, man. You know he's an asshole. He didn't leave either of us alone for months before Seb signed. He's the best agent in the business, but only because he's a jerk." He beeps his horn as a fan tries to block the car. "Are you hung up on the money? Damn, they're offering you the world, especially since you're almost thirty. And with what they just paid Seb, I can't believe how much they're willing to give you."

"It's not the money," I say, letting out a long breath. "I told you I don't know if I want to play anymore."

"You really want to go back to school? That's crazy. You already finished four more years of college than the rest of us. What percentage of players have a degree? It has to be less than five."

"It's not a competition." I sit up when we finally get past the last of the fans. "I've got different goals. I want to go to law school. I have since I was a kid."

He flips open his sunroof as we leave the stadium parking

lot. "How are you going to get into law school? You said your college grades were marginal."

"Marginal at UCLA. It's a good school. And I was playing baseball full-time. If I could concentrate on school, I'd get good grades."

"Your dad's going to kill you if you leave before your playing days are over."

"Maybe not—"

"Seriously, man?" He starts flipping through channels on his sound system. "I've known him since the prospect league. He expects you to play until they have to take you off the field in a wheelchair."

I glare at him. "I'm almost thirty-fucking-years-old. Maybe it's time to do what I want to do."

"Damn," he says, turning up the music, "don't kill the messenger. I'm not telling you what to do, but you know how your dad's going to react. Do what you want. I'll miss you, but you have to do what's best for you."

"You're going to more than miss me. You're going to lose it. You know I'm the only one who can talk you down when they're hitting your fastball."

"It's a good thing that rarely happens then." He shoves my shoulder. "Man, cheer up. You've been in a bad mood for months. And don't bring this attitude to the wedding. You're the only person who I can have fun with down there."

"The only person? Are you forgetting your wife's coming with us?"

"Nope," he says, "trying really hard to, though."

Chapter Five

RAINE

"Mo looks so much like you." I try to focus on the baby instead of Mack's intense eyes.

"Yeah, he's my twin." He smiles as Mo looks up at him.

"Look at his smile. He loves you. Do you spend a lot of time with him?"

"As much as they'll let me. I can't get enough of him." He kisses Mo's head as he starts to tap him on the back. "Now, are you done trying to distract me?"

"What?" I say, giving him my best innocent look.

He shakes his head. "Raine, my daughter is the master of distraction. She has been since she was about three. She's never fooled me once, so do you want to stop trying, and just tell me why you were talking all that nonsense about men not looking at you?"

I cross my arms and frown at him. "Were you listening at the door?"

"You already know I was. Start talking. You're not leaving

this room until you tell me why you're thinking bullshit like that." He points at the chair again—this time with the sternest look I've ever seen. "I've always given Millie great advice—including advice about men. Let's have it."

"From what Millie's told me," I say, sitting down, "the only men advice you gave her was not to start dating until she was thirty."

"And I stand by that. Since she failed to follow it, now I'll give it to you. No man's worthy of you. Don't be in a hurry."

Mo lets out a healthy burp. "Good job, Mo-Mo," Mack whispers. He's the cutest grandpa. I can't even imagine how sweet he was with Millie when she was a baby.

"How did Millie try to distract you when she was little?" I pull my legs up on the chair and rest my head on my knees.

Mack laughs as he lays Mo on the floor for a diaper change. "Every time she did something she wasn't supposed to —before I even had a chance to say anything—she'd pet my head and say, 'Daddy has pretty hair.' There wasn't much chance I was going to discipline her anyway, but when she did that, the chance was zero. She's had my number since day one."

"Yeah, Millie's never had a problem getting any man to do what she wants him to do."

"I doubt you have that problem either." He looks up for a second and then back down as Mo starts kicking his feet. "I've seen the way these guys jump when you ask for anything."

"Yeah, I'm cool professionally, but personally," I say, pausing for a second, "I'm so awkward around guys. When they show interest in me, I fall apart."

"So, tell them that."

"Tell them that I'm awkward? That doesn't seem to be a good way to attract a guy."

"What I'm saying is be upfront with the guy—tell him when a man starts showing interest, you get nervous. Believe me, the guy's nervous, too. It'll make him feel at ease."

"Or make him run in the other direction."

"And if he does that, let him run. He's not worth your time." He picks up the newly diapered Mo and leans against the wall. "Any guy—I don't care how confident he is—is nervous when he approaches a woman. No one wants to be rejected. So diffuse the situation. Tell him you like him, but you might be awkward for a while. That would be endearing to me, and to any guy who's worthy of you. Be honest. It'll help you lighten up a little bit."

"That's what Millie tells me, but I'm not like her. She's always been so free and easy with guys."

He looks up at me with his eyebrows raised. "Free and easy are not words I'd like to associate with my daughter."

"No, not like that. I mean she's so confident and carefree, and with the way she looks, she's never had a problem attracting guys."

"Raine, you're beautiful, so don't even come at me with that shit. No, wipe that pouty look off your face because it's not up for debate. You're a beautiful woman. If anyone made you feel like you weren't, they need to be out of your life, and I'd also like their names and numbers, so I can speak with them privately."

"So would you like to call my parents right now then?" I say, forcing out a laugh.

"I'll gladly call them if they've made you feel for a second that you're less than the amazing woman you are—"

"No, it's not that. They've always been supportive." I look at the ceiling. "It's just that they're so reserved about everything. You know? They're so conservative. They always pushed me in that direction and I let them. I didn't have one carefree second when I was growing up. I think I'm the only person alive who didn't rebel against their parents as a teenager."

"I rebelled against my mom from day one, and honestly, it wasn't much better." He hugs Mo tighter and starts rocking him. "How much has Millie told you about my mom?"

"Enough," I say, looking down.

"Yeah, she wasn't a very nice person," he says. "Look, she tried to make me feel bad about myself every day of my life. She blamed me for her situation. She hated that she got pregnant when she was a teenager. She never let me forget it. She was always picking at me, making me feel like I wasn't good enough."

"Picking at you about what?" I sit up straight. Suddenly, I'm feeling very protective of him.

"Everything," he says, rubbing his eyes. "She tried to make me feel bad about every part of myself—from the way I acted to the way I looked."

"The way you looked? How? You're so hot—"

I throw my hands over my mouth. His eyes start twinkling as he tries to suppress a laugh.

"Oh my God," I mumble through my fingers. "I didn't mean to say that out loud."

34

"All good," he says, smiling. "You're just making an old man feel good about himself."

"Ugh," I groan. "Stop it. You're always so perfect. Be an asshole for once."

"Stop making me out to be someone I'm not. You know damn well I'm not perfect," he says. "Raine, you're my favorite friend of Millie's by far and that's partially because you're so confident. This is the first time I'm seeing any insecurity from you and it's bullshit. Knock it off."

I pull my legs tighter to my chest. "How'd you get so confident? I mean growing up with your mom."

"I'm confident now, but I wasn't always. I was a sensitive kid. My mom did a number on me, but thankfully, I had enough good people around me that I survived her. It was actually her best friend who encouraged me to go into the navy. She knew it would help build my confidence."

"And it obviously did."

"Professionally, for sure, but I didn't really find myself— my real self—until Millie was born. Being her dad was the thing that finally balanced me."

"What do you mean 'balanced' you?"

"I'm like you. With the way my mom was, I was serious, conservative, guarded. I didn't want to make any mistakes and disappoint anyone else in my life." He pauses for a second and shakes his head. "And that serious demeanor transferred well into my military life. But then Millie came along—this sweet, innocent little girl. She reminded me of the person I was deep down. I was determined to give her everything my mom never gave me. I always encouraged her to be herself, and when she was growing up that was a carefree, sunny, butterfly-chasing girl. Just watching her enjoy life brought out my real person-ality—the gentle side."

"I love how you are with her," I say, smiling wistfully at him. "You have the best relationship."

"Yeah, we do, but my point is that I didn't have that with my mom, and I survived it. It's never too late to find yourself —the person you want to be, not the person your parents want you to be."

"And what if I don't know who that person is?"

"You do—down deep somewhere you know. You've just been hiding her for so long that you can't see her right now, but you know. I agree with what Millie told you. Go down to the island and let loose a little. Be exactly who you want to be." He holds his hand up as I start to talk. "I'd like to clarify. I agree with most of what she said. Maybe pass on the baseball players and find a nice, respectful man instead."

"Did you stand at the door and listen to our entire conversation?"

"SEAL training plus Dad training. I'm always lurking around corners," he says, laughing. "Now go outside and get a head start on your vacation. Be free and enjoy yourself. I'm going to try to get the little man to sleep."

When I get to the door, I turn around and look at him. He's rocking Mo and singing softly to him.

"You forget something?" he says, smiling as he looks up at me.

"Has Millie ever told you what I'm known for at work?"

"I don't think so," he says, rubbing his beard. "Tell me."

"I'm always right." I lean against the door frame. "Par-tially because I was born with incredible intuition, but also because I'm a great analyst. When I get the right information, I don't miss. I always make the right call. Do you believe me?"

He nods. "Absolutely. I would never doubt your analysis for a second."

"Good," I say, locking my eyes with his. "Then believe me when I say you're perfect. I knew it the second I met you, and all the intelligence I've gathered since then has confirmed it."

"Raine—"

"No! Stop," I say, pointing at him. "You don't get to say anything. You told me you would never doubt my analysis. I'll be very offended if you go back on that."

He smiles and nods. "Can I just say thank you then?"

"I'll allow it." I push myself off the door. "Thanks for the talk. It helped more than you know."

"Any time," he says as I walk out. "I mean that, Raine. I'm here for you any time you need me."

"I already told you that you're perfect," I yell as I continue down the hall. "Stop trying for bonus points."

I hear him chuckling as I head back outside. Millie looks up at me from the poker table as I walk out.

"All good?" she says, swatting Butch's hand as he tries to grab some of her chips.

"Yep," I say, patting her shoulder. "It's perfect."

Chapter Six

ALEX

As I walk into my house, the smell of tostones fills the air. My housekeeper, Rosa, knows they're my favorite. I won't let her make them for me while we're in season because I try to eat healthy—except for the chicken fingers, of course.

"The season's not over yet, Rosa," I yell, stopping in the foyer to let the intoxicating smell of fried food fill my nostrils.

"One more game," she yells back. As I turn the corner into the kitchen, she turns around and points the spatula at me. "That's nothing. I want to feed you something other than baked chicken, rice, and vegetables before you leave to go home. Your mother will think I starve you."

She scoops the rest of the tostones out of the frying pan and sets the plate in front of me. I grab one and drop it quickly when it burns my fingers.

She hands me a fork, shaking her head. "They just came out of the skillet. Sometimes you're the smartest person I know and sometimes the dumbest."

I spear a tostone off the plate and dip it into her homemade hot sauce.

"Damn," I say as I savor the mix of sweet and spicy, "your sauce is still the best I've ever tasted. Are you ever going to tell me what spices you put in it?"

"If I give you the recipe, you won't need me. And I won't tell your mother that you like my sauce better than hers—or that you cuss."

"I appreciate it." I grab the glass of sweet iced tea she slides across the counter. "Sugar and fried food? Really, Rosa? Are you trying to kill me?"

"Your post-game smoothie is in the refrigerator," she says, pointing over her shoulder. "The mangoes were so fresh at the market this week, so I used them instead of strawberries. It's banana/mango—"

"And kale?" I grab another tostone on the way over to the refrigerator.

"Yes, I put your disgusting weeds in it." She sticks her tongue out. "They make it taste like dirt."

"Thank you." I kiss the top of her head as I pass by. "Is Ant here today? I thought I heard the leaf blower when we drove up."

She wipes her hands on her apron. "Yes, he's trying to get the yard in shape before you leave."

"It's already in shape," I say, taking a long drink of the smoothie. She's right it tastes like fruit-flavored dirt. "I swear he grooms every blade of the grass individually."

"Probably. He's obsessively detailed," she says, rolling her eyes. "He doesn't get that from me or his father. It drives us crazy most days."

She puts an entire roasted chicken on my plate and dishes out a side of rice and vegetables from the stove. "How are you not tired of eating this?"

"It's a good recovery meal for my body," I say as I tear into the chicken. "And the way you cook it, it always tastes different."

"I try, but I won't miss cooking it in the off-season. Between you and Seb, I'm about tired of chicken. Are you still heading out on Wednesday?"

"Yeah, but not to Puerto Rico," I say, switching from Spanish to English. "Switch to English. You said you wanted to practice."

She sighs, but switches. "You're not going home?"

"I decided I'm going to Seb's wedding, so St. John first and then home."

"Ah, I'm glad you're going to the wedding!" She claps her hands together. "Sophie will be so happy. I like her. She's sweet, but very feasty, too. She'll keep Seb on his toes."

"Feasty?" I look up from my plate.

"Yes. It's like spirited, right?"

"Do you mean feisty?" I grab a piece of paper and pen off the counter and spell it out. "Like this?"

"Yes, but I think it should be pronounced feasty," she says. "I'll never be fluent in English. How did you get so good?"

"Your English is fantastic, Rosa," I say, patting her hand. "And I've been bi-lingual almost since birth. Remember? My uncle grew up in Ohio. I spent a lot of time with him and my aunt when I was a kid."

"Plus, you went to college here. That makes a big difference. Are you still trying to help me get Antonio to apply for college?"

"Come on, Rosa," I say as she puts another heaping scoop of rice on my plate. "Ant doesn't want to go. Give him a break. College isn't for everyone. He makes good money from his business."

"But you're smarter than anyone I know. I want him to be like you."

"He's smart—very smart. And college doesn't make you smart. It just teaches you about something you didn't know, but reading can do that, too."

"Yes, I know you love your books. I have to dust ten more every time I clean. That's why you're still single. You'll never find a woman as smart as you."

"I can and I will—eventually."

She grunts like she does when she disagrees with me. "Speaking of women, are you taking that horrible Cecelia to Seb's wedding?"

I drop my fork on the island with a loud clank. "What? I'm not taking her. Who told you that?"

"She did. I saw her at Manny's house today. She and Miss Caroline were talking about what they were packing."

"I'm not taking her," I snarl as I walk over to rinse my plate. "I made that clear to Caroline about an hour ago."

She shoos me away from the sink. "She'll show up like she always does, and you'll give in because you're too nice. They talk about what a turnover you are—"

"I think you mean pushover, and I've told you, if you're going to work for multiple players, you can't be sharing our private conversations between the households," I say, pointing at her. She rolls her eyes again. "And I'm not a pushover. I'm nice. Being nice isn't a bad thing."

"You know you're the only person I share information with," she says, pulling a plate out of the refrigerator. "I would never tell Caroline anything about you or anyone else. She's a gossip."

She uncovers the plate to reveal a cheesecake topped with fresh pineapple—my favorite dessert.

"Rosa," I groan. "Come on. You're killing me. Cut me off the tiniest slice of that. And you better not be talking to anyone about me. You know how private I am."

"And what gossip am I going to tell them about you, Alex?" she says as she lops off at least a quarter of the cake and shoves it in front of me. "Alex spent all weekend in bed with three—books. Gossip is supposed to be sexy or at least interesting."

"Reading's sexy as hell—"

"To no one except you," she says as she ladles extra pineapple on the mound of cheesecake in front of me. "And that's the second curse word you've used since you've been home."

"There are women out there who like to read." I take a bite and close my eyes for a second. Her cheesecake tastes like pure heaven. "I just haven't found the right one yet."

"Yes, I'm guessing the women I find in your bed some mornings don't even know how to read."

I open my eyes and look at her sternly. "Rosa, be nice."

"I'm nice to people who deserve it." She takes a bite of the cheesecake and nods like she approves, and then points the fork at me. "You're too nice to everyone, all the time."

"Again, being nice is not a bad thing, but just so we're clear, Cece's not coming to the wedding with me. I told them not to bring her to the airport. If she comes, I won't let her on the plane."

"We'll see, but I'm guessing if there's an open seat on the plane, her very large butt will be filling it."

"Rosa!"

"What's up, Alex?" I hear the patio door opening and turn around to see Rosa's son, Antonio, leaning in. His T-shirt is covered with grass. "Good game today."

"Thanks, bruh. Please get in here and eat some of this cheesecake before your mom tries to force-feed me the entire thing."

"Antonio!" Rosa snaps as he tries to take a step inside. "If you bring one piece of grass into this clean house, I'll ground you—"

"I'm twenty-one, Momma. You can't ground me anymore."

"Would you like to test me?" Rosa says, raising the knife she's holding. "Sit at the patio table outside. I'll bring you a plate."

"And I'll bring you a beer," I say, heading to the refrigerator to grab a six-pack.

"You know beer is bad for you, too, but you drink enough of that to fill your entire swimming pool," Rosa says as I walk toward the patio door.

"Beer is mostly water, Rosa—"

"And sugar from the carbohidratos."

"Carbohydrates," I say, not turning around. "Don't cheat by using Spanglish."

As I walk out on the patio, Ant jerks his feet down off the chair he had them resting on.

"It's my chair, Ant, not hers," I say, laughing. "Put your feet back up. You work hard. You deserve a rest."

He keeps them on the ground. "It's funny that you think you run this house when my mom's around. My dad's delusional like that, too."

Rosa comes out of the house and places a regularly sized slice of cheesecake in front of Ant.

"You missed some dead flowers on the hydrangeas," she says, pointing across the patio.

"I haven't gotten to that side yet." He takes a swig of beer. "I'll do it when I'm done here."

Rosa makes a beeline to the hydrangeas and starts pulling off the dead flowers.

"Hey, Ant. What are you doing this weekend? You want a free trip to St. John?"

"For Seb's wedding?" he says, looking over at me with his mouth full of cheesecake.

"You can go to the wedding if you want, but just to take a break, you know? You deserve a vacation."

"You're asking me so Caroline's sister won't come on the trip, right?" He laughs as he shoves another bite in his mouth.

"Damn, how do you know about that? Did they tell you, too?"

"Bruh, they don't talk to me," he says, shaking his head.

"They barely look at me. They talk in front of me, though. I don't think they know I understand English."

"What? You were born here. How do they not know you're fluent in English?"

"They barely know my name. Caroline's called me Anthony more than once. And I think the sister thinks my name is Andrew."

"Sounds about right." I drain the rest of my beer and pop open another one. "So Cece really thinks she's coming on this trip with me?"

"It's all they've been talking about since Manny told them about the trip like a week ago. They've been coming home with shopping bags every day full of vacation clothes."

"Well, she's not coming with me, so either you take the extra seat on the plane or it'll be empty."

"Caroline will fire me if I take her sister's place on the trip—"

"Her sister doesn't have a place on the trip," I growl. "And Manny's the only one making any money in that house. It's his decision whether you work there or not."

"You're not as smart as I think you are, Alex, if you think Manny makes any decisions in that house," Rosa yells from across the patio. "Caroline has the pants in that family."

"Wears the pants, Rosa," I yell and then lower my voice. "Damn, she has ears like a bat. How'd you get away with anything when you were growing up?"

"Shit," he whispers. "You think I got away with anything with her as my mom?"

"Don't think I don't hear you both cursing because you try to whisper now," Rosa says, swarming our table. She jerks away Ant's unfinished plate. "You can have dessert when you clean up your dirty mouth, Antonio."

Ant waits until the kitchen door is firmly closed behind her and then looks at me. "You know what? I could use a little time to myself. I'm in. When do we leave?"

Chapter Seven

RAINE

Before Millie left to go back to San Diego, we went shopping for "island clothes." We bought about ten things—each one showing more skin than the next. I'm comfortable wearing exactly zero of them. But I promised her I would try to tap into my carefree side, so this morning as I head to the airport, I'm wearing a canary yellow sundress with a plunging neckline. My carry-on is an enormous straw bag with a parrot sewn into the weaving. The parrot's yellow bill matches my dress to a tee. My hair—that's perpetually in a top knot or ponytail—is flowing over my shoulders pushed back by the extremely large sunglasses that Millie said were my 'crowning glory.'

As I pull up to the airport, I immediately spot Butch. He's leaning against a wall with a duffle bag at his feet. He's wearing his favorite cap—a well-worn navy trucker hat with a large red and white rooster on the front. It's paired with a gray Lynyrd Skynyrd T-shirt and army green cargo shorts. He's scanning every cab that pulls up, tapping his fingers nervously on the wall. I'm sure he's been here for at least an hour. Even retired, I know he's still going by SEAL time. He lets out a long breath when he sees my head pop out of the car.

"Okay, damn," Butch says, giving my body a slow scan as he walks over. "I see what you're doing for me here—"

"I'm not doing anything for *you*," I say as I try to maneuver my severely overpacked suitcase onto the sidewalk. "This is the way I always dress when I'm off-duty."

"Bullshit," he says, coughing into his hand.

"You don't know what I do when I'm not with you guys."

"When are you ever not with us? You've spent the better part of five years attached to us—almost literally."

"I have time off," I say, tugging at the neckline of my dress as I try to keep the parrot bag on my shoulder. "I go out—with people—I mean, sometimes I do."

"When's the last time you've gone out with anyone except us?" He points at me as I start to open my mouth. "And Millie counts as one of us."

I stick my tongue out at him as I start rolling my bag into the terminal. He grabs it from me and picks it up.

"Damn, girl. What do you have in here? Did Millie crawl in before you left this morning?" He leans down and whispers into the bag, "Millie? You in there? Knock twice if you can hear me."

"Stop," I say, trying to grab it back from him. "I packed a few books."

He holds the bag further away from me. "What books? Like briefing books? You know you can't take those out of secured areas."

"Not briefing books," I say, rolling my eyes. "Book books. Like for pleasure. I'm on vacation."

He lifts the bag again. "Did you clear all the shelves at the library? We're only there for a long weekend."

"I read fast," I say, grabbing for my bag again. "Give it to me! That's agency rule number one for being embedded with SEALs—don't expect them to carry anything for you."

"That's because when we're on a mission, we kind of need our arms to be free. We're not on a mission right now. I don't have to get to my weapon."

"Oh my God," I whisper as I grab his arm. "Do you have a gun on you? You can't carry on the plane anymore. You're a civilian now."

"Don't remind me," he growls. "I feel like I have a body part missing. And I'm carrying your bag because for the duration of this trip, you're my girlfriend. I'm a gentleman."

"Fine," I say, taking my boarding pass out of the parrot bag. "But it has wheels. You don't have to carry it."

"I like carrying things for you," he says, blowing me a kiss. "I'd carry you if you'd let me, baby."

"Baby? No!" I turn around and point at him. "Absolutely no more of that."

I hear him laughing as he follows behind me. "Ok, honey then or maybe sweet cheeks."

"Oh my God," I say, not looking back. "Asking you to be my plus-one was the worst idea I've ever had."

When we get to our row in the plane, our seatmate's already sleeping, his head pressed against the window with his legs sprawled out into the middle seat's leg space.

"I'm assuming you want the aisle," I say, looking over my shoulder at Butch.

"You assume correctly, but let me take care of that for you first."

He rams his duffle into the guy's legs. The guy snaps awake and glares at us, but he pulls his legs back into his third of the space.

"Sorry, brother," Butch says in his deepest Southern drawl. He has a pronounced accent from his Georgia roots, but he only turns it up this much when he's trying to act folksy. "I was trying to fit this bag under her seat. Guess I'm going to have to put it in the overhead."

I sit down and smile at the guy. He doesn't smile back.

"Good work," I whisper to Butch as he sits down. "You've already made your first enemy on this trip."

"Naw, I'm pretty sure the TSA guy at security didn't like me much either." He tries to slide his enormous legs under the seat, but ends up hitting his knees hard on the seatback in front of him. The woman sitting there turns around and shoots daggers at him.

"That's number three."

He shakes his head. "If you want to count something this weekend, how about you count the number of ladies who make it back to my room?"

"Eww!" I say, slapping his arm. "No one wants to know that number."

"You're just mad because you know you can't beat me at

something."

"I don't want to beat you at that."

"Bullshit. You want to win everything. You're the most competitive person I know." He stops for a second and looks at me—a scary twinkle in his eyes. "Maybe we should have a little bet on who can *entertain* the most new friends when we get to the island."

"I'm not making a sex bet with you," I say, shoving his hand away as he tries to shake on the bet. "You're such a practiced whore. It wouldn't be fair."

"I'm not a whore," he says, laughing when he sees my eyebrows shoot up. "I'm just an expert at my craft."

"Whore." I turn away from him toward the window. Our seatmate is suddenly wide awake and listening to our conversation.

"You're just jealous," Butch says, nudging me on the shoulder.

"Shh. Lower your voice." I nod my head backward. "Not everyone needs to hear this conversation."

"When's the last time you've been with a guy?" he says, not lowering his voice at all. "Like for a date or anything."

I cross my arms and frown at him. "You're not dating anyone either."

"I don't want to be dating anyone, but I'm damn sure having sex." He pulls a toothpick out of his T-shirt pocket and starts chewing on it. "I'm just saying, there's nothing wrong with letting loose a little bit every now and then. You're always wound so tightly. This weekend might be the perfect time to relax and have some fun. When are you going to see these people again?"

"I'm going to see you again," I say, sinking into my seat.

"And I've already told you, I'm the best wingman ever created, and part of that is keeping my mouth shut. You know, the whole "what happens in Vegas, stays in Vegas" rule. I've got you. No judgment. Let it all hang out. And let me tell you, that little dress you're wearing is a great start to that."

I punch his leg as I pull the ends of my hair over my cleavage. "Stop looking at my boobs."

"Don't show them to me if you don't want me to look. I'll make sure no one else is looking, though. Unless you want someone to look. Maybe we should have a signal, like pat your head or something if you want a guy to look."

"I hate you."

"There's a fine line between love and hate, Raineth."

I push myself back up as the plane starts to move. "And what signal should I use if I want you to leave me alone?"

"Patting the head is good for that, too. It says, 'Butch, please leave me alone so I can get with this guy.'" He starts patting his head to demonstrate. "And you didn't answer my question from before. When's the last time you've been with a guy?"

"That's none of your business."

"That long, huh?" he says, tapping his chin. "Do you not like sex? Are you anti-sexual?"

"I think you mean asexual and I'm neither asexual nor anti-sexual, thank you. I'm just not a whore, like you."

"Girl, just because I like to have sex doesn't make me a whore—"

"Please," I say, looking at my phone as we take off. Right on time. "You're all whores. Seriously. Every SEAL I've ever met is an active whore. I'm convinced there's a class on it in BUD/S, like "How to be a SEAL whore 101."

"It's not 101. That's an advanced-level course," he says. "You have to take the prerequisite "How to Identify a Frog Hog" first."

"I hate you."

"Don't hate the player, baby, only hate the game."

"Hey." The guy next to me taps my leg. "Your buddy's right. Sex is good for the soul. I have as much of it as I can. In fact, if you want to get a head start on your weekend, I'm a certified member of the mile-high club—"

In a split second, Butch has unbuckled both of our seatbelts and lifted me over him into the aisle. He pounces into my seat and leans toward the man until he's an inch from his face. The man's pressed so hard against the plane wall that I think he might bust through it.

"Put your headphones on and try not to get the back of this hand before we land," Butch snarls as he raises his enormous hand and holds it right in the guy's face. "Look at her again and you're leaving this plane on a stretcher. You understand me?"

The guy nods vigorously as he grabs his headphones from around his neck and slides them over his ears. Butch turns back to me as I slide into the aisle seat.

"You're retired now," I say, buckling my seatbelt. "You don't have to scare people out of their minds anymore."

"Didn't I tell you?" he says, patting my leg. "Scaring people is going to be my retirement hobby."

Chapter Eight

ALEX

As we pull into the private airfield to catch the chartered flight to the island, we see Manny, Caroline, and Cece leaning against their car. Caroline and Cece are wearing enormous straw sun hats, short, strapless sundresses, and sandals with towering heels. They'd look like twins if it weren't for Caroline's porn-star-sized fake boobs.

"Fuck," I say, taking a deep breath and blowing it out forcefully.

"Told you," Ant says, pulling his baseball cap over his eyes. "Why don't you let her go? You can say I'm here to take your car back home."

"I'm not taking her." I park in the spot the furthest away from them. "You do what you want to do, but she's not getting on that plane with me."

When I get out of the car, Cece's running across the tarmac toward me. Her sundress is simultaneously slipping further down her chest and rising further up her thighs with every stride she takes. You'd think seeing a woman almost naked would turn me on, but it's making me feel nauseated.

"Alex! This trip's going to be so much fun!" She closes in on me and tries to throw herself into my body.

"What's up, Cece?" I say, holding out my arms to block her from reaching me. "I didn't know you were coming on the trip. Whose guest are you?"

She pushes my chest and laughs. "Stop! Don't try to be coy, Alex. You know I'm coming with you."

Manny and Caroline make it over to us. Caroline looks right at me and smiles. "I'll occupy most of her time, so you can meet women. Although she's going to have to stay in your room. If you have sleepovers, maybe go back to the women's rooms."

Manny shrugs as I glare at him. "Shame to let a free trip go to waste."

"I'm not letting it go to waste," I say, motioning to Ant to get out of the car. He opens the door slowly. "Ant's coming with me."

"What?" Caroline spins around to look at him. He sinks back down in the seat. "Very funny, Alex."

I walk over and pull Ant out of the car. "He's coming with me. If Cece wants to go, she'll have to find another seat."

"You're taking a gardener to St. John with you?" Caroline says, looking at Manny for backup. He looks at me, his eyes pleading.

"Nope. I'm taking my friend." I grab our luggage out of the trunk and hand Ant his bag. "Wheels up in about thirty minutes. See you on the plane."

"Alex! Do not get on that plane with him!" Caroline yells

as I push Ant forward. "This is ridiculous. Manny, I'm not getting on the plane without Cece. Stop! Everyone stop!"

I hear the clicking of heels following us. I don't turn around. An airport coordinator is checking people in at the base of the boarding stairs. "Names, please."

"Alejandro Molina and my guest, Antonio Reyes."

"Alex!" Caroline tugs at my arm. "Stop! You're being ridiculous."

The coordinator scans the list and looks up at me. "I have an Alex Molina plus guest."

"Same person," I say, handing her my ID. I motion for Ant to hand his to her.

Caroline grabs Ant's ID and throws it on the tarmac. "This isn't his guest. He's trying to be funny. He's bringing my sister," she says, pointing back at Cece who has her hands over her face, sobbing loudly. I notice her peek between her fingers a few times to make sure we're all watching.

Ant picks up his ID. I grab it and hand it back to the coordinator. "He's my guest. Can we board?"

"Yep. All good." The coordinator looks from me to Caroline. "Ma'am, we're wheels up in less than thirty minutes. This is your last chance to board if you're going."

"Alex! Stop! I mean it," Caroline screams as we start up the stairs.

"Well she's definitely going to fire me," Ant says as we start down the aisle to our seats.

I give Jack a fist bump as we pass him and his wife on the way back. "No worries, I'll pay you double what I pay you now."

"Naw, you don't even have to do that," Ant says, glancing

out the window as we get to our seats. He cringes as we both watch Caroline throw her bag at Manny as he starts toward the plane. "I don't want to work for her anymore. I'm tired of cleaning up her dog's poop. That thing's the size of a loaf of bread, but I swear it poops like a horse."

"Fucking thing bit me the last time I was over there," I say, looking up at the flight attendant as she lowers a tray of mimosas to us. I grab two. "Thank you, ma'am."

"Nice," Ant says as I hand him one. He holds up the champagne flute and admires it. "They serve OJ in fancy glasses on this plane."

"It's a mimosa, dumbass. Champagne and OJ."

"I've never had champagne." He clinks my glass and downs it in one gulp. "Cool."

Manny walks onto the plane. I think for a second that he's alone, but then Caroline bursts through the door. She whips off her sunhat and focuses her eyes on me. I glance out the window just in time to see Cece's head disappearing into Manny's car.

Caroline walks slowly down the aisle. She switches her glare from me to Ant when she gets to our row.

"You're fired," she says, shoving the back of his seat, "and so is your mother."

Ant nods. "Sounds good."

"And neither of you," she says, pointing between us as she continues down the aisle, "should ever talk to me again."

"Nice, asshole," Manny whispers to me. "Not only do I have to deal with that attitude for the entire trip, but Cece now has the keys to my Aston. I know she'll drive it the entire weekend. She's going to smoke in it and she'll probably try to park it at her trash apartment. I'll be lucky if I get it back at all."

"Are you really worried about your car when your wife just fired Ant? Not to mention firing Rosa—who's been like a mom to you."

"I'm trying to keep the peace," Manny whispers. "I'll pay you on the side or something, Ant, and Rosa, too."

"We're good, brother," Ant says. "We both have so much business right now. Sophie introduced us to a lot of her clients."

"Manny!" Caroline screams from the back of the plane.

He closes his eyes. "This trip is going to be from hell."

"Still not too late to kick her off," I say, pointing to the front of the plane. "They haven't closed the door yet."

"Don't tempt me," Manny says as he continues to his seat. "Yes, honey. I'm coming. No need to yell."

Ant grabs another mimosa off the tray as the attendant passes us. "So do you need me to stay close when we get there or can I take out on my own? Maybe explore the island a little."

"Do what you want, but when you're doing this *exploring*, make sure you wrap it up. If you come back home with some kind of dick disease, Rosa will probably kill me."

"No probably about it," he says, chugging his drink. "She'd straight up murder both of us."

"You're supposed to sip a mimosa. It's not a tequila shot."

"Oh, damn, do they have tequila on the plane?" he says, waving his hand at the attendant. "I'd like to do some shots."

"Put on the brakes, Ant," I say, grabbing his arm and lowering it. "This isn't spring break. Stay sober-ish at least until we get to the resort, then you can drink as much as you want."

"I'll probably hit some townie bars when I get there. I'm not going to be able to afford the drinks at the resort."

"I'm certain I shouldn't tell you this," I say, sighing, "but Seb's paying for everything the entire weekend—drinks, food, whatever."

Ant sits up straight in his seat. "What? Seriously? This might be the best weekend of my life. Are we sharing a room?"

"If I had to share a room with you, you wouldn't be on this trip. You have your own."

"I love this weekend so much already—my own place, free everything," he says, glancing around the plane. "You got your eyes on any of these women?"

"All of the women on this plane are taken, so eyes to yourself."

"All good," he says. "I'll find someone when we get there. Are you hooking up with Allie while we're down there? She talks about you non-stop when she's at Seb and Sophie's house."

I rub my hands over my face. I'm beginning to regret asking a twenty-one-year-old to come with me on the trip. "You're as bad as your mom. Don't share information between the households. It's going to get you fired."

"I already got fired," he laughs. "And that's because I'm your date to the wedding. You owe me. Maybe introduce me to Allie if you're not interested. She's sexy as hell."

"I'm not interested in her," I say, closing my eyes as the plane takes off. "And you don't need me to do groundwork.

Introduce yourself. Or have Sophie do it. She lives to set people up."

"Yeah, Sophie's awesome. She's so nice to me. And speaking of sexy, good God—"

My eyes snap open. "Ant," I say, putting my finger in his face, "don't let Seb catch you looking at her or you'll lose another client and probably a few limbs. He's crazy protective."

"I'm careful," he says, grinning, "but you can't ask me not to look. Holy fuck."

"Asking you to be my guest was maybe the worst decision of my life. You're either going to end up diseased, passed out drunk in some ditch or Seb's going to kill you with his bare hands. I wonder if I asked the pilot nicely if he'd turn the plane around."

"No such luck, brother. The only way off now is with a parachute."

"Don't tempt me." I grab a book out of my bag. "Now leave me alone for a while so I can read."

"You read out in public like this?" He looks around the plane. "Where your friends can see you?"

"I'm reading a book, Ant, not whacking off."

"I think I'd rather have someone see me whack off—"

The flight attendant stops at our row just as he's saying it. She tries to cover the disgust that fills her face. "May I get either of you anything?" she says, glaring at us.

"Yeah, I'll take a parachute if you can pry open one of the doors for me," I say. "But if you can't, I'll take a beer and keep them coming."

Chapter Nine

RAINE

"May I get you something to drink?" The flight attendant barely looks up as he hands us each a bag of pretzels.

"Yes, sir, you may," Butch says, ripping his bag open with his teeth. "I'll have your finest mass-produced beer—Miller, Budweiser—dealer's choice. And my beautiful girlfriend will have a vodka tonic with just a splash of orange juice. Please and thank you."

Butch pulls my hand up and kisses it. I pinch his nose hard. The flight attendant looks from me to Butch and shakes his head.

"I'm sorry, sweetie," Butch laughs as he drops my hand and looks back at the flight attendant. "Make the vodka Tito's if you have it. She gets very testy if I don't order her liquor correctly."

The flight attendant lets out a long exhale as he starts making our drinks.

"He hates you, too," I whisper. "And you're getting a little too into this whole boyfriend thing."

"Oh Rainey, this is just the beginning." He squeezes my leg. "I can't wait until I have a proper audience."

"How much do I have to pay you to turn it down by at least fifty percent?"

"I'll turn it all the way down if you agree to my proposed wager." He takes his beer from the flight attendant and guzzles half of it before setting it down on his tray.

"I already told you I'm not making a sex bet with you."

"Okay," he says, grabbing the pretzels off my tray and ripping into them. "It doesn't have to be a quantity bet. How about just one guy? If you hook up with one guy while we're on the island, you win the bet."

"That's still a sex bet," I say, lowering my voice as the flight attendant looks right at me. "And I don't want that kind of pressure. Millie told me to be carefree for the entire trip. That will make me too anxious."

"We can still be carefree and have some fun—"

"Not we," I say, taking a sip of my drink. "Me. Millie wants me to be carefree. No one wants to see you being carefree."

"I don't know, girl. Once people meet Island Butch, they're going to fall head over heels in love with him."

"Island Butch?" I shudder. "What the hell is an Island Butch? He sounds terrifying."

He takes the pretzels off our seatmate's tray and starts to open them.

"Stop," I say, trying to wrestle the bag out of his hand. "What if he saw you take them?"

"You think he's going to challenge me about anything? He won't open his eyes until we land." He pours the pretzels into his mouth. "Even if he's awake. He won't risk glancing at you by mistake."

"Remind me never to take a SEAL on a personal trip again," I say, massaging my temples. "Will you turn down the bravado a little bit? You're exhausting."

"Sorry, sister. The bravado dial's set permanently on high." He pats my leg. "You know what they say? No such thing as a former SEAL."

"This is going to be the longest weekend of my life."

"And it's just getting started. I'm not sure what to even expect from carefree Raine."

"Actually, I made a list of the carefree things I want to do while we're there."

"A list? Seriously?" He stretches out, sprawling his legs wide. "I don't think you're doing carefree right."

"How would you know anything about carefree?" I say, draining the rest of my drink.

"Let me see the list." He reaches for my bag.

I slap his hand. "Stay out of my bag."

"Fine, but you need to put our bet on the list? That's carefree objective number one."

"We don't have a bet."

He takes off his baseball cap and runs his fingers through his long, messy hair. "Okay, how about this? You land one guy before I land ten women and you win the bet."

"Ten!" I scrunch up my face. "We're only there for three nights."

"Darling, if you think you can only have sex at night, I

know what part of your problem is already," he says, downing the rest of his beer. "And besides, you know what a great multitasker I am. Who says I'm limited to one woman at a time?"

"Ahh," I groan. "Please stop. I don't want to hear about your sexual preferences. Maybe the bet should be I land one guy, but you're limited to only one woman."

"Oh, holy hell, no. That's not even possible."

I rub my chin as I lock my eyes with his. "Why do you cycle through so many women? Are you scared to put in the work of keeping someone satisfied for more than one night?"

His eyes narrow into slits. "Don't try to analyze me, Agent Raine."

"Why don't you say it louder?" I glance around the plane. "I don't think the pilots heard what I do for a living."

He shakes his head. "I only said *agent*. You could be a travel agent for all anyone knows. Your whole cloak and dagger thing's secure. And I still don't know why you can't tell anyone what you do for a living. Is that something the *travel* agency requires of you?"

"Stop avoiding my question. Why do you run from real intimacy by burying yourself in forgettable women?"

"Damn! Was that your question?" He lets out a long whistle. "We're on vacation. Ease up a little bit, tiger."

"Classic avoidance technique," I say, tapping on his arm.

"I've been married and divorced twice. You know that. I'm not good at relationships."

"Or," I say, holding my hand up, "you chose the wrong women. Maybe if you start concentrating on quality versus quantity, you can find the right woman."

"You're still analyzing. Stop it." He strokes his beard as he thinks. "For this weekend, I'll limit myself to eight women."

"Three."

"Six. Final offer. And to be clear, that's not having sex only six times. I'll have to go back to them multiple times on the trip, but I'll keep it to the same six women."

"Gross," I say, rubbing my face. "Okay, but if you go over six different women, I win. And I already know I'm going to win because there's no way in hell you're going to be able to do that."

"No, that's not the bet." He holds up his empty beer can to the flight attendant who nods at him. "You have to land a guy to win. It's not just about me staying under my number."

"Define 'land,'" I say slowly.

"For this trip, "landing" means spending one night with said man," he says, grabbing his fresh beer from the attendant. "And I have to have proof."

"Eww, no. How am I supposed to prove it to you?"

"Pictures are nice."

I shove his leg. "Stop being a pervert. Landing means kissing a guy—sex optional. And you can take my word for it. When have I ever lied to you?"

"That's professional Raine. She's as honest as they come," he says. "I'm not too sure about this new personal Raine. I think she would lie just to get me to shut up."

"Seriously, lying to you makes you shut up? How am I just learning this five years into working with you? I would have lied to you the entire time if I would have known that's all it took to keep you quiet."

"Do we have a deal or not?" He holds out his hand for me to shake.

"I have an addendum," I say, pushing his hand away. "You can't tell any of the women that you're a SEAL."

"Seriously?" He looks at me under a severely furrowed brow. "Do you think the only reason I get women is because I'm a SEAL?"

"No," I say, holding his stern look, "but it certainly doesn't hurt."

"All right. I won't play the SEAL card, but in return. I get to choose your target man."

"What? No," I say, leaning away from him. "You'll choose some guy who's way out of my league, so you can win the bet."

"There's no man who's out of your league. In fact, just the opposite is true," he says, pointing his finger right in my face. "And I'm going to choose someone who I think is probably way more terrifying to you—someone who you're attracted to and even worse, someone who's attracted to you."

I grip the armrests as anxiety shoots through my body. "Well that just sounds horrible. I'm already stressed out and we haven't even landed."

"Do we have a deal?" He holds out his hand.

I push it away again. "What do I get if I win the bet?"

"Hopefully an exciting and very satisfying night with the gentleman that I choose for you. Is that not enough?"

His eyes narrow as my face scrunches up again.

"Wait," he says, finally lowering his voice to a whisper. "Are you a virgin? Do we need to have the sex talk?"

"I'm not a virgin," I say, rolling my eyes. "I just feel like if we're betting, there should be a prize at least."

"Oh, there will be prizes, plenty of prizes—"

"Shut up," I say, shifting in my seat until I'm inches from his face. "Here's what I get if I win the bet: You promise me that when we get to San Diego, you'll let me set you up with a normal woman, someone who's a real possibility."

He pushes my face back and looks away. "I told you I'm not looking to date anyone."

"Because you're scared to put yourself out there," I say. "We're not that different, Butch. We just handle it in different ways."

He turns around to look at me and nods. "If that will make you finally shake on this bet, yeah, go crazy, set me up."

"We have a deal." I hold my hand out, he pushes it down.

"If I win," he says, "you have to ask Culver if he banged the waitress at The Baja Grill."

"What?" I say, my mouth hanging open. "You're insane. He's our boss. Not to mention he's scary as fuck."

"He's not really our boss anymore," he says, nodding his head, "but he's definitely scary as fuck. That's why none of us have the cajones to ask him. Come on. You want to know if they slept together—"

"Of course I want to know, Butch, but why does the smallest person on the team have to ask him?"

"You're the only one he wouldn't hit," he laughs.

"Are we sure about that?"

"I guess we'll find out when you lose the bet."

"Then I'm winning because I'm not asking him that."

He holds out his hand again. I blow out a long breath. "Fine," I say as I shake it.

His lips form a terrifying grin. "I can't wait to choose your man."

The flight attendant stops at our aisle. "Ma'am, may I get you another drink?"

"Yes, please. And keep them coming," I say, pulling my hand away from Butch. "I'm going to need all of the liquor if I'm going to get through this trip."

Chapter Ten

ALEX

After I checked in at the resort, I headed over to Seb and Sophie's villa. It's the only house in a small, private bay on the south side of the island—about a twenty-minute drive from where everyone else is staying.

The villa sits so close to the beach that it almost looks like the infinity pool is connected to the ocean. The patio's surrounded by a lush forest of palm and mangrove trees with dots of white frangipani flowers jumping out at their bases. The rich, ginger smell reminds me of my childhood home.

Seb's three friends from Michigan were already here when I arrived. Stone and Ricky are sitting on the edge of the pool. Paul's floating on a raft. Sophie's sitting between Seb's legs on the steps, leaning back against his chest. His arms are firmly wrapped around her, as usual.

We've been hanging out for about an hour, but I can tell by the way Seb's started kissing Sophie's neck that he'd like to have some alone time with her.

"Okay," Sophie says, standing up. "I'm jumping in the shower. I'll leave you guys so you can have some male-bonding time."

Seb pulls Sophie back down on his lap. "Baby, you don't have to leave."

"I know," she says, kissing him, "but I need to clean up if I'm going to be ready to go to the airport to get Raine. Maisie's picking me up in an hour."

"I'll drive you to the airport." His hand slides down until it rests on her butt cheek that's just barely covered by her bikini. "I don't want you two going on the ferry alone."

"If you want to," she says, hugging him, "but we can handle it."

He nuzzles his face into her hair. "I know, but isn't Raine bringing her boyfriend? He might like having another guy there."

Sophie laughs. "She's bringing a guy who she says is her boyfriend, but he's probably not."

"What?" I say. "Why would she lie about having a boyfriend?"

"So I won't try to play matchmaker. She hates it when I try to set her up."

"Oh look at that," I say, rolling my eyes. "I have something in common with her already. Maybe you should set me up with her."

Sophie spins her head around and looks at me. "Maybe I should. You have a lot in common. She's wicked smart just like you. You might like her if you can get her nose out of whatever book she's reading."

"She likes to read?" I say and then realize I said it out loud. I point at Sophie. "No setups! Promise me."

"Yes, she likes to read. I've never seen her without a book." She taps her lips with her fingers. "Hmm. Who else have I never seen without a book?"

"Seb," I say, slapping some water his way. "You promised to talk to her about this."

"I can't help you if you're going to encourage her."

"I was joking." They're both smiling at me—their faces pressed together. "Sophie, stop setting me up—with her or anyone else."

She looks back at Seb. "Do I have to stop?" she coos.

He starts kissing her neck again. "You don't have to stop anything, ever."

"Are you just saying that to make me feel good?"

His hands start moving up and down her back. "No, baby, I have other ways to make you feel good—"

"Oh my God. Enough!" I say, splashing them again. "There are other people right next to you. Get a room."

Sophie laughs as she wriggles out of his grip and stands up again. "Sorry, Alex. It's still new."

"It's not that new," Ricky snarls. "Start getting sick of each other already. It's annoying."

"What he said," I say, nodding at Ricky.

She pats the top of my head as she walks by. "I'm setting you up with Raine."

"Sophie!" I yell as she walks away. "Do not set me up again."

"I can't hear you," she says, dismissing me with a wave of her hand.

I look at Seb for support, but his eyes are fixed on Ricky.

"You get a good look?" Seb says, glaring at him.

Ricky hasn't taken his eyes off Sophie's butt since she stood up. Honestly, I took a quick look, too. It's impossible not to look when it's that perfect.

"Man," Ricky whistles as he turns back toward us after Sophie disappears into the villa. "How do you expect me not to look at that? Especially when she's wearing that little bikini."

"Not only do I expect you not to look at it," Seb growls, "I also expect you not to talk about it. Let me catch you looking again and you're on the next plane back to Michigan."

"I think it's about time we left Seb and Sophie alone," I say, draining the last of my beer. "I'll take you guys back to the resort if you don't have a car."

"What?" Ricky looks over at Seb. "We're not staying here with you? We always stay with you."

"You're not staying here," Seb says as he stands up and starts to follow Sophie into the villa. "Even you're not that stupid. This is our wedding weekend. Lock the front door behind you. We'll see you over at the resort for the party tonight."

"What's wrong with you?" Stone shakes his head as he looks at Ricky. "You know how protective he is of his people and it's on another level with Sophie. You better watch yourself or you're going to get a beat down harder than the one he gave you in eighth grade."

"Come on, Stone. You looked—"

"Brother," I interrupt, "we all looked. The key is a quick look and then divert your eyes. Look. Divert. Look. Divert."

"That's bullshit," Ricky says, popping open another beer. "I miss the Seb that used to look with me."

"You think he isn't looking at that?" Paul says. "Not only does he look at it all day, every day, he's probably inside the house now pressed up against it. You see how they are in front of other people. I don't even want to think about what they do when they're alone."

Ricky sighs. "I want it to go back to pre-Sophie when we all hung out as single guys."

"Paul and I are married, dipshit," Stone says. "Are you forgetting about those two women who were sitting next to us on the plane?"

Ricky makes a grunting noise as he takes another drink of his beer.

"Where are your wives?" I say, looking at Ricky over my sunglasses. He's pouting like a five-year-old kid.

"They're back at the resort by the pool," Paul says. "They always give us a little male bonding time with Seb."

"Male bonding, my ass," Ricky snaps. "Why didn't Sophie go over and hang out with the women while we're here? It's bullshit. We don't get any alone time with Seb anymore."

"It's not going back to pre-Sophie, Rick," Stone says. "You're the only single one left. I mean, except for Alex."

"Then it's up to us, Alex," Ricky says, lowering himself into the pool. "I was a great wingman for Seb. I'll transfer my services over to you."

"Yeah, that's a hard pass." I shake my head at him. "Sorry, man. I don't need a wingman. And you're in town for Seb's wedding, so it's not going to go back to pre-Sophie."

"Maybe," he says. "I'm still trying to convince him to

slow it down. They haven't even known each other for a year. There's no need to get married so quickly."

"You're delusional," Paul says. "You see how they are with each other. He's not slowing that down. If anything, he wants to marry her today instead of waiting for Saturday."

"I'm not the only one who thinks he's moving too fast," Ricky says, turning to Stone. "You told him you thought the way they met was shady—"

"I thought that—past tense," Stone says, glaring at him. "Then I got to know her. She's cool and she's great for Seb. You need to give her a chance."

"I second that," I say. "If anything, she's too good for him."

"We'll see. I've known Seb longer than any of you. I think he might change his mind and call off the wedding," Ricky says, shrugging as he chugs the rest of his beer. "Who's this friend they're picking up at the airport? Like Renee or something?"

"I think it's Raine," Stone says. "Seb said they grew up together in Chicago."

"Has anyone seen a picture of her?" Ricky asks.

"I don't think it matters what she looks like, Rick. She sounds way out of your league," Paul says. "Sophie said she works for the State Department."

"Oh that's cool," I say. "What does she do for them?"

Everyone turns and looks at me. "Uh, not sure," Paul says, "but Soph said she travels a lot, speaks a bunch of languages, so probably some kind of envoy."

"Damn, she already sounds way more interesting than any woman I've met in years."

"Interesting?" Ricky looks at me like I'm crazy. "You can't be serious. She sounds boring as hell. She'll probably want to talk about politics and shit."

"I don't know," I say. "That sounds kind of great to me. Maybe someone with a little more substance."

"Substance takes too long," Ricky says. "We're just here for the weekend."

"Yeah, like I said, you're good, Rick. No one wants to talk to you about world events," Paul says. "She's definitely out of your league. Maybe try something from the college friends' group. Some of them seem stupid enough to tolerate you."

"I hate this weekend so much already," Ricky says, looking over at me. "Alex, let me know early who you have your eyes on, so I won't waste my time there."

"Sorry, man. This isn't going to be that kind of friendship. We're not in this together." I stand up and throw my car keys to Stone. "I think I'll go to the airport with them. Will you take my car back to the resort?"

"Yeah, I've got you." Stone stands up and nods toward the house. "I wouldn't go in there for at least a half-hour, though—"

I hold up my hand. "I learned my lesson on a road trip earlier this year. I had the room next door to them. I never want to hear those sounds again. My butt is firmly planted on this patio until I hear Maisie's car pull up."

"Maybe wear headphones, too," Pauls says, shaking his head. "We'll see you over there tonight."

"Sounds good," I say, pointing at Ricky. "Don't let him drive my car."

"We don't let him drive." Stone laughs as they walk away. "We barely let him in the car at all."

As they walk through the gate, my mind switches back to Raine. In the last five minutes, I've learned that she likes to read, she's smart, she has an interesting job, and she makes up fake boyfriends so Sophie won't try to find her a match. She sounds perfect and honestly, I've never wanted to be set up with someone so badly in my life.

Chapter Eleven

RAINE

As the wheels touch down, my anxiety level goes straight up. Not only am I regretting the stupid bet I made with Butch, but I'm also a little stressed about seeing Sophie and Maisie again.

Sophie and I have known each other almost literally since birth. She was born two days after me at the same hospital. Our families have lived next door to each other for almost thirty years. Despite being opposite in looks and demeanor, the neighbors called us "the twins" when we were growing up because we were practically glued to each other's sides.

We met Maisie in kindergarten and became an inseparable trio until high school. Sophie and Maisie went to the public high school in our neighborhood while I headed to an all-girls, private school across town.

From the first day of freshman year, I had a full schedule of AP classes, so I spent most of my time studying. By contrast, they were involved in every extracurricular activity possible. While I was in the library, they were at football games, dances, and student council meetings.

Sophie and I still saw each other most weeks. We'd catch up on our driveways if we got home from school at the same time. Occasionally, we'd have a double date with Dak—the guy she set me up with my freshman year—and whatever guy she was dating at the time. But overall, we kept heading in different directions until she and Maisie ended up in Miami for college and I went to Georgetown.

We still see each other on the occasional holiday back in Chicago, but I hadn't seen either of them in almost two years when Sophie called to invite me to her wedding. I didn't even know she was engaged—much less to one of the most famous athletes in the world. At least that's what my mom tells me.

Mom normally wouldn't know a baseball from a hockey puck, but apparently Seb helped her carry groceries into the house when he and Sophie were in Chicago visiting her parents. Now, Mom's his number one fan. She was even wearing his jersey the last time I talked to her on FaceTime.

As we walk out of the airport's secured area, I run ahead of Butch and climb on a bench to peek out of the terminal window. I immediately see Sophie in front of the airport. I'm assuming the guy whose lap she's sitting on is Seb. Maisie's standing a few feet from them—talking on the phone.

Butch looks out the window. "I see Seb Miller. I'm assuming the one he's almost inhaling is Sophie."

"Yeah, that's her," I say, sighing. "Have you ever seen a more beautiful couple?"

"As a matter of fact," he says, wrapping his arm around

my waist and lifting me off the bench, "I'm looking at a more beautiful couple right now."

"What?" I say, squinting at him. "Who?"

He shakes his head. "Did you already forget we're supposed to be a couple?"

"No!" I say, trying to sound convincing.

"You work for the CIA. How are you so bad at this? You're going to blow your cover within the first few seconds."

"I am not," I say, throwing my shoulders back. "I'm on vacation. I forgot for a second. I'm good now—locked and loaded."

"You're so far from that right now. Seriously, girl, breathe. I've seen you keep your focus in the most stressful life-or-death situations at work. How are you letting this get to you?"

"It's not getting to me. I just haven't seen Sophie and Maisie for a while. I'm excited—"

"Terrified is more like it." He grabs my shoulders and steadies me. "This is kind of fun. I've never seen you so scattered. Let's make it interesting. I've got a hundred that says you blow your cover in the first five minutes."

"No deal," I say, pushing him away from me. "One bet with you per vacation is plenty."

"That's fine," he chuckles. "I'm good with just winning the one. And speaking of that bet, when you see the guy you want to target, our signal is head patting. Do you think you can remember that part?"

I let out a long, shaky breath. "You know, maybe we should just turn around and go back home?"

"We're not doing that." He points at me. "Stay right there. I have to use the men's. When I get back, we're going out there together to start our carefree vacation. Do you under-stand me?"

"No," I say, shaking my head forcefully. He stops it, grabs my chin, and nods it up and down.

"Yes, Butch," he says in a falsetto voice. "I understand your command and I'll do anything you want me to do."

"My voice doesn't sound like that," I say, swatting his hand away. "And I'm not doing anything you want me to do. In fact, I'm not doing anything you want me to do."

"There she is," he says, walking backward into the bath-room. "Welcome back, Trouble. I thought I'd lost you there for a second."

As he disappears, a man walks out. "Trouble, huh?" he says, raising his eyebrows. "How'd you get that nickname?"

"Many hours of putting in the hard work."

"Nice," he says, grinning. When I see his gleaming, white teeth pop out of his beautiful caramel skin, I take a quick breath. He holds out his hand. "You okay?"

I nod, but I can't seem to make words come out of my mouth. He's the most beautiful man I've ever seen.

"Okay, well, welcome to the Virgin Islands, Trouble. Have you ever been here?"

"Nope." I finally get out a word. "My first time. I guess I'm kind of a Virgin Islands virgin."

He grins at me again. This time I notice a dimple on his left cheek. I really want to touch it. "A virgin, huh?"

"Ignore me, please," I say, looking up to the ceiling. "Sorry. My humor's usually not that cheesy. It's been a long day."

"It's fine," he says, still smiling. "I thought it was cute.

Have fun on the islands."

My eyes are glued to him as he walks through to the baggage area. He has a wickedly perfect body—about six feet tall with wide shoulders, a thin waist, and chiseled arms. And as he turns the corner, I notice a very muscular butt that's highlighted beautifully by his bright pink swim trunks. I stare at the door for a full minute before someone taps me on the shoulder.

"Are you in a trance?" Butch says, shaking my shoulders. "What's wrong with you? Why are you sweating? It's not that hot in here."

"Nothing's wrong," I say, spinning around to him. "Are you ready?"

"I need to call my mom real quick. She called me three times while we were in the air."

"Your grandma again?"

"Probably. You know she's been declining for a while now." He squeezes my hand. "I'm fine. Really."

"I'm sorry, Butch. I'll give you some space. Meet me by the luggage carousel."

"Okay, but don't try to lift your bag without me," he says, looking up from his phone. "I don't want to find you crushed under your suitcase."

"I'm stronger than I look." I curl my arm to show off my muscles.

"What are you trying to show me there?" He squints his eyes. "Your arms are smaller than my toothpick."

"Only a couple of days into retirement and you already need glasses," I say, still flexing as I back out of the room. "My arms are jacked."

He rolls his eyes as he turns around and walks in the other direction. "Hey Mom," I hear him say as I head toward the baggage carousel.

My suitcase is already on the belt and about ready to disappear into the back area. I sprint over and grab the handle. I'm pulling on it as hard as I can, but I'm losing the battle until another hand grabs it.

"Here, let me get it for you," a man says from behind me as he lifts the bag with ease and puts it down next to me. "Damn, that's heavy. Do you want me to help you out to your car with it?"

"No, I don't need a porter," I say, not looking at him. I try to grab the handle as my parrot bag slips from my shoulder—spilling its contents across the floor.

"Oh, uh, I'm not a porter," he says as he crouches beside me.

I finally look at his face. It's pink swim trunks guy. His glowing smile's still in place.

"Oh, wow, yeah, that's probably not an approved porter uniform. Sorry," I say as he puts the last of my things back in my bag and hands it to me.

"All good," he says, nodding toward my bag. "I noticed you're reading Half-Blood Prince. Is this your first time reading the Harry Potter series?"

"What? No," I say, my mouth falling open. "They've been out for like twenty years."

"Sorry," he says, laughing. "I didn't mean to offend you. So you're reading them again?"

"Just re-reading this one. It's the best book in the series."

"That's not true," he says, scrunching up his face. "The

Prisoner of Azkaban is way better."

"What?" I take a step back from him. "Stop embarrassing yourself. That's just a bad take."

"Hmm." He lifts my suitcase again and does a few curls with it. His huge, beautiful bicep jumps out of his T-shirt. "Feels like you packed the entire series in here. Maybe we can read them together on the beach and decide which one is the best."

"Uh," I say. "My boyfriend's just over there."

"The scary-looking guy's your boyfriend?" he says, putting the bag back down. "The one I passed going into the restroom?"

"That's him," I say, "but he's friendlier than he looks."

"That would almost have to be the case because he looks downright terrifying." He holds his arms in the air as he takes a step backward. When he raises them, his T-shirt comes up a little revealing a six-pack that flows down into his swim trunks like a finely carved set of stairs. "Understood. You're taken. I'm backing away slowly. Have a nice vacation, Trouble. Yellow's a good color on you, by the way."

"Yeah, you, t-too," I stutter, my eyes glued to his abs. "I mean the having a good time part, not the yellow part. Although yellow might be a good color on you. I can't be sure until I see you wearing it."

"Next time we meet," he says, grinning again, "I'll make sure I'm wearing yellow so you can tell me. I might even get a big parrot bag like that."

"Maybe get a bag with a shark on it to match the sharks all over your swim trunks," I say, pointing at them. I pull my hand back when his eyebrows shoot up.

"You got a good look at my trunks, huh?" He purses his lips hard, trying not to laugh. "You're very observant."

I look down as my face starts to burn. "Yep, it's a blessing and a curse."

"Okay then, Trouble. It was nice to meet you. My name's Alex, by the way."

He smiles at me again before he turns around and walks toward the arrivals area. I'm frozen in place, watching his beautiful backside walk away when I hear something behind me. I turn around to find Butch staring at me.

"What?" I look up at him. "Did you say something?"

"Yes. Are your ears clogged from the plane?" He points to my bag. "Didn't I tell you to let me lift your suitcase?"

"It's good. Some guy lifted it for me."

"What guy?" he says, scanning the room.

"I don't know. Some guy. He's gone now. And you don't need to be suspicious of everyone anymore. You're retired now, remember?"

"Old habits, die hard, sister. Let me live." As we start walking, his eyes fix on something. "You didn't tell me your friends were both with baseball players."

"They're not. Only Sophie. Maisie married her high school sweetheart. He's some kind of financial thing."

He turns me around so I'm looking at them as they walk into the terminal. "Well, those two guys are both baseball players. The tall blondish guy is Seb Miller. The other one— wearing pink shorts—is Alejandro Molina. They both play for Miami."

Chapter Twelve

ALEX

As I walk out of the luggage area, I take one more look at Trouble. She's still looking at me. She looks down at her suitcase quickly and rolls it in the other direction. I start to walk away, but it's hard to take my eyes off her. She can't be much over five feet, but she seems larger than life for some reason. From the way she carries herself, I can tell she's confident, but she also seems kind of awkward. It's a weird—and adorable—mix.

I glance over at her boyfriend who's on the phone. He's not much taller than me, but he's ripped from head-to-toe. His face is shielded by a baseball cap he has pulled low over his eyes. All I can see clearly are his nose—which looks like it's been broken a few times—and a very unkept beard.

As he talks on the phone, his eyes do a constant sweep of the room. On this sweep, he sees me looking at him. His eyes fix on me so hard that I'm surprised his glare doesn't knock me to the floor. I return the look for a second before I head back to the waiting area. When I get there, Seb, Sophie, and Maisie have finally made it inside.

"We thought we lost you, man," Seb says. "Were you preening in the bathroom mirror again?"

Maisie hugs me around the waist. "Alex doesn't have to preen. He always looks this beautiful."

I squeeze her shoulders and put my head on top of hers. I must look like I'm enjoying the hug too much because Seb grabs her left hand and holds it up to me.

"Happily married," he says. "Catch and release, brother."

"Fine." I give her shoulders one more squeeze before I let her go. "Where's your husband, by the way? Did he make it down?"

"No," Maisie says. "He's back home. It's his busy season at work."

"He trusts you down here with baseball players all over the place?"

She sighs as she smiles up at me. "We started dating when we were sixteen and never broke up once. We even survived going to college across the country from each other. We're hopelessly in love."

"Another happy couple," I mutter. "I've got to get new friends."

"Ricky's looking for a new leader," Sophie says. "I don't think he knows what to do without Seb around all the time."

"Hard pass," I say, my teeth clenched.

Seb looks up and laughs. "Ricky's getting to you already, huh?"

"He's fine—"

"Liar." Maisie points at me. "Ricky's the opposite of fine.

He's a pain in the ass. I'm still convinced that he's actively trying to break up Seb and Sophie."

"He's not trying to break us up," Sophie says, grabbing Maisie's arm. "Stop saying that. If anyone's trying to break us up, it's Savannah."

"Yeah, but Savannah's trying to separate you so she can get with Seb."

"Mae, stop. Please," Seb says, pulling Sophie into his arms. "I'd rather date Ricky than Savannah."

"I think Ricky would be okay with that," I say. "He's always been a little too into you. And I agree with Maisie that he's trying to break you up. This afternoon he said—"

"Good luck breaking us up," Seb says, laughing as he kisses the top of Sophie's head. He gives me a quick, but stern look that tells me Sophie doesn't know about Ricky's active campaign against the wedding.

"I wonder where Raine is." Sophie looks at her phone again. "Her plane landed like twenty minutes ago. Do you think she ditched us again?"

"Probably," Maisie says. "When's the last time you talked to her?"

"We texted this morning. She said she was headed to the airport. I'll text her again."

"Maybe her *date* backed out on her," Maisie says, using finger quotes. "She probably panicked and missed the flight."

"Why the air quotes?" I ask.

Maisie turns to Sophie. "What are the chances you think she's dating him?"

"Is there less percentage than zero?" Sophie says. "She's bringing him so we won't try to set her up. He's a beard."

"A beard?"

"Yeah, you know," Maisie says, turning to me, "a disguise, a fake boyfriend."

"So if I bring a lady beard to these events, you'll leave me alone?" I say, looking at Sophie.

"Not a chance. You're way too good of a catch to waste your time with a beard."

"Baby," Seb says. "Give him a break. Sometimes it just has to happen—like with us."

"Oh my God," Maisie says, pushing his shoulder. "Do you think you'd be with her today if I hadn't interfered? You both were being stubborn idiots until I forced the issue."

"Yeah, you're not wrong—" Seb says, jerking his head back as Sophie busts out of his arms.

"Raine!" she screams. Before I can even look up, Sophie's bolting across the airport. She collides with someone with such force that they both tumble to the ground. Maisie arrives a second later and throws herself on top of them. As the pile shifts around, I see a peek of bright, yellow material. My heart starts racing as I quickly realize that Trouble is Raine.

Raine's boyfriend gets to the pile at the same time Seb jogs over. He reaches down and pulls Maisie and Raine up as Seb untangles Sophie. I inch over toward them as I try to give my mind time to process that the woman I was hitting on is Raine.

"You teach her that tackle move?" The boyfriend says to Seb as he steadies Raine. "I thought you played baseball, not football."

"I do," Seb says as he puts his hands under Sophie's arms and pulls her to her feet. "That's the first time I'm seeing her open-field tackling skills. Makes me love her even more. I'm Seb Miller."

"I know who you are. Big fan," the boyfriend says, shaking Seb's hand. "Butch Harrison."

Sophie hugs Butch. "It's so nice to meet you, Butch. I'm Sophie. Raine has told me absolutely nothing about you except that you're a Navy SEAL and you met while you were working together."

"I—" Raine says.

Butch slides his arm around Raine. "It's nice to meet you, too, Sophie, and frankly, I'm one of those people you can't quite describe. It's better to just meet me in person."

"You must be Raine," Seb says, smiling as he shakes her hand. "Sophie's told me so much about your time growing up in Chicago. I met your mom the last time we were there."

"Yeah, Mom won't quit talking about you," she says, smiling. "You've made her a dedicated baseball fan—or a dedicated Seb Miller fan anyway."

Seb turns around and pulls me from behind him. "This is my buddy Alex Molina. He plays for the team, too."

Raine looks around Seb and finally sees me. Her eyes get wide. "Uh—"

"Hey, Trouble," I say, smiling at her. "Sorry, I'm not wearing yellow. I didn't know we'd be meeting again this soon."

"You two know each other?" Butch says, his steely eyes staring at me from underneath the bill of his cap.

"We just met. I helped her with her bag," I say, looking down at her. "I didn't realize you were the famous Raine at the time."

"What? Did you think my real name was Trouble?"

"Maybe just hoping it was," I say, trying to control the grin that keeps growing on my face.

"Aww," Sophie says, slipping her arm through mine. "You have a nickname for her already."

"Stop," I whisper, squeezing her arm tight against me.

Raine glares at Sophie as she grabs Butch's hand.

Maisie points at their hands. "So how long have you two been dating?"

Butch puts his arm around Raine's waist and lets his hand slide down to her butt. He squeezes it. "I don't know, babe, like six months, right?"

"Oh my God!" she says, throwing his hand down and slapping him across the chest. "Don't ever squeeze my butt again."

Sophie and Maisie laugh and high-five each other. They both cross their arms and look at Raine.

"We're not dating, okay? We're just friends. I brought him so you two wouldn't try to meddle in my love life as usual."

"Way to keep your cover," Butch says, swatting her butt. She slugs him on the shoulder. "Good thing you work for the State Department and not the CIA or something. You'd make a horrible spy."

She sticks her tongue out at him. "I could have done it if you hadn't touched my butt."

"Hate to break it to you, but couples touch each other's butts," Butch says. "Seb hasn't taken his hand off Sophie's butt since we got here."

"And I don't plan to." Seb smiles as he spreads his hand out further. "Unless she asks me to—"

"Never. I want you to touch it more often." Sophie tilts her head up for a kiss.

"Who do they remind you of?" Butch says, nudging Raine.

"Millie and Mason," she groans. "I think they're just as cute and I didn't think that was possible. Another happy couple. I've got to get new friends."

Everyone spins around and looks at Raine.

"What?" she says. "I was joking."

"No, it's just that Alex said that same thing about five minutes ago," Maisie laughs. "Almost to the word."

"Aww, look you two are already thinking alike—"

"Sophie," Raine says, grabbing her shoulders. "Stop. I'm sorry, Alex. She's obsessed with setting me up with any single man who's within a hundred feet of me."

"It's fine," I say. "She tries to do that with me, too. I mean with women, though. I'll protect you from her."

"Mae," Sophie says, grabbing Raine's arm and pulling her into a group hug with Maisie. "Alex wants to protect Raine."

"Oh my God, stop. Sophie!" Raine laughs as she tries to break out of their hug.

"Sorry, man," Seb whispers to me. "I did tell her to stop."

"I'm guessing from the way Alex is looking at Raine he doesn't much want her to stop," Butch says, gnawing on the toothpick that's dangling from his mouth.

"Do you have all of your bags?" Seb says, looking at Butch. "We should probably get going. The party starts in two hours. We don't want to miss the next ferry over to St. John."

"Yeah," Butch says. "Just two bags. My duffle and her enormous trunk filled to the brim with books."

"Books," Sophie whispers as she grabs my arm again.

"Stop." I bump her with my hip.

"Here, I'll grab Raine's bag," I say, reaching for her suitcase. Butch gives me a wry grin. "I mean unless you want to carry it, Butch."

"Naw, you're good."

"I'm just trying to be polite," I say, staring at him.

"Is that what you're trying to be?" he says, locking his eyes with mine. His face is still tight, but I think I see a slight twinkle in his eyes.

"Butch," Raine says. She pulls his chin toward her as she starts tapping on her head.

"What's wrong, Raine? Why are you tapping your head?" Butch says, smiling. "You got a headache or something?"

"No," she says, her eyes getting wider as she continues to tap her head. "I'm just trying to pop my ears from the flight."

"Is that what you're doing?" Butch laughs as he puts his arm around her and pulls her toward the exit. He puts her in a headlock and starts messing up her hair.

"Stop it," she says, laughing as she tries to break his hold.

I let them get out of earshot before I whisper to Seb, "Didn't she say they weren't dating?"

"Yeah," he whispers, "but from the look Butch gave you, you'd better keep your eyes—and hands—to yourself until we're sure."

"I might have my eyes and hands removed to be safe," I say as I start rolling Raine's bag toward the door. "I'm not looking to die on this trip."

Chapter Thirteen

RAINE

After we drop Seb and Sophie off at their private villa, Maisie, Alex, Butch, and I head to the resort. Alex is driving with Butch riding shotgun. I can tell by their tense shoulders that they're still feeling each other out, but at least they're talking —something about Alex's new contract with his team.

I turn toward Maisie as we wind through a narrow, heavily vegetated road "Did Sophie tell me her friend was reserving the entire resort for her wedding guests?"

"Yeah," she says. "It's kind of like a soft opening for the resort to get the staff ready for the grand opening next month. Roman and his husband, Michael, bought it a few years back. They've renovated it into an exclusive forty-suite resort. It's gorgeous."

"It's pretty amazing that he's giving it to her exclusively. He's a former client, right?"

"Former client and now one of her best friends. He and Michael adore her."

"What's not to adore?" I say as I take her hand. "She seems really happy with Seb. Do you approve?"

"Highly approve," Maisie says, nodding. "The highest approval rating I could give anyone. Seb's wild about her and he treats her like the goddess she is. They're great together."

"Yeah, that's the feeling I get. They seem perfect—like you and Ryan."

Maisie squeezes my hand. "They are perfect, but how about you? Are you interested in anyone?"

Alex looks at me in the rearview mirror. When my eyes meet his, he looks back at the road.

"Uh, not really," I say, lowering my voice. "You know I work a lot. I don't meet that many guys."

"Well you're on vacation now, maybe you'll meet someone here," she says, pushing the back of Alex's seat. "Isn't that right, Alex? Vacation is a great place to meet people —not to mention weddings. This weekend is made for finding that special someone."

"Very subtle," he says, reaching his arm into the back seat and slapping Maisie's leg. "Sorry, Raine. She's not as bad as Sophie, but she's bad enough."

"Just trying to be helpful—"

"Oh look, we're at the resort," Alex says. "No more time for playing matchmaker."

He brings the van to a quick stop in front of the valet stand.

"Good afternoon," the valet says as he opens our doors. "If anyone's checking in, the reception desk is to your left as you walk into the lobby. I'll bring your bags to you."

"That's all right, chief," Butch says, grabbing our bags from the back. "We're good."

"Let him take the bags if he wants to," I whisper.

"No one touches my stuff, except me," Butch growls.

"Seriously? This is your carefree side? Let me know when Island Butch arrives."

I leave him to wrangle the bags as I walk into the open-air lobby. The smell stops me in my tracks. I take a deep breath. The sweet scent of lilies is mixing perfectly with the salty ocean air. Everywhere I look bougainvilleas are draping over trellises and falling into the lobby in waterfalls of pink, red, yellow, and purple buds. Deep green palm plants surround a small fountain in the middle of the lobby. Teak wood couches with plush, white cushions peek out from every corner of the room. I feel relaxed for the first time in five years.

"What's up, Alex? You good?" I turn around to see a man walking toward us—dressed head-to-toe in black.

"Damn, Joe. You're in the Caribbean," Alex says. "Could you not add a little color to your wardrobe?"

"You know I don't like to stand out."

"Actually you stand out like a sore thumb here," Alex laughs. "Hey, I didn't see you over at Seb's this afternoon. You're usually glued to his side."

"Yeah, he's been keeping me at more of a distance since he met Sophie," Joe says with a little growl to his voice.

"You know it's not personal," Alex says. "He doesn't mean anything by it. He just likes alone time with her. Speaking of Sophie, this is her friend Raine—uh, I don't even know your last name."

"Raine Laghari," I say, holding my hand out to Joe. "I grew up with Sophie in Chicago."

"Nice to meet you, Raine. I'm Joe, the head of security for the team."

"And this is my friend Butch Harrison," I say, pulling Butch into the group.

"Butch," Joe says, shaking his hand, "I can spot another military man from a mile away."

"Yeah, Navy," Butch says. "You?"

"I was a Marine. You a SEAL?"

"Was. Just retired," Butch says, nodding. "Maybe I'll get into your line of work—protect some ballplayers."

"I'd hire you in a second, but I'm not sure we need your kind of firepower. It's a pretty easy gig. A lot of the time I feel like a glorified babysitter."

"It got a little more serious for you this past year, though," Alex says. "I mean with all that stuff about the Randalls. Have you heard anything from them since they sold the team? Seb said they were suing you."

"They were trying," Joe says, "but they withdrew the suit. They've got their hands full with the criminal stuff. A lot of women came forward with complaints after that story ran in the newspaper."

"I read about that," Butch says. "The team owner's son was sexually harassing female staff, right? Do you think any of the charges will stick?"

"I'm not sure—probably a few," Joe says. "I think the son, Gentry, might be looking at some light jail time. Regardless, their family's reputation is ruined. The team's minority owners forced the dad, Gary, to sell. And the board of directors at his transportation company asked him to step down as CEO. If he doesn't do it voluntarily, I think they'll vote him out. Honestly, I stopped following it. I want to forget about them."

"Yeah," Alex says. "We all do. Seb said they even came after Sophie for a hot minute—"

"What?" I say, my eyes narrowing. "Who came after Sophie?"

"Uh," Alex says. "I'm not sure I was supposed to say anything about that."

"You already did," I say, locking my eyes with his. "Finish it."

"Sophie was the one who exposed the Randalls," Alex says, lowering his voice. "Gentry harassed her when she was working for the team. She gave the information to the media."

"Did he hurt her?" I hiss.

"No," Joe laughs. "More like she hurt him—gave him a black eye and a hard blow to his balls. She's tougher than she looks."

"Yes, she is." I nod. "Are they still coming after her?"

"I think Roman put an end to that," Alex says. "Maybe ask her more about it. We've probably said too much already."

"Roman? The guy who owns this resort?" I say, squinting as my mind tries to process all of this new information. "What does he have to do with anything?"

Joe steps forward and whispers, "I think Roman is, uh, connected, shall we say. He's a cool guy, but I wouldn't want to get on his bad side. He protects Sophie like one of his family. I'm certain that he had a conversation with the Randalls about leaving Sophie alone."

"Huh. All very interesting," I say, grabbing Butch's arm. "Well, Butch and I should check in. Nice to meet you, Joe. We'll see you guys around."

As I pull Butch toward the check-in desk, he whispers, "Look at that, the island air's already making you soft. All that intelligence you just received and you're not even interested in pursuing it?"

"You know me *way* better than that. I'll be pursuing every last piece of that information," I whisper as I hand the front-desk attendant my ID. "I've been taking care of Sophie since we were kids. No one gets close to her. Will you keep an eye on her for me?"

"That will definitely be my pleasure."

"Not in a weird way. I'm being serious," I say as I grab our room keys. "Watch her. I'm probably overreacting, but it sounds like she might have gotten in the crosshairs."

"I've got you," he says as he does a quick sweep of the lobby. "No one gets close to her except Seb."

I hand him his key. "I'm room sixteen. You're twenty-four."

"Looks like you're that way and I'm on the other side," he says. "Did you purposely ask for our rooms to be across the resort from each other?"

"No, but the universe is clearly on my side."

"So from the vigorous head tapping you did at the airport, I'm guessing you'd like Alex to be your target man for the bet."

"What?" I say, looking up at him. "No, definitely no. I was just trying to get you to be nice to Sophie's friends."

He nods as he strokes his beard. "You're not attracted to him?"

"Of course, I'm attracted to him, Butch," I say, taking a step back. "Did you look at him? I mean, I'm sweating just thinking about him, but he's a stunningly gorgeous professional athlete. That's too big of a mountain to climb, especially since we're just here for the weekend."

"I don't know, sister. I think that mountain would like to be climbed—by you. He was flirting pretty hard."

"He was not," I say, shaking my head. "He was just being nice because I'm Sophie's friend."

"All right, if you say so." He takes another sweep of the lobby. "I'm going to get a nap in before the party. You want me to walk you to your room?"

"No, I'm good," I say, grabbing the handle of my suitcase. "Pick me up at seven."

"The party starts at seven. I'll be at your room by at least six-thirty."

"We're not on military time anymore. We're on island time."

"What the fuck is island time?" He starts walking away and then turns back around. "It sounds like something made up to torture me."

"I thought we were both supposed to let loose this weekend," I yell after him. "Or do you have double standards?"

He taps his phone a few times and makes a beeping sound. "All right. If that's what you want, Island Butch is officially activated. There's no putting him back in his bottle now."

As he walks away, I glance at the room number directional

sign on the wall. It's pointing me down a small flight of stairs toward the oceanfront rooms.

"Hey," I hear from behind me. "Let me carry the suitcase down the stairs for you."

I turn around to see Alex rushing toward me.

"Hey," I say. "Uh, I was going to look for an elevator—"

"No need," he says, smiling as he grabs the suitcase and lifts it down the five stairs.

I follow him. "Thanks. I'm usually a better packer than this. I wasn't sure what to bring. It's been a while since I've had a vacation."

"Well for a beach vacation all you really need is a swimsuit."

"Typical guy thing to say. Thanks for the packing tips, though."

He rolls the bag away from me as I try to grab the handle. "I'll help you to your room," he says, motioning me ahead of him.

"Oh, I'm just a couple of rooms from here."

"That's too bad," he says. "It won't give us much time to talk."

I look up at him as we reach my room. He's still smiling, but his eyes are really intense all of a sudden.

"Uh, thank you so much," I say, turning away from him quickly as I swipe my key card. "You've saved me more than once today."

"It was my pleasure. You want me to lift it onto a luggage rack or something?"

Before I can answer, the room door next to mine flies open. A woman in a tiny red bikini bounds out.

"Alex!" she screams as she throws herself into his arms. "I thought I heard you out here. How did you find out where my room is? I was just about to text you."

Chapter Fourteen

ALEX

"I didn't know this was your room," I say, pushing Allie back as she practically tries to hump me. "I was helping Raine to her room. I guess she's next door to you.

Allie whips around to look at Raine. "And who is Raine?"

"Raine Laghari. She's a friend of Sophie's from Chicago." I take another step back from Allie as she tries to put her arm around my waist. "Raine, this is Allie Williams—another friend of Sophie's—but I'm forgetting how you know her. College?"

"My last name is Williamson," Allie says, ignoring Raine's outstretched hand. "And Sophie and I worked together at a PR agency right after college. I don't blame Alex for not remembering, since I told him that right after we had sex."

"Wow," Raine says, taking a step back into her room. "That's my cue to disappear. It was nice to meet you, Allie. Thanks for your help, Alex. You two have fun."

"Raine, wait," I say as she slams the door.

I grab Allie's arm and pull her away from Raine's room. "What the hell, Allie? You know I'm a private person. Don't say shit like that, especially in front of people you don't know."

"Alex," she says, laughing. "It's not like everyone doesn't know we're dating—"

"We're not dating. How many times do I need to tell you that?"

"Okay, then hanging out, but we did have sex and I'd like to have more of it—a lot more." I block her as she tries to hug me again. "Why are you mad at me? You're hurting my feelings."

"I don't mean to hurt your feelings," I say, letting out a long breath. "And I'm not mad at you, but I told you last week, I'm not looking for a serious thing."

"Neither am I," she says as she grabs a beach bag out of her room and slams the door. "I'm headed down to the pool. Walk down there with me and say hi to the girls."

"I need to go to my room and get ready for the party."

"It's a pool party," she says, pointing to my swim trunks and then linking her arm through mine. "You're already ready. Come on, you were mean to me. This will make me feel better."

"Fine," I say, sighing as she starts pulling me toward the pool.

I glance back at Raine's door as we turn the corner. Maybe Rosa was right about me being too nice. I'm probably going to need to do something about that.

"Where were you this afternoon?" Manny says as I walk across the pool deck to a group of my teammates. "We looked for you to play golf."

"I headed over to Seb's place and helped them pick up some of Sophie's friends from the airport."

"So you'll do favors for anyone except for me apparently," Caroline says, glaring at me. "If Cece were here, I wouldn't have been a golf widow all afternoon."

"Caroline, you need to get over the Cece thing," Manny says. "And I wasn't gone that long. You weren't even here when I got back."

"I told you I went shopping," she hisses. "You're going to lose a lot of money on this trip. When I get bored, I spend."

"You spend all the time—bored, excited, in your sleep," Manny says. "One of these days I'm going to quit playing and you're going to have to learn to live within a budget."

Caroline rolls her eyes. "So Seb can give little Sophie an all expenses paid wedding at an exclusive Caribbean resort for a hundred of their friends and family, but I have to work within a budget?"

Manny rubs his hands over his face. "I've told you, it's not a competition. And Seb makes way more than I do—"

"Way more than all of us do," Jack says. "All of us combined. And y'all need to lighten up on Sophie. She's cool."

Jack's wife, Casey, grabs his arm. "Jack has a crush on Sophie."

"I don't have a crush on her. I'm just saying, you could lighten up on the rookie hazing. Maybe invite her to one of your Wife Wednesday happy hours or something."

"Jack," Caroline says, "the title has "wife" in it for a reason. We don't accept random girlfriends. They come and go like the wind."

"They're getting married in two days," I say. "She's about as close to a wife as she's going to get."

"I don't see a wedding ring on her finger yet," Caroline says, pointing to her ring.

"What? That diamond on her finger that's the size of a small planet isn't enough?" Manny says.

"No, it's not. That's just like a dinner reservation," Caroline says, linking her arm with Casey's and pulling her away from us. "They arrived at the restaurant, but we'll see if they actually eat the dinner."

"Damn," I say, blowing out a breath as I watch them walk away. "They really don't like Sophie."

"What gave it away, Einstein?" Jack says. "Those two have been coming at Sophie since day one. I keep telling Casey to get to know her, but she lets Caroline whip her up into a fury."

"Can we please quit talking about our wives? Anything has to be more interesting than their mean girl pity party," Manny says, turning toward me. "Who was that little thing I saw you walk in with? Her ass is something else."

"The redhead?"

"Do you have more than one beautiful ass following you around?" He holds up his hand. "No, don't answer that. It'll make me too depressed."

"That's the Allie woman Sophie set me up with. I told you about her. We had a couple of dates and she started stalking me after I didn't call again. She's the one who showed up to my autograph-signing event and tried to sit at the table with me—like she was my wife or something."

"Yeah, right," he says. "I remember now, but you didn't say she looked like that. That's worth a few more dates, right?"

"Not at all. She's a fame whore. She doesn't know the first thing about me. She wants to date me for the attention and the money." I nod toward Caroline and Casey. "You two know what I'm talking about—you married women just like her."

"Fuck you," Jack says, laughing as he walks away. "We're playing poker later tonight in Will's room if you want to stop by. Despite your bad attitude, I'll still take your money."

"Shit," I say, "like either one of you has ever beat me. You know I have the best poker face around."

"I'm happy to try again," Manny says, following Jack, "but I'm hoping you'll be occupied with something more interesting than us."

"Everything's more interesting than you," I yell after him. He flips me off without looking back.

I do another scan of the party to try to find Raine. I've been looking for her for at least an hour. I still don't see her.

"You looking for someone, Alex?" I turn around to see Roman and Michael closing in on me.

"If you're looking for me," Michael says, hugging me, "I'm right here, honey."

"You know I'm always looking for you, Michael," I say, squeezing him. "Didn't we agree that we're party partners for life?"

"Yes," he says, slipping his arm through mine. "You

desperately need me to bring you out of your shell. You'd hide in a corner all night if it weren't for me."

"Maybe he wants to hang out in a corner," Roman says. "Not everyone can be as socially extroverted as you."

"No one's as socially extroverted as Michael." I motion to the bartender for another beer. "That's why I need his help."

"I'm glad you made it down," Roman says. "Sophie said you were on the fence."

"Is there anyone who can say no to Sophie?" I say, taking a long drink.

"If there is, I haven't met him," Roman says as he motions toward the hotel. "What do you think of the place? It's not quite perfect yet, but we're close."

"It's beautiful," I say. "My room's like a palace. The tub's the size of a small swimming pool."

"Room enough for two," Michael says, pulling me closer. "Do you have your eyes on any of the ladies?"

"Stop being nosy," Roman says, pulling him away from me.

"It's fine," I say. "Actually, there is one I have my eyes on—"

"Hey, Alex, you seen Raine?" Butch walks up from behind me. I jump when I hear her name.

"Hey, uh, no. I thought you were picking her up at her room." I look around the patio again to see if I can find her.

"Yeah, when I got there, Sophie and Maisie were in her room. They told me they were having a girl chat and that I had to leave—like I wanted to stay for that anyway."

"Butch, this is Roman Garcia and his husband, Michael. They own the resort," I say. "This is Butch Harrison, he's—"

"Raine's guest," Roman says, shaking Butch's hand. "Sophie was so excited you two were coming to the wedding. Welcome."

"Appreciate it," Butch says. "This is quite a place you have here. I've never stayed anywhere close to this nice."

"Well you're welcome back any time," Roman says.

"Any time," Michael echoes as he scans Butch's body slowly.

"My brothers and I are going deep-sea fishing tomorrow if you want to join us," Roman says to Butch. "I've never met a Southerner who doesn't like to fish."

"And you still haven't," Butch says, laughing. "My damn accent gives me away every time."

"Yeah, you've got quite the drawl," Roman says. "Alabama?"

"The hell you say." Butch throws his hand over his chest. "This is pure Georgia, right here."

"Well, Georgia, we'd love to have you along. I caught a monster barracuda the last time we were out. Damn thing fought me for more than an hour."

"I'd love to go out with you," Butch says, rubbing his hands together. "Let me check with Raine to make sure she's covered tomorrow."

"I'll keep an eye on her."

"I bet you will," Butch says, spinning his head to me. He looks back at Roman and Michael. "I think Alex has a little crush on Raine."

"Wait, I thought you were dating Raine," Michael says, pointing at Butch.

"That's none of our business, honey. It was nice to meet

you, Butch," Roman says, pulling Michael away. "We're leaving at eight tomorrow morning if you want to join us. Meet us at the front desk."

"Roger that," Butch says. He turns back to me. "Do you have a thing for Raine or not?"

"Look, man, if you two are dating or thinking about dating or thinking about thinking about dating, I'll steer way clear of her."

He rubs his hand over his beard. "We're not dating and we'll never date. She's like a little sister to me."

"Then yeah, I think she's interesting—way more interesting than anyone I've been around recently."

"Even that little redhead who was wrapped around you like a boa constrictor about a half-hour ago."

I straighten up quickly. "I'm not with her—at all."

"Does she know that?" he says, his eyebrows raising almost to his hairline.

"I've told her."

He holds up his hand. "Look man, I'm not telling you how to do your thing. In fact, I don't care at all, but if you're looking at Raine as another notch on the bedpost, you need to keep looking. She's way too good for all that and I'll kill any man who hurts her."

"I—"

"Nope," he says holding up his hand again. "I'm not her dad, and you and I aren't friends. Do what you want, but if you come at her, it better be with pure intentions. I won't warn you again. Are we clear?"

"Crystal."

"Now, what's the redhead's name? If you aren't into her, I can distract her for you."

"Allie," I say, "but I'd steer clear. She's a little crazy."

"Aww, brother," he says, chucking my shoulder as he walks away, "I like them a little crazy—at least for one night."

Chapter Fifteen

RAINE

"It's a pool party, Raine," Sophie says, sighing. "You have to wear a swimsuit."

When I hesitate, Maisie jumps over to my suitcase and starts rifling through it.

"Raine," she says, looking up at me, "why are there at least ten books in here? You're not studying the entire trip like you did on our eighth grade spring break."

"I'm not in school anymore, Mae. I don't need to study," I say, grabbing the book she's holding up. "They're pleasure books—vacation books."

"This one's called *Criminal Profiling: The Forensic Science*," she says, pulling out another one.

I grab that one, too. "Like I said, pleasure books. Sophie, make her leave me alone."

Sophie's rubbing suntan lotion on her arms when I look back at her. She's taken off her sundress to reveal a skimpy white bikini.

"Oh my God," I whine, "put your body away. Why does it look like that? It's the reason I don't want to wear a swimsuit."

She tilts her head and raises her eyebrows. I swear she's been doing that same thing since we were five, and every time she does it, I know I'm about to do anything she asks me.

"Get your swimsuit out now, Raine," she says, pointing at my suitcase. "If you didn't pack any, you can wear one of mine."

"Like I have anything on my body that could fill up even a part of your swimsuits." I grab my one-piece out of the suit-case—stuffing the tiny bikini Millie made me buy to the bottom of the bag—and head to the bathroom to change.

"Really?" Maisie yells after me. "Can you still not change in front of us? We've known each other more than twenty years."

"Leave me alone, bossy," I say, closing the door and locking it.

"If you come out of there wearing a wetsuit, I'm getting the scissors," Maisie says, banging on the door.

When I'm done changing, I peek out. They're sitting on the bed, staring at the door. I pull the towel tighter around my chest and walk out slowly.

Sophie leaps off the bed and pulls the towel off me. She gasps. "Oh my God! That suit's adorable. It's so low-cut. Look, Mae, Raine has boobs."

"Quit," I say, slapping her hands away. "Is it too much?"

"It's just right. That emerald green color is gorgeous on you," Maisie says, bouncing off the bed and turning me toward the mirror. "Look how hot you are. Seriously, I don't think I've ever seen this much of your skin."

"Millie made me buy a bunch of new clothes before we left," I say, pulling on the suit to try to make it cover more of my breasts.

"Who's Millie again?" Maisie says, flopping back down on the bed.

"My best friend—"

"Excuse me?" Sophie says, pulling her sundress back on. "I've held that title since birth. She can get in line."

"My best friend from my work life then."

"Does she work at the State Department, too?" Maisie asks.

"Uh, no, not exactly," I say, grabbing the matching cover up out of my bag. "Let's get to the party. The guest of honor shouldn't be late."

"When has Sophie ever been on time for anything?" Maisie laughs. "So I noticed Alex looking at you in the rearview mirror when we were driving over here this afternoon. I think he's into you."

"He is not. He just likes to make eye contact when he talks."

"He was making a lot of eye contact with your ass as we were walking out of the airport," Maisie says.

"And he was all tongue-tied," Sophie says. "I've never seen him nervous around a woman."

"That was probably Butch," I say. "He makes people nervous until they get to know him. He's soft and squishy underneath all the bravado."

"So do you have something with Butch or not?" Maisie says. "Because Alex is definitely into you."

"I don't have anything with Butch," I say, grabbing their hands and pulling them off the bed. "And it's almost seven-thirty. We're ridiculously late."

"All right," Sophie says, "but we need more alone time to talk about Alex and other things. Seb and I are having a very small group over to our place tomorrow afternoon. Will you come over? Bring Butch if you want."

"Of course. Who else is going to be there?"

"Just our families, Maisie, Seb's Michigan boys." She pauses for a second as she wraps her arm around my shoulder and whispers, "and Alex."

"Oh-h-h-h," Maisie says like she's having an orgasm. "Al-l-l-ex."

"Grow up!" I say, laughing as I try to get out of their group hug. "Stop it! Both of you. Right now."

"Sophie!" As soon as we walk into the party, a voice screeches at us from a table to our right. I look over to see Allie and a woman in a bright orange swimsuit waving us over to a table of women.

"God," Maisie whispers, "does she own any piece of clothing that's not that horrible orange color?"

"Savannah," Sophie says, disdain dripping from her voice. "I told you I'm not playing Truth or Tequila at my bachelorette party. My wedding, my rules. And this isn't even a bachelorette party. It's a welcome reception."

Savannah, the one in orange, walks toward us—one hand

on her hip, the other hand shoving a bottle of tequila into Sophie's face. Maisie pushes the bottle back.

"I'm not playing either, Van," Maisie says. "It's Sophie's weekend. We're lucky she even invited us to her wedding. You know how big weddings horrify her."

"Yeah, what happened with that?" I say, looking at Sophie. "You've said since you were little that you wanted a private wedding and then a big party afterward."

She shrugs and looks away from me. "I guess things change."

"Sophie," Savannah says, holding up the bottle again, "we need more people to play. Quit being an asshole as usual."

"I'll take Sophie's place," I say, pushing the bottle away from her again as I stand between Sophie and Savannah. "Just teach me the rules. I'm a quick learner."

"And who are you?" Savannah says, taking a step away from me when she sees my cold eyes.

Allie walks over. "This is Raine. I met her this afternoon. Alex was *helping* her to her room."

"Alex was doing what?" Sophie turns me around and smiles—her eyes wide.

"Sophia," I say, pushing her toward Maisie. "You have guests to greet. Please go away. I'll take care of your drinking game obligations."

"You don't have to rescue me anymore," Sophie says, kissing the top of my head. "I'm a big girl now."

"It's been my job since we were born. I'm not stopping now. Mae, take her away, please."

"Okay," she says, grabbing Sophie's hand, "but we're talking about Alex helping you to your room later."

"No, we're not," I yell as they walk away. I turn back around to Allie and Savannah. "So, do you need another person to play this game or what?"

"Maybe. Can you hold more than one shot a night or are you a weakass, little lightweight like Sophie?" Savannah says, taking a seat at the table.

"I'm not a weak anything," I say, grabbing the bottle and taking a long drink. "And if you keep talking shit about my girl, we're going to have a problem."

Savannah glares at me. "Meaning?"

"Fuck around and find out," I say, looking at the other women around the table for emphasis as I sit down. "So are you all college friends?"

"I told you how I knew Sophie an hour ago," Allie says, rolling her eyes. "Do you have a memory problem?"

"I wasn't talking to you, Allie. There are other people at the table."

"Yeah, most of us are college. Hey, I'm Serena. That's Taylor and Ava. How do you know Sophie?"

"We grew up together in Chicago."

"Has she always been as big of a pain in the ass as she is now?" Savannah says, pouring herself a shot of tequila.

"Damn, Savannah. You're a slow learner," I say, turning toward her, my arms crossed. "I'm trying to figure out why you're at her wedding. Do you even like Sophie?"

She slams the shot. "She's fine. She just always has to get her way."

Taylor grabs my arm. "She's jealous of Sophie. She has been since the second she met her."

"It's more than jealousy," Serena laughs. "Savannah wants to be her, especially now that she has Seb."

"I'm not jealous of her," Savannah says, pouring another shot. "And I definitely don't want to be her. Have you heard how she talks to Seb? It's so cringy. Seriously, it's only a matter of time before he gets sick of it. I'd be surprised if they even make it to the altar on Saturday."

"Hmm," I say, tapping my lips, "it sounds like you're rooting against the marriage."

"I'm not rooting for or against anything. I don't care either way. I just don't like the way she talks to him."

"Please, he's way worse than her. He's always cooing baby talk to her," Ava says. "And you're just jealous that he doesn't talk to you like that, Van."

"You've got a little crush on Seb, huh?" I say, laughing as I look at Savannah who's glaring at Ava.

"I don't have a crush on Seb." She whips her head toward me. "I'm happily married."

"It's cool," I say. "Crushes are fine as long as you don't mistake them for reality. And Seb seems awesome—very crush-worthy."

"Whatever," Savannah snarls. "Can we just start the game?"

"Let's go," I say. "But fair warning, I never lose any game."

"You're a lot of talk for as small as you are," Savannah says, pointing to the bottle. "I'm doubting you're even going to make it through the first round."

"Like I said," I say, grabbing the bottle, "fuck around and find out."

As I start chugging, a hand from behind me grabs the bottle and pulls it away from me.

"That's plenty for you," Butch says as he pulls me up by my arm. He points at Savannah. "What's your name? Samantha? Believe me, you don't want to fuck around and find out. Raine's small, but deadly—like a murder hornet."

"My name's Savannah, not Samantha," she says, scowling at him. "Is this your boyfriend, Raine? Or does Sophie have some hidden family from the redneck south?"

"Da-a-a-mn," Butch says, throwing in an extra dose of Southern twang, "you've got a mouth on you, Stephanie."

"My name's Savannah!"

"No one cares what your name is," Butch says as she stands up and tries to grab the bottle back from him. He holds it over her head and out of her reach.

"The only way you get a swig is if you let Uncle Butch pour it for you," he says, tilting the bottle. "Open up."

She jumps out of the way—an annoying pouty look on her face. I want to slap it off her.

"Give me the bottle." She holds her hand out as she takes another step back.

Butch lunges toward her and pours a little tequila out. I jump over, push her out of the way, and catch the tequila. Most of it goes into my mouth. I lick the rest off my chin and look at Savannah. "I'm fast, too. Small, deadly, and fast. Come at me again. I dare you."

Savannah sits back down. "No, thank you. I'd rather not see or talk to either of you for the rest of this trip."

"Same, sister. Same," I say, taking a step toward her. Butch picks me up around the waist and starts to carry me away. I look back at the table. "It was nice meeting you Serena, Taylor, and Ava. Not so much you though, Savannah."

"Damn, girl," Butch laughs as he puts his hand over my mouth. "I leave you alone for thirty minutes and you're already causing trouble. Settle down there, little Murder Hornet."

Chapter Sixteen

ALEX

"So I hear you helped Raine to her room this afternoon," Sophie says as she glides up next to me and snakes her arm through mine.

Maisie closes in on me from the other side. "Very romantic, Alex."

"It's cute that you two think you get to set me up again," I say, grabbing them both around their shoulders and squeezing them to me, "because the last woman you set me up with happens to have a room right next to Raine's. She busted out of her door the second she heard my voice and told Raine we slept together."

"Who? Allie?" Sophie says, looking up at me. "How did that even come up in the conversation?"

"It didn't come up, Sophia," I say, directly into her ear before I release them both. "I told you Allie's crazy. She was trying to mark her territory when she saw me talking to another woman."

"Damn," Maisie says, letting out a long breath. "That's some stalk-ish shit. Soph, didn't she tell you last week she had given up on Alex?"

"Yeah. I told her to move on and she said she had—"

"She hasn't moved on," I say, leaning down to get directly into Sophie's face. "I'm trying not to hurt her feelings since she's your friend, but I'm on the verge of losing it with her."

"Okay," Sophie sighs. "I'll tell her to back off again. I don't know why she's being like this—"

"You won't tell her anything," I say, putting my finger in her face. "You'll stay out of it. I'll handle it from here."

"Why does it look like you're yelling at my wife?" Seb growls as he runs over to us. He pulls Sophie away from me.

"Almost wife," Sophie says, tapping him on the chest.

"Right," Seb says quickly. "Fiancé. Why does it look like you're yelling at my fiancé?"

"He's not yelling at me. He's lecturing me and I kind of deserve it."

"Yes, you do," I say, pointing at her and then looking at Seb. "Take your woman away from me, please. She's meddling in my love life again."

"Gladly." He sweeps her up into his arms. She giggles as he dips her backward and starts kissing her neck. "Come on, baby. Let's get away from the grouch. My parents want to introduce you to some of their friends."

"I'm sorry, Alex," she says as Seb starts to carry her away. "I had no idea she was really being a stalker. I'll quit. I promise."

"Is this Allie again?" Seb says, turning back around. "Why

does she still think she's in the game? Grow a pair and tell her you're not interested."

"People in perfect relationships don't get to give advice," I say, motioning them away from me. "Leave."

Maisie tugs on my arm from behind me. "So let's talk more about Raine—"

"You go away, too," I say, turning her toward Sophie's mom who's yelling her name. "You're wanted over there."

"Fine," she says, smiling as she points toward the beach, "but in case you're interested, Raine's sitting over there—all by herself."

I whip my head around and see Raine sitting alone in a row of lounge chairs in the sand.

"Hmm," Maisie says, tilting her head as she walks backward away from me. "That was a pretty quick reaction time for someone you're not even interested in."

I shake my head. "I'll give you any amount of money you want if you don't tell Sophie I just did that."

"Not enough money in the world, buddy," she says, smiling. "All kidding aside, Raine's amazing. Truly. She might be a lot of work, but she's worth every bit of the effort. Believe me."

I nod as I watch her walk away.

"You want to bring her a drink?" I hear from behind me. I turn around to see the bartender nodding toward Raine. "The little one over there—black hair, green dress. She's drinking a piña colada."

"Were you listening to our conversation?" I say as he hands me a fresh beer.

"Yeah, sorry, man," he says, pulling a pitcher out of the mini-refrigerator. "These parties are boring. I entertain myself by guessing who's trying to hook up and what the odds are that it will happen."

"Oh, yeah. What odds are you giving me with her?"

He shakes his head as he starts pouring the piña colada. "Low, man. I mean you're a professional baseball player and you're a good-looking dude and all, but I overheard her talking to some guy earlier. I only understood every other word of what she was saying. I think she's crazy smart."

"Bruh, give your boy some credit. I'm smart."

"Yeah, you're not Raine smart, though," Butch sidles up to the bar from behind me.

"Why are you everywhere?" I say, turning to him. "Seriously, man, are you duplicating? Are there two of you now wandering around trying to make my life more difficult?"

"Naw, man. I'm an original. No duplicates." He grabs another beer. "And I'm not trying to make your life more difficult. Just being real. Raine's a genius."

"See?" the bartender says. "I was right. Low odds, man. Good luck, though. I'm rooting for you. She's cute and I think she's got some nice assets underneath that dress. I just got a peek—"

"That's plenty," I say as I throw my arm against Butch's chest. "Really. Stop—before this man kills you."

He takes a step back when he looks at Butch's face. He hands me Raine's drink and then looks down quickly.

"Any advice before I head over there?" I say, turning to Butch.

"She's a tough nut to crack," he says, taking a long pull off his beer. "She's a weird mix of confident and awkward. She freezes up if she thinks a guy's into her. Maybe just buddy up for now."

"We're only here for a long weekend and I'm not looking for any more buddies."

"Huh. Well, you don't seem like a complete asshole, so I think I can help you out. Raine and I have a bet, and she hates to lose more than anything in the world."

"What's the bet?"

"She has to put herself out there with one guy and I have to keep my count under six women." He looks at me and smiles. "And I get to choose her guy."

"I don't want her interested in me because she wants to win a bet. And I definitely don't want to know what 'put herself out there' means."

"It means she has to try," he laughs. "If I choose you for the bet, at least she'll put in some effort instead of freaking out and running in the other direction."

"Hmm," I say, nodding, "how about I let you know if I need the extra help?"

"All right, brother," he says, patting me on the back. "Now if you'll excuse me, I need to get started on finding my six women."

I turn back to Raine. She's pulled her legs under her dress and is resting her head on her knees, looking out at the ocean. I head over there.

"Hey," I say as I get closer to her.

She jerks her head up and starts coughing as she spits out a little of her drink.

"You okay?" I reach down and give her a light pat on the

back. "You've got to watch those frozen drinks. Sometimes you get an ice chunk."

"I'm good," she says, coughing again. "You just made me jump. I thought I was hidden over here."

"You are, pretty much, but I thought you could use another drink. Of course, that's before I knew they were a choking hazard for you. Who are you hiding from?"

"Sophie and Maisie," she says, peering around the edge of the chair back toward the party. "They never stop."

"Never," I say, handing her the drink. "And if you're hiding from them, can I hide with you?"

She laughs and pats the chair. "Yes, but hurry up and sit down. If they see us together, it's only going to encourage them."

"Then let's make sure to keep our heads low," I say, dropping down into the chair. "Hey, sorry about this afternoon. That was awkward. I went out with Allie a few times. That's it. I don't want to go out with her again. I'm not into her at all."

"That's none of my business," she says, slurping the last bit of her drink through a straw and then starting on the new one. "You didn't have to tell me that."

"I wanted to tell you, though," I say, smiling at her. "I don't have a girlfriend. I'm not seeing anyone."

She laughs. "Does Allie know that?"

"Does Butch know he's not your boyfriend?"

"He's not my boyfriend," she groans. "I thought I made that embarrassingly clear at the airport."

"He acts like he is. Are you sure?"

"I'm sure. Believe me, there's no interest either way there."

"That's good. Then you're available?"

Her eyes shoot wide open. She spins her head away from me and looks back at the ocean. "It's so pretty down here, right?"

"Okay," I say, patting her leg. "We can do small talk. Yep, it's beautiful. I grew up in the Caribbean, so this is a little like home for me."

"Where'd you grow up?" She keeps her eyes fixed on the ocean.

"Puerto Rico. My family still lives there. I left when I was seventeen to start college here."

She looks back at me. "That's cool. What college?"

"UCLA. Where'd you go?"

"Georgetown."

"Great school," I say, nodding. "What'd you major in?"

"Political science. You?"

"Social sciences."

"Is that a normal major for a baseball player? I don't know much about sports." Her face scrunches up. She has a cute little line that forms above her eyebrows when she does that. I noticed it this afternoon.

"You don't need a college degree to play baseball. Most guys go straight from high school to the minor leagues."

"Really?" She taps her fingers on her lips as she processes the information. "I had no idea. Why didn't you?"

"I've always had a larger goal in mind. I mean, baseball got me into college, and I'm grateful for that," I say, looking out at the ocean, "but eventually I want to go back to school—law school."

"Nice. When do you plan to do that?"

"That's all I've been thinking about for the last few months," I say, running my hands roughly through my hair. "It's stressing me out. Do you mind if we talk about anything else right now?"

"Okay. We can do small talk."

I look back at her and laugh. "You're quick."

"You have no idea," she says. "Why don't we talk about Harry Potter? Who's your favorite character?"

"I'm a Snape fan—"

"Me, too!" she says, a wide grin breaking out over her face. "Snape's the biggest badass in the series, besides Hermione, of course."

"God," I say, leaning back in the chair, "I had the biggest crush on Hermione."

"Who didn't? I was Hermione for like five straight Halloweens until Maisie made us all go as the Spice Girls one year."

"Wow," I say, laughing. "Please tell me there are pictures of the three of you as Spice Girls."

"All of the evidence has been destroyed."

"Which spice were you?"

"Posh."

"I see you more as Ginger," I say, rubbing my chin. "She was the leader, right?"

"I'm a little scared you know this much about the Spice Girls."

"My big sister loved the Spice Girls. She made me listen to them with her," I say, shuddering. "I had to grab my little brother and offer him to her as a sacrifice so I could escape to my room and read. I'd hide behind the bed, so she couldn't find me."

"I did that, too!" She sits up straight—her eyes dancing as she looks at me. "My mom would knock on my door every fifteen minutes when I was reading. She never understood why I wanted to spend that much time alone."

"Same. When the last Harry Potter came out, I literally barricaded myself in my room and didn't come out until I finished it. I missed a baseball practice. My dad was so pissed. I'm still not sure he's forgiven me for that."

The line forms over her eyebrows again. "For missing one baseball practice?"

"Yeah. I had scouts coming to my practices from about age eight on. It wasn't a great idea to miss a practice if you wanted to get recruited."

"Did you want to get recruited?"

"Yeah, I mean, I wanted to go to college and a baseball scholarship was the way to do that, you know?" I look over at her. She's smiling at me. "I got a scholarship from UCLA and played there four years before I got drafted into the league. Another reason my dad was mad at me."

"What? He was mad at you for going to college?"

"I had an offer from a major league team right out of high school with a pretty big signing bonus. He wanted me to take that."

"Why didn't you?"

"We're getting close to that thing I don't want to talk about—"

"Okay," she says, nodding at me as her eyes narrow, "but I have ways to make people talk."

"I bet you do." I take a drink of my beer and smile at her. "Do I get to choose which way you use?"

Chapter Seventeen

RAINE

"What?" I scoot away from him. "Wait, are you flirting with me?"

He pulls his head back like I slapped him, but then starts laughing. "Well, I'm damn sure trying to, but I guess I'm not doing a very good job if you can't tell."

I scoot further away. "Why? Why are you flirting with me?"

"What?" he says, squinting. "Why am I flirting? Is that a trick question?"

I look back at the party to see if Sophie and Maisie are watching. "Did they tell you to?"

"Who?" He looks over his shoulder to try to see where I'm looking.

"You don't have to hit on me. Really. It's cool. I'm good—"

"Raine, whoa," he says, putting his hand on my leg and

squeezing it. "Take a breath. If you're not interested, I understand. It's no big deal."

When I feel his hand on my leg, a burst of heat rages through my body with such intensity that it makes me jump.

"Oh, God," he says, pulling his hand away. "I'm so sorry I touched you. Do you want me to go away?"

"No!" I say, grabbing his arm. He pulls his head back again, smiling a little. I try to get my voice under control. "I mean, no. You don't have to leave and you can touch me. No, I mean if you want to, you can touch me, but you don't have to touch me—"

"Raine," he says, putting his hand on my shoulder to stop my shifting, "what's happening right now?"

As he says it, Mack's voice runs through my head. *Be upfront with the guy—tell him when a man starts showing interest, you get nervous.*

I look up at Alex as he starts massaging my shoulder.

"What's going on?" he says, smiling. "Tell me."

I take a long, slow breath and blow it out. "Look, I have a pattern. When hot guys show any interest in me, I kind of fall apart. I get really awkward."

He smiles as his hand slides down my arm. "So you think I'm hot, huh?" he says, taking my hand.

"Really?" I try to pull my hand away. He holds it tighter. "I put myself out there and that's the only thing you took away from it?"

He looks down at me. "I have a pattern, too. I make jokes when I'm nervous."

"You're nervous?"

"Yeah, I'm nervous. I don't want to look dumb in front of you. You're really smart. It's intimidating."

"What?" I say, tilting my head. "No, it's not. You're smart, too."

"I'm okay, but I'm just saying, I'm nervous, too." He squeezes my hand again. "And I'm glad you told me that. It makes me feel better."

Before I can answer him, I hear a screech from behind us that can only belong to Savannah. "Alex!"

"God, I think it's Savannah," I say, pulling my hand back and ducking behind the chair. "I got into it with her earlier. Hide me."

"You got *into it* with her?" He looks at me with his eyebrows squishing together. "Like you fought with her?"

"Yeah, it almost came to blows."

"What?" he says, shaking his head. "Seriously? I can't take you anywhere."

"Don't try to hide from me, Alex," Savannah says as she closes in on us. She shakes the chair a few times. "I could see your swim trunks from across the party."

"What's up, Savannah?" Alex says, sitting up. He turns his body sideways to try to block her from seeing me.

"And who are you hiding behind you?" she says, taking a few steps to the side so she can look around him. "Oh look. It's my friend Raine. You're so small that I almost didn't see you."

"I think I've already warned you what kind of damage this small body can do," I say, starting to stand up. "Any time you're ready."

"Really?" Alex grabs my arm and pulls me back down. "Who are you right now? Put your butt back on this chair."

"Fine," I say, sitting back down as I keep my eyes locked on Savannah.

"Do you need something, Savannah?" Alex says as he turns back toward her.

"Yes, we need you," she says, trying to grab his arm. He pulls it back. "Alex, you promised you'd play beer pong with us. Allie needs a partner."

"Uh, maybe later. I'm good here for now," he says, glancing back at me.

"Don't let me keep you," I say, smiling. "Beer bong awaits."

"Pong," he says, laughing. "It's called beer pong. Have you never played?"

"She has not," Butch says, closing in on us from the other side. "And neither have I, but we're game."

Alex looks up at him and shakes his head. "Again, why are you everywhere? Do you just appear whenever you sense you can cause the most trouble?"

"That's pretty much my job description," Butch laughs. "What do you say, Sandra? Do you have room for another team? Raine and I would like to play."

"I thought I told you I didn't want to see you for the rest of the trip," Savannah hisses at Butch.

"And I don't want to be this beautiful," Butch says, grabbing me under my arms and pulling me up. "So we both have problems. Let's go, Alex. Get your ass up. We've got games to play."

"I'm not really in the game-playing mood right now," Alex says, staring at Butch.

"But I am," Butch says, grinning broadly. "I just *love* to play games."

Alex stares at him for another second and then looks at me. "Fine. Raine, do you want to be my partner? I'll teach you how to play."

Butch puts his hand over Savannah's mouth as she starts to protest. "Raine's my partner. I think Susanna said Allie's looking for a partner, though."

Alex glares at Butch. "You're looking for a beat down, brother."

"Come at me," Butch laughs as he pulls me away from them. "We'll meet you up there."

"Why are you making me play a drinking game?" I whisper. "What about our five years of friendship makes you think I would enjoy that?"

"It's a good way to flirt without having to think about it too much," he says. "Alex is your target for the bet, by the way."

"What?" I say, pushing him away from me. "No. I don't want him to be a part of our bet."

"I get to choose the target. It's him," he says, putting his arm around my shoulders. "He's into you, Raine. Maybe lean in a little bit and encourage him. Let's play a stupid drinking game and let him see your fun side."

"Have you ever played beer pong?"

"I don't play games when I want to drink, but it's called beer pong, how hard can it be?"

He grabs my hand and pulls me to the table where Seb's

friend Ricky is yelling at someone to chug. He gives Serena a double high five. They must be partners.

"I guess we have to throw the balls in the cups or something?" I whisper to Butch. "Are you a good shot?"

"Are you really asking me that right now? Do you think any of these idiots are a better shot than me?"

"We're not shooting the cups with guns. We're throwing balls at them. I would think professional baseball players would be pretty accurate at that."

Allie grabs Alex's hand and pulls him up to the table. His eyes are fixed on me.

"Our turn," she says as Alex pulls his hand away from her. "Who wants to take us on?"

"We will," Butch says as he pushes me up to the table. "We just need the basic rules. It looks like a shuffleboard table to me. Do we try to knock the cups over?"

Allie rolls her eyes. "Oh good God, why don't you forfeit so we can get to a real opponent?"

"Naw, I don't surrender, Abby. Lay down the basic rules and let's get this thing started."

"First my name's Allie—"

"Don't care," Butch says as he grabs one of the cups on our side and chugs the beer out of it.

"Butch, you have to wait until the game starts to drink," Ricky says as he refills the cup.

"I already don't like this game," Butch growls. "Give me the other rules."

"Overall rules," Alex says, looking right at me. "Throw the balls into your opponents' cups. If you get it in, they have to drink. If you can get another ball in that cup before they're done drinking it, that's a death cup and the game's over. You can toss the balls straight in or bounce them on the table first and then in. If you get a bounce shot in, your opponents have to drink two cups, but they can swat a bounce shot away—so high risk, high reward. You want me to go over them again?"

I laugh. "No, I think we've got it. You good, Butch?"

"Locked and loaded, Murder Hornet. Let's play."

"Murder Hornet?" Alex smiles. "New nickname?"

I shrug as I grab a few balls off the table. "You can go first. You'll need a head start."

"Okay. I see how we're playing. A little trash talk." Alex throws a ball in the air and catches it behind his back. "Oh, and one more thing, whoever gets the ball in the cup gets to choose who drinks that cup, and I'm coming after the Murder Hornet hard—all night long."

He slings a quick bounce shot our way. Butch swats it hard, sending it crashing into a spectator's head.

"Oh!" Alex's teammate Manny grabs him around the shoulders and almost tackles him. "He slapped you into tomorrow!"

"Damn," Alex says. "Nice reaction time."

"He's a fucking Navy SEAL," Ricky laughs. "How do you think he's not going to have quick reaction time?"

Allie looks up. "You're a Navy SEAL?"

"Yes, ma'am," Butch drawls out, smiling at her. "I am."

I turn to look at him. "Didn't we agree that you couldn't drop the SEAL bomb?"

"I didn't drop it, sister," he says, pulsing his eyebrows. "Ricky did."

"Clever. You tell the biggest talker at the party so he'll drop it for you."

"I need to win the bet," he says. "I want to know if Culver slept with that waitress."

"I hate you."

"Are we playing or not?" Allie whines from the other end of the table.

I lob a ball and watch it splash down into a cup.

"Nice shot," Alex says, nodding. "You're a fast learner."

"Step up your game, Alejandro," I say in Spanish. "Or it's going to be a really long night for you."

"Damn," Manny says, looking at Alex. "She's bi-lingual, too—"

"Aw, man," Butch says. "Raine hasn't been bi-lingual since she was about eight years old. How many languages do you speak now? About five, right?"

"Five fluently," I say, looking at Alex. "A couple more conversationally. I believe I just got a ball into a cup and I would like Alex to drink it."

Before Alex can pick it up, Butch throws another ball into it.

"Death cup, right?" he says. "I think we just won."

Alex takes a step back—his mouth wide open.

"Better close that mouth," I say, pointing at Alex, "before I pop a ball in there, too."

"Oh, damn. Can I borrow that phrase later tonight?" Butch says.

I slap him across the chest without taking my eyes off Alex. He's still staring at me—wide-eyed with a little grin coming to his face.

I let out a whistle. "Man, I hope you play baseball better than you play beer pong because you suck at this game."

"Who's up next?" Butch says, pointing to the spectators. "And I think it's time we started putting a little money on these games."

Chapter Eighteen

ALEX

After we lose another game to Butch and Raine, I stand to the side and watch them take on Stone and his wife. Raine tries to swat one of Stone's bounce shots off the table, but gets her arm caught in the sleeve of her dress. She chugs two cups and then yanks off her dress and throws it on a chair.

The entire male population around the table almost passes out en masse. I'm guessing none of us had any idea what was hiding under her dress. Her bright green swimsuit is cut almost down to her navel—revealing a good portion of her perfectly rounded breasts.

"Good Lord, Raine," Butch says, looking down at her. "If you're trying to distract Stone, good work. I'm not even sure he can breathe right now."

I don't know about Stone, but I definitely can't breathe. She grabs a ponytail thing from her wrist and twists her hair on top of her head as she looks up at Butch, "You know I play to win. Center back, double shot. Let's go."

Raine throws a lob toward the cup and Butch throws a clothesline a second after her. Both balls land in the same cup one right after the other. It's the second time they've aced that move. They work well together—too well. It's making me a little jealous until Raine glances around the table. Her eyes stop when they find mine. She sees me looking at her and smiles.

I walk over and whisper, "When you're done playing, can we get a little more alone time?"

"What? Are you done? Don't you want a rematch?"

"A rematch alone with you, yes," I say, taking her hand. "With beer bong, no."

"It's pong, Alex," she says, her eyes twinkling. "Beer pong. Don't you know anything?"

I stroke my hand up and down her arm. "I don't like games that much."

"Okay, Romeo," Butch says, shoving me away, "I need my partner back. I have money on these games."

"I'll find you later," I say, backing up, my eyes still firmly fixed with hers.

When she looks back at the table, I see Allie trying to make her way over to me. I head quickly in the other direction to look for Sophie. I find her where she always is—wrapped up in Seb's arms. This time, they're leaning up against a wall, talking to our agent.

"Seb, I just need ten minutes alone with you," Jeff says, his voice tinged with frustration. "Sophie doesn't mind."

"Don't speak for her," Seb snarls. "And I mind. We've talked about everything we need to—"

"Seb, I don't mind," Sophie says, trying to push through

the circle Seb's arms have formed around her. He pulls her tighter to him.

As I get closer, I see Jeff's normally jovial face is strained and angry. I've never seen him upset with Seb. Of course, the millions he made in commissions off Seb's last contract would make anyone happy.

"Hey, Soph," I say, reaching out my hand to her. "I need to borrow you for a second."

She grabs my hand. As I start to pull her away, Seb switches his glare from Jeff to me.

"Damn, Seb," I say, dropping her hand. "I just need to talk to her for a second. I promise I'll return her in the condition in which she was received."

Seb shakes his head. "Yeah, sorry, man. That look wasn't meant for you."

"I need another drink," Sophie says, rising on tiptoe to kiss Seb. "Babe, we'll be at the bar when you're done here."

"You've got two minutes," Seb growls at Jeff as Sophie pushes me away from them.

"What's going on there?" I whisper as I wrap my arm around her.

"I have no idea," she whispers, "but none of it's good. Jeff seems like he's always in a bad mood. He's on an all expenses paid trip in St. John. You'd think he could lighten up a little bit. Is he always like that?"

"Not really. He's like one of the guys normally." I motion to the bartender for another beer. "What do you want, Soph?"

"May I have a mai tai, please?" she says, smiling at the bartender.

"A woman as beautiful as you can have anything she wants," he says, smiling back at her. "I mean, anything—"

"No," I say, pointing at him as I pull Sophie a few steps away from the bar.

"I guess Jeff doesn't like me," she says. "There are a few of Seb's boys that aren't comfortable with a woman being introduced into the group. Thank you for not being one of them."

"The only people who are uncomfortable when a wife or girlfriend comes in are the ones who stand to lose money from —or access to—the player. I don't need Seb's money and I don't want any more access to him."

"I'm not trying to take anyone's money or access."

"I'm not saying you are. In fact, I know you're not, but Seb's changed since he met you—in my opinion, for the better. He's so much happier now. But you know, some people don't want other people to be happy. They lose a little bit of their purpose in that person's life—their control over them. You know?"

"Yeah, I guess," she says, sighing. "That's kind of messed up, though."

The bartender whistles at me—holding up Sophie's drink. I grab it and pull her further away from the crowd.

"I need to talk to you about something," I say, locking my eyes with hers. "And what I'm about to say can't be repeated or used against me in the future. Do you agree to these terms?"

"Intrigue. You know how I like that," she says, sipping on the straw and nodding. "Agreed."

"Tell me more about your friend Raine."

"What?" She takes an exaggerated step back, her hand

flying up to her chest like she's about to pass out. "Do you like her?"

"Settle down," I say, closing the distance between us again as I swivel my head to make sure no one's listening to us. "I'm just asking for some information."

"What information?" Her eyes are almost as wide as her mouth. "Are you attracted to her? Oh my God. This is amazing. Are you going to let me set you up?"

"I don't need you to set me up. I can do my own work. Just give me the basics. You know, is she seeing anyone? Like Butch or anyone else. Does she want to be seeing anyone?"

She puts her hand over her mouth as her eyes start to fill up.

"Sophie, stop," I say, rolling my eyes. "This was a bad idea. Never mind."

She grabs my arm as I start to turn around. "No, it's not a bad idea. It's an amazing idea. Raine's smart and funny and sweet—just like you. You'd be such a good match. And she's not dating Butch or anyone else."

"Does she want to be dating anyone?"

"I'm not sure," she says, frowning. "Her job keeps her really busy, and the long-distance thing might be a hard way to start a relationship, but you should get to know her while you're down here and see what happens. I think she's perfect for you."

"Who would be perfect for Alex? Me?" Allie walks up to us and slides her arm through mine.

"Allie," Sophie says, taking her hand. "Let's go find the girls."

"No, Soph, I need to talk to Allie alone."

"You heard him, Sophie," Allie says, kissing my arm. "He needs to talk to me alone."

I pull my arm away from her. Sophie's looking back and forth between us. "Soph, seriously, go. You don't need to be a part of this."

"A part of what?" Allie says, jerking her head up to look at me. "Are you breaking up with me?"

"We're not dating, Allie," I say, nodding Sophie away from us one more time before I look down at Allie. "I don't need to break up with you, but I want to make it clear that I'm not interested in anything more with you. I thought I had already made that clear, but obviously, I haven't. I'm sorry if that hurts your feelings."

"So, what?" she yells, her arms flying in the air. "You sleep with me and then you're done?"

"It's not like that," I say, putting my hand up to try to calm her down. She slaps it away.

"You were using me all this time?" She flips her eyes to Sophie. "Nice guy to set me up with, Soph. Did you know he was this much of an asshole? I thought we were friends."

"Allie, we are friends," Sophie says. "And Alex isn't an asshole. It's just not a connection. It happens."

Allie's glaring at her. "Savannah's right. You've changed since you met Seb. You don't care about anyone except yourself."

"Whoa, whoa, whoa," I say, stepping in front of Sophie. "Allie, we're down here for her wedding. Back off."

"Fuck you, Alex. Don't talk to me again." Allie starts to walk away, but turns back around and points at Sophie. "That goes for you, too."

145

"This isn't Sophie's fault," I say to her back as she runs toward a group of women.

"No, Alex. Stop," Sophie says, tugging on my hand. "It's fine. I'm kind of growing out of that friendship anyway. Really. I'm not even sure why I invited a lot of these people down here. They're just adding stress and drama, as usual."

"I'm sorry. You shouldn't have to deal with that on your wedding weekend."

She shrugs. "When Seb and I started dating, he told me how fast he had to tighten his circle when he became famous. I'm kind of there right now. I'm not famous, of course, but I still have the overwhelming urge to start shedding everyone except the people who bring me positive energy."

"Yeah, I went through that a few years ago. It's not easy. In fact, it sucks, but when you get rid of negative people, you start to feel better almost instantly."

"That's what Seb keeps telling me," she says, nodding over my shoulder. I turn around to see Allie and a few other women staring at us. "He told me not to invite any of them, but I felt like I had to for some reason. I won't invite them to the next thing. I think it's time to start cutting."

"You want me to kick them out? I worked as a bouncer for a minute in college. The bar owner fired me because he said I was too nice, but I'm willing to give it another try."

"No, you're good," she says, laughing. "I'm about done with this party anyway. I'm going to find Seb and see if he wants to head back to our place. You're coming over tomorrow, right?"

"Yeah, like around noon?"

"Yep, my brothers are barbecuing. Just a small group—the people we really wanted to invite to our wedding."

"Looking forward to it."

"Hey, will you make sure Raine has a ride over? I think Butch is going out fishing with Roman."

"Yeah, I've got her—"

"I bet you do," she says, her eyes starting to fill up again. "This might be my most successful set-up yet."

Chapter Nineteen

RAINE

"Hey, I'm done for the night," I say to Butch as we finish off our fourth team.

He hands me half of the money we won. "Yeah, no real competition here anyway. It's getting boring."

"Do you see Sophie?" I stand on a chair and look around. "I need to talk to her."

Butch does a quick sweep of the party. "I don't see her. Do you want me to help you look?"

"No, I'm good. I'm sure you can find something else to occupy your time." I nod toward Ava who's had her eyes glued to Butch all night.

"Yeah, that seems like as good a place as any to start," he says, patting my arm. "Call me if you need me."

I walk around for a bit until I see Seb's head above a line of palm plants separating the pool area from a walkway. Since he's rarely without Sophie, I head over there, but when I get closer, I see he's talking to a man.

"Seb, you're not thinking clearly," the man says. "If Sophie loves you, she won't mind signing a prenup—"

"What do you mean if she loves me?" Seb snarls. "Man, fuck you. I'm not asking her to sign a prenup or anything else. You've already talked to me about this once. I told you to leave it alone."

"I'm doing my job—"

"Your job is to get me contracts, Jeff. That's it."

"My job is to put as much money in my athletes' pockets as possible," Jeff says, lowering his voice. I tiptoe to the other side of the palms as he continues, "and then to make sure the money stays there."

Seb shoves the palm next to me. It hits me in the face. I drop to my hands and knees as he looks over to see what he hit. I curl up in a ball and press my back up against the planter.

"You want to put more money in my pocket?" Seb says in a deep and menacing tone. "How about giving me back some of that five percent you made on my contract? Two-hundred million. What's five percent of that? Ten million or so you put in your pocket?"

"Seb." Jeff's voice is starting to shake. "I'm just saying, this whole thing has moved so fast. If you want to get married this soon at least take some precautions. Protect yourself in case anything changes."

Seb pushes the plant again. A palm frond hits me on the head. "If you bring this up one more time, the only thing that's going to change is my agent. Do you understand me? End of discussion."

"Seb!" I glance up to see Seb's head moving away from Jeff. "Let me talk to Sophie about it. She won't mind."

Seb spins back around and runs at Jeff. I peek through the plants in time to see Seb throw him against a wall. "If you talk to Sophie about this or anything else, all of your clients will need a new agent because I will flat out kill you. Don't talk to her. Don't look at her. And if you can't get behind this marriage in the next thirty seconds, leave this fucking island and never contact me again."

Seb shoves him one more time and then turns on a heel and starts back toward the party. Jeff takes a deep breath and leans heavily against the wall. I stay hidden until I think Jeff's gone. As I start to stand up, he flies around the corner.

He comes to a quick stop when he sees me. "Who the fuck are you?"

"That's none of your business," I say, jumping to my feet.

As I try to walk around him, he grabs my shoulder and pushes me against the wall. "Everything's my business."

He's got me trapped at the end of the hallway. He's not very big—maybe five foot, nine and slightly built. I think about trying to plow through him, but I know I can't take him.

He grabs my arm and glares down at me. "How long have you been standing here?"

I yank my arm away from him. "Long enough to figure out what a dick you are."

I take out my phone and try to call Butch. Jeff tries to grab it.

"Who are you calling?"

I pull it behind me. "My mom. She worries if I don't call her every hour. Now, get the fuck out of my way."

"Who do you think you're talking to?" He steps in front of

me as I try to get around him again. "You better forget everything you just heard or—"

"Or what?" I shove him on the chest to try to get him to back up. It doesn't work. "You don't even know who I am."

"I can find out who anyone is." His shoulders start arching toward me like he's a vulture about ready to swoop down on his prey.

I hit him again—this time with my fist balled up. I think it hurts my knuckles more than it hurts his chest, but he takes a step back.

"I can find out who anyone is, too," I say, trying to stretch up as tall as I can. "I'll tell you what I do with people when I find them if you tell me. I bet mine's much worse."

"What the fuck?" Seb says as he comes charging down the hallway. He grabs Jeff and pins him up against a wall with his forearm. He looks back at me. "You okay?"

"I'm fine."

"Seb, she was eavesdropping on our conversation."

"I wasn't eavesdropping—not on purpose," I say, looking up at Seb. "But I overheard the conversation. Sorry. I got caught and didn't know how to escape."

His strained expression lightens as he looks down at me. "Don't worry about it. How much did you hear?"

"The prenup stuff."

"Are you going to tell Sophie?" He takes his arm off Jeff's chest.

"No, but you should. She told me how you guys met—the secret you were keeping from her. Don't hide things from her, even if you're doing it to protect her. Sophie's tough."

He nods. "I know she is. I'll tell her."

"What's going on here?" I look around Seb to see Alex headed down the hallway.

"Our agent had Raine trapped in the hallway when I got here."

"Excuse me?" Alex grabs Jeff by the collar and pins him back up against the wall. "What the fuck, Jeff?"

"He's your agent, too?" I look over at Alex and shake my head. "Damn, you guys know how to pick them."

"He's my agent for now," Alex says, looking back at me. "Did he hurt you?"

"No, nothing like that. He's mad that I overheard his conversation with Seb."

Alex looks up at Seb. "I'm sure she didn't mean to—"

"I'm not pissed at her, but I'm about ready to punch him," Seb says, pointing at Jeff. "Don't you ever fucking touch Raine again."

Alex shoves him harder against the wall. "You touched her?"

"Finally!" Sophie says as she turns the corner. "Seb, I've been looking for you. Wait, what's wrong? What's happening?"

Seb steps in front of her to shield her from Alex and Jeff. "Nothing, baby. Everything's fine. Are you ready to go back to our place?"

"Yes, but tell me what's happening. You look mad."

"It's nothing you need to worry about." Seb turns his head to look at me. He nods as I raise my eyebrows. "But I'll tell you everything in the car. Let's get out of here. Alex, will you make sure Raine gets back to her room safely tonight?"

Alex grabs my hand and pulls me next to him. "Yeah, I've got her."

Sophie looks at me, her eyes wide. "Why do you need someone to get you back to your room safely? Is someone trying to hurt you?"

"Well, Savannah for one," Alex says, laughing as he looks down at me. "Have you fought with anyone else tonight?"

"Wait, what?" Seb says. "Did you get into a fight with Savannah tonight? And more importantly, did you win?"

"Oh, I won," I say, throwing my shoulders back. "She's all talk."

"God, please tell me there were punches thrown."

"Seb, stop," Sophie says, pushing his chest.

"No punches," I say, shrugging, "but the weekend isn't over yet."

"I think Raine might have just passed Maisie as my favorite of your friends, Soph."

"Stop!" I hold my hand up to Seb. "Keep that shit to yourself or there damn well will be punches thrown, and I don't think I can take Maisie."

"Understood. Come on, Soph. Let's start saying our good-byes, so we can get out of here. We'll see you both tomorrow." He stops and points at Jeff who has backed up into a corner. "You're not invited to our house tomorrow. Close friends only."

As we watch them walk away, Jeff turns back to me. "Who are you? Do you work for a competing agency?"

"I don't know about competing," I say, smiling at him, "but I definitely work for an agency."

"Who? Octagon? Are you trying to get Seb away from me? Or Alex?" He grunts. "Good luck with that."

"What the fuck are you talking about?" Alex pushes Jeff back. "She's a friend of Sophie's. She doesn't work for a sports agency."

"I don't care who she is," Jeff says, glaring at me. "She overheard me talking to Seb about having Sophie sign a prenup."

"They're already married, dumbass," I say. "It's too late for a prenup."

Jeff's face drains of color. "What did you say? Did Sophie tell you that?"

"She didn't have to. I've known her since we were kids. This," I say, waving my hand around, "would be her nightmare wedding. Believe me, we're just here for the after-party."

"They're not married," he says, taking a step back toward me. Alex pushes him back. "Seb would have told me."

"Check for their marriage license if you don't believe me. Start with Florida, but I'd check Michigan, too. I'm guessing they got married at his lake house at some point. She loves that place."

Jeff takes a quick breath. "They were up there over the All Star break. He said he was hurt and couldn't play in the game—"

"There it is," I say, smiling. "Sounds like a secret wedding plan to me."

"Fuck!" He dials his phone. "Look for a marriage license for Seb and Sophie in Michigan. It would have been over the All Star break."

Alex looks down at me. "Do you really think they're already married? Or are you just fucking with him?"

"I know they're already married. I've been able to read Sophie since we were little. But don't get me wrong, I'm enjoying fucking with Jeff, too."

"No, she didn't sign a prenup!" Jeff screams into the phone. "How did you not know it was happening that week? You're supposed to be on top of these things. I don't care who you have to wake up. Find someone in the fucking state of Michigan who can confirm or deny it."

"Are we done here?" Alex says, putting his arm around me. "You promised me some more alone time."

He starts pulling me down the hallway. As we pass Jeff, I whisper, "You're too late, Jeff. It looks like Seb loves Sophie more than he loves you."

Jeff glares at me and then charges in the other direction.

Alex shakes his head. "Am I going to have to watch you every second of this trip to make sure you don't get into a fight?"

"Probably," I say, looking up at him. "Is that a problem?"

"No, I was pretty much planning on doing that anyway." He takes my hand and starts pulling me away from the party. "Come on. I know a place where we can get a little privacy."

Chapter Twenty

ALEX

"Really?" She pulls back on my hand. Her eyebrows are raised when I turn around. "A place where we can get a little privacy? Is it your room?"

"It's not my room," I say, smiling. "Unless you want it to be my room, then it's definitely my room."

"I don't want it to be your room," she says as the line over her eyebrows deepens again. "Yet."

"Yet, huh? Then it's not my room—yet. Come on." I grab her hand again and pull her toward the front of the resort. "I explored a little when I got here. There's a private bay just through those trees."

As I start to guide her through the narrow sand pathway, she squeezes my hand tighter. "I can't see anything," she whispers, pulling back a little bit.

"It's only a few hundred more feet," I say, crouching down in front of her, "but crawl on my back, so you won't step on a snake."

She jumps on my back so hard that I almost fall over.

"What kind of snakes are there down here?" she says, wrapping her arms and legs around me as I stand up.

"I don't think there are any snakes down here. I just wanted you on my back."

"That's very sneaky," she says, pushing my head. "Not funny."

"Do you want me to put you down?"

"I didn't say that," she says, locking her ankles in front of me. "I'll stay up here in case you're wrong about the snakes."

I wrap my arms under her legs and hoist her higher on my body as I continue to weave through the palm trees. We finally come to the opening.

"Look. All to ourselves," I say as she straightens up and looks over my shoulder.

"Wow," she says, inhaling quickly, "it's so pretty. The moonlight makes it look like there are a bunch of sparkly diamonds on the water."

"Do you want to swim out there and see for ourselves?" I whisper as she lays her chin on my shoulder.

"I don't know," she says. "I'm a little scared of swimming in the ocean at night."

"What?" I nudge her head with mine. "That's the best time to swim—floating in the warm water, looking up at the stars. There's nothing like it."

"Yeah, but sharks and stuff."

"Sharks and stuff?" I say, laughing. "You know, sharks stay in the ocean around the clock. They don't just get in at night."

"I know, but you can't see them at night."

"What are you talking about?" I say, nodding out to the deeper water. "Of course you can. There's Samuel right over there."

"Samuel?" She starts pushing away from my body. "Really? That's your shark's name?"

"What?" I say as I set her down gently. "I didn't name him. His parents did."

She looks up at me and rolls her eyes. "Maybe we can just wade in a little bit for now and work our way up to swimming."

"Sure," I say, pulling my T-shirt over my head. "We can take it slow."

When I look back at her, she's staring at my chest.

"You good?"

"Yep," she says. "I'm just not sure I want you to see my body now that I've seen yours. Good Lord, Alex, do you work out every minute of every day? Your chest is ridiculous."

"Thank you," I say, laughing. I lean down and whisper into her ear, "And did you forget that you stripped at the beer pong table? I've already seen your body."

"What?" she says, frowning at me. "That was for competitive reasons. My dress was getting in my way. You weren't supposed to look."

"Everyone looked. Believe me—everyone. You have an incredible body."

"Hmm," she says, narrowing her eyes. "That's cheating, but fine."

She pulls her dress over her head and throws it on top of my T-shirt. She walks out until the water's up to her knees. As she reaches up to let her hair out of the ponytail, her suit rides up—revealing a nice portion of her butt. It looks so soft and smooth. I want to run my hands all over it.

"Are you coming in?" she says as she turns back to me. "I'll hold your hand if you're scared."

"Yes, I'm very scared," I say, walking out to her. "Hold my hand, please."

She laughs as she reaches down and runs her hand through the water. "It's so calm here. Why isn't the surf stronger like it is over at the resort?"

"There's a huge sandbar a couple of hundred feet out. It's blocking most of the big waves." I grab her hand and pull her deeper into the water. "Let's go out there."

She pulls back a little when the water gets waist-deep for her.

"You want me to carry you?"

"Maybe." She looks up at me. "Can we just stay here for a second?"

"Sure," I say, lowering myself onto my back until I'm floating. I stare up at the stars for a minute before I say, "Hey, I have something to confess to you."

She looks down at me. "You're dating Allie, aren't you?"

"No," I say, standing back up. "Definitely no."

"You're dying then." She takes a step toward me. "Oh my God, are you dying?"

"I'm not dying. And I'm not dating anyone."

"You're not dating anyone," she says, nodding, "but you're married, right?"

I grab her shoulders. "You know, this might be easier if you just let me tell you."

She pushes me back and crosses her arms over her chest.

"I'm a little concerned that you didn't deny the marriage thing right away."

"I'm not married. Butch told me about the bet you have with him. That's my confession."

"What?" she says, taking a step away from me. "Oh my God, Alex, it's just a stupid bet. Butch is always playing and he—"

I hold my hand up to stop her. "Just tell me one thing: Are you hanging out with me so you can win the bet?"

"No!" She throws her arms down in the water—splashing both of us. She shakes her head. "I swear."

"Hmm," I say, rubbing my hand over my mouth. "Butch said he got to choose the guy for you. Has he chosen yet?"

"Yes," she says, wiping the water off her face. "It's you, but I told him I didn't want it to be you. I don't want you to be a part of this stupid bet."

"Well," I say, frowning, "I don't want him to pick another guy for you, so it might as well be me. What do you have to do to win the bet?"

"Uh, I forgot what we said. Oh, I have to kiss whatever guy he picks for me."

I lean down and give her a quick kiss on the lips. "There. You won. Can we stop talking about the bet now? Maybe I can even kiss you for real at some point."

She looks up at me for a second—her eyes wide—then she laughs and looks out at the ocean. "I don't know. If that's all the better you can kiss, I'm thinking about giving Samuel a try."

I sweep her up into my arms and start walking out into the

deeper water. "Did you hear that Sammy? Raine wants to kiss you."

"Alex! Stop!" She wraps her arms tightly around my neck as the water hits her butt. "Seriously, Alex. Stop. We're too deep."

I stop when the water's almost covering her. "We're fine. I'm a great swimmer. I grew up in the ocean. Lie back and look up at the stars. It'll calm you down."

She puts her head back in the water and looks up at the sky. "Don't let go of me."

"I won't," I say, pushing my hands more firmly into her back and legs as I hold her up. "It's pretty right?"

"Yeah," she whispers. "I never see this many stars in D.C."

"How long have you lived there?"

"Too long," she sighs. "Almost ten years between there and Virginia, but I'm moving out to San Diego for a while."

"Really?" I say, floating my body up underneath hers. "Did you quit your job?"

"No. I just have a special assignment out there for a bit."

"What kind of assignment?"

She glances over at me. "It's so pretty down here, right?"

"Okay," I laugh. "We can do small talk."

She unhooks herself from my body and starts treading water. "I'm sorry. I really can't talk about my job much."

"It's okay."

A little surge of water bobs over her head. She surfaces and reaches out to me. I grab her hands and pull her into my body. As she wraps her arms around my neck, I put my hands under her butt and lift her onto my waist.

"I don't want to talk that much right now anyway," I whisper as she wraps her legs around me.

As I start kissing her neck, she wiggles higher on my body. Her breath is exhaling right into my ear. I let my lips travel across her face until they land on her open mouth. Her tongue immediately comes out to touch mine. I grab the back of her head and pull it into mine as I push her mouth open wider.

"Was that kiss better?" I say as my mouth starts running down her neck.

"Better," she says, moaning a little as my hand reaches into her swimsuit and cups her breast.

My mouth travels quickly down her body. I start licking her nipple as the water caresses my chin. She lets out a larger moan as I close my mouth over her breast and start sucking.

"Alex," she says, running her hands over my head, "I feel like I'm going to pass out. I don't want to drown."

"I won't let you," I say as my mouth crosses over to the other side of her body and pushes her swimsuit to the side.

As I grab her nipple lightly with my teeth, she shudders. "I'm serious. I can't do this in the water. It's like sensory overload."

"Get on my back," I say, turning around so she can climb on. "I'll swim us out to the sandbar."

"No, we should go back in," she says as I keep getting deeper. "Really. Let's go back to the shore."

Her arms wrap around my body as I start to swim faster. As my feet hit the sandbar, I hoist her up on my body and walk the rest of the way until we're out of the water. I lay her down in the sand.

"We don't have to do anything you don't want to do," I say as I lower myself on top of her.

She starts breathing heavily as I pull the straps of her swimsuit down. I bury my head between her breasts again—paying each one a little attention before I start licking down her body. I yank the rest of her suit down to her knees.

She groans loudly as my lips get below her stomach. I run my tongue through her forcefully—from bottom to top—and then start exploring. I'm only down there for a few minutes before she starts shaking and moaning. I keep going until she screams out my name. When her body stops shaking, I start working my way back up.

Chapter Twenty-One

It's only eight in the morning. I didn't get back to my room until two, but I'm wide awake. I can't stop thinking about Alex. Last night feels like a magical dream. It was so perfect that I'm beginning to question whether or not it happened.

I'm tired of tossing and turning, so I decide to head down and grab an early breakfast. When I come out of my room, I see Serena walking down the hall.

"Hey. It's Serena, right? I'm Raine."

She laughs as she walks over to me. "Oh, I remember you. You almost took Savannah's head off last night."

"I—"

"Don't apologize. I'm not mad about it. Savannah needs a good slap down now and then."

I smile as I pull my door shut. "It definitely seems that way."

"You got back to your room last night about the same time we did."

I look down at my phone quickly. "Oh yeah, I didn't notice you."

"I'm sure you didn't. Alex was sucking pretty hard on your face."

I grimace as I look up at her again. "Oh, wow. Uh—"

"You don't have to explain. Believe me, if I were single, I'd be going after that hard. He's so fucking sexy." She lets out a little whistle. "Have fun. Just don't catch any feelings or you'll be his next victim."

"His next *victim*? Is that you talking or Allie?"

She shakes her head. "I'm not friends with Allie. I barely know her. But woman to woman, Alex gets around—a lot."

"Okay," I say, nodding. "I appreciate the heads-up."

She turns around and starts walking toward the beach. "No judgment. Just know he's a player—in every sense of the word."

My head starts spinning as I watch her walk around the corner. What did she say? Don't catch any feelings. Unfortunately, I think it's a little too late for that. He's all I've thought about since I saw him at the airport yesterday. I want to go back into my room and bury myself in my bed, but last night's vigorous activity has left me famished. I need breakfast. When I get into the lobby, I see Butch pacing—his face drawn tight underneath his cap.

"What are you still doing here? I thought you were leaving at eight."

"Yes," he says, his teeth clenched, "I thought that, too. Apparently, Roman's on that island time you warned me about."

"It's only eight thirty." I pull him over to the drink station and pour him a glass of water. "Deep breaths, buddy."

"There's fruit floating in that water," he says, pointing at the oranges and lemons in the pitcher. "I like my water to taste like water."

"Island Butch is a complicated man, isn't he?" I squint at him as I take a long drink. "Why don't you grab some breakfast with me while you wait?"

"I had breakfast two hours ago," he growls, looking over at Roman who's talking to a few people by the check-in desk.

"You can come over to Seb and Sophie's with me if you don't want to wait for them."

"Definitely not. Fishing over everything." He looks down at me—his eyes finally softening. "And I wouldn't want to get in the way of you and your boy toy. You don't look like you got any sleep."

"Oh, you know, I always have a problem sleeping in a new bed," I say, looking away.

"Which bed were you trying to sleep in—yours or Alex's?"

"What?" I look up at him blankly.

"Nice try. Your poker face sucks. Don't think I didn't see him leading you out of the party."

"He was walking me back to my room."

"I bet he was. Just tell me one thing: did you win our bet?"

I plop down on a couch. "You know what? I'm going to forfeit the bet. You win."

"Wow," he says, sitting down next to me and patting my leg. "You did win. I'm proud of you. Any pictures?"

"Shut up," I say, shoving his shoulder. "I don't want to talk about it."

"Oh, but I think we should talk about it." He strokes his beard as looks at me. "Hmm. I think you really won. Sex?"

"Leave me alone."

"Wow, look at carefree Raine go," he says, grinning. "I'm just as proud as I can be—"

"Excuse me." We both look up as a porter closes in on us. "Do you know who Sophie Banks is? I'm supposed to give her this note."

"She's going to see her later today," Butch says, nodding to me. "She'll deliver it."

"No." The porter pulls the note away from him. "I'm supposed to give the note directly to Miss Banks. No one else is supposed to see it."

"Butch, quit being funny," I say, standing up. "I'm Sophie Banks."

The porter takes a step back. "They told me Miss Banks was tall and blonde. You're short with dark hair."

"You know, I tried the whole blonde thing. It didn't work for me," I say, shrugging. "And tall is a matter of perspective. I'm Sophie Banks."

He starts to walk away. "I don't think so—"

"Butch."

Butch jumps up, grabs the porter by the neck, and shoves him behind a wall of plants. He snatches the note out of his hand and gives it to me.

"Never doubt the word of a lady," Butch snarls as the porter grimaces from the pressure on his neck. "Are we done with him?"

"No, but don't break his neck," I say, smiling at the porter. "Yet."

I rip the envelope open. The message is written in capital, block letters—like an old-time ransom note.

SEB'S CHEATING ON YOU.
HE HAS BEEN FROM THE START.

I turn the note toward Butch.

"Naw," he says. "I've only known him for a day, but he doesn't seem like the type at all. And it looks like a five-year-old wrote that."

"Who gave you this note?" I say, looking back at the porter.

"I don't know. I didn't get a good look."

His face twists up as Butch increases the pressure on his neck again.

"Was it a man or a woman?"

"Woman."

"Taller or shorter than me."

The porter scans my body. "Is anyone shorter than you?"

"Really?" I say. "You're going to try comedy when my friend can break your neck in a couple of moves."

"It's really only one move," Butch says to me as he starts to demonstrate on the porter's neck. "It has a twist, though, so sometimes it looks like two if you don't get a smooth break."

"Taller," the porter says quickly. "A lot taller, but she might have been wearing heels."

"Hair color?"

"She had on a big hat and sunglasses." A bead of sweat rolls down his forehead. "I didn't get a good look at her."

"Is she a guest of the resort?"

"Maybe," he says, looking down. "I didn't see her arrive or anything."

"You didn't see her arrive, but you saw her leave?"

He hesitates as he looks up at Butch. "I need to get back to work."

"You're not leaving until she says you can leave. Answer the question."

"The lady gave me a twenty to keep it to myself—"

"And I'm going to let you live if you keep talking," Butch says. "Which is more important to you?"

"After she gave me the note, she got into a sports car out front and drove away with a guy." He looks up at Butch. "And I don't know what the guy looked like. I didn't really look at him."

"Because you were looking at his car," I say, smiling. "What kind of car was it?"

He hesitates. "I didn't get a good look."

"Butch."

The porter winces again. "It was a red BMW convertible of some kind, but I noticed it because the dashboard was high and the guy was slung down low in the seat. I'm not sure how he even saw to drive."

"Very nice. We're done. If this woman gives you another note, it comes to one of us." I point at Butch. "If you give it to anyone else, I'll have him hunt you down. Do you understand me?"

He nods vigorously.

"Let him go, Butch."

Butch gives him one more menacing look before he releases him.

"Who do you think gave him the note?" he says as we watch the porter run away from us.

I look at the note again. "I think some troll's probably just fucking with Sophie. Like maybe Savannah."

"Seb's friend Ricky was talking some trash about her last night, too," he says, leaning back on the wall. "You want me to come with you today to keep an eye on things?"

"No, go fishing. This feels more petty than dangerous, but maybe subtly pump Roman for information about the team owners coming at Sophie. Don't tell him about this, though. I don't want him involved. He's too emotional about Sophie."

"And you're not emotional about Sophie?"

"You already know my emotion gets funneled into action," I say, looking up at him. "When we find the person who sent this note, we're putting them down."

"Roger that," he says, turning me around so I can see Alex walking toward us.

Just seeing him again almost takes my breath away. My mind snaps back to when he was inside me—my hands grabbing at the beautiful muscles in his back. His eyes are fixed on me as he makes his way across the lobby.

"Hey," he says gently as he tries to take my hand. "Good morning."

"Good morning," I say, pulling my hand away.

He looks at Butch and then back at me. "Am I interrupting something?"

"Not at all," I say, pointing back toward the drink table. "Butch was just complaining about the fruit that's floating in the water."

Butch looks at me—his eyes narrowing. "I'm just saying that water should taste like water."

"Did you change your mind about the fishing trip, Butch?" Alex says, his eyes still firmly fixed on me.

"Nope," Butch says, motioning across the lobby to Roman. "In fact, it looks like they're finally ready to go. Roman said we're coming over to Seb and Sophie's after we're done fishing, so I'll see you over there."

"Okay," I say, my voice getting higher as I look up at him. "Have fun. Catch a big one or whatever."

His eyes narrow further. He always knows when something's wrong with me. "You good?"

"Yeah, I'm fine. Seriously. All good. I'll see you over there."

"Okay," Butch says, walking away backward. "Alex, keep an eye on her. Don't let her fight with anyone. Except for maybe Savannah. And if that happens, make sure you send me a video."

Alex nods at him and then turns back to me. "What's wrong? Are you having second thoughts about last night?"

"Not at all. I'm just a little tired. I didn't get much sleep."

He slides his arms around my waist. "I told you that you'd sleep better on my chest, but you wanted to go back to your room."

He tries to kiss me, but I pull back.

"Raine, what's wrong?"

"Nothing's wrong," I say, looking around the lobby. "There are just a lot of eyes everywhere down here."

He pulls me back into an alcove and presses me against the wall. "We're all alone here," he says, planting his lips firmly on mine. "I missed you."

"For the six hours we've been apart?" I take a deep, shaky breath as he runs his hands up and down my back.

"Every second of it," he growls. "Maybe we can go back to my room and pick up where we left off."

I push at his chest. "I was going to get breakfast."

He starts kissing my neck. "We can get room service," he whispers.

"Alex, no." I push him again. This time he takes a step back. His face tightens as he looks down at me.

"Tell me what's wrong." His eyes are so intense that I have to look away. "Raine, what's changed? What's happening?"

When I don't answer, he grabs my hand and starts pulling me toward the restaurant. "Come on. Let's get breakfast."

"Maybe we shouldn't eat together in public," I say, pulling back on his hand.

He spins around. "Wait. Do you not want to be seen with me in public?"

"That's not it."

His eyebrows draw together as he takes a step back toward me. "Or maybe you won the bet, so you're done with me now."

"Alex, that's not it. It's just—I'm a private person. And this whole resort," I say, waving my hand around the lobby, "is like college spring break or something. Everyone's in each other's business."

His face melts a little bit. "Then let's get breakfast somewhere else. I'll drive us over to Cruz Bay. We can find something there and talk about what's going on with you right now."

"Okay," I say slowly, "but I'm really hungry. And I get combative when I'm hungry."

"More combative than this?" He laughs as he grabs my hand and pulls me over to the drink table. He hands me a banana. "Will this hold you until I can properly feed you?"

I nod. As he starts pulling me toward the valet, he looks over his shoulder. "Okay, then let's go before someone sees us together. I wouldn't want to be on the front page of the St. John newspaper or something."

Chapter Twenty-Two

ALEX

When we get to the valet stand, one of the porters sees Raine and spins around so quickly that he crashes into a bench and almost falls over the top of it.

"You okay, man?" I say as I reach out to steady him.

"Yeah," he says, not taking his eyes off Raine. "Do you need your car?"

I look back and forth between them. Raine's trying to act normal, but her eyes aren't blinking as she looks at him.

"That's my Jeep right there." I motion over to the parking area. "Alex Molina. Just give me the keys. We can walk over there."

He starts fumbling through the keys and finally grabs mine. He hands them to me without looking up.

"Thank you," I say, putting my arm around Raine's shoulders as I guide her to the parking lot. "What was that about?"

She looks up at me—trying to keep her face neutral. "What was what about?"

"You're not a good liar. Why's the valet scared of you? Did you get into a fight with him, too?"

She nods over to Savannah who's staring at us as she walks toward the lobby with her husband. "Can we go?"

After I drive out of the resort, I pull over under a clump of palm trees. "What's going on this morning? We're not leaving here until you tell me."

"Alex, I'm hungry—"

"Eat the banana. I'm not driving any further until you start talking."

She sighs, but takes a big bite of the banana and then hands me a piece of paper out of her bag. "The porter was trying to deliver this note to Sophie this morning. Butch and I intercepted it."

I read it and look up at her. "That shit's not happening. Seb isn't cheating on her. No way."

"Yeah, I don't think so either."

"Who gave this note to him?"

"We're still working on that," she says, finishing her banana, "but I don't think we're dealing with a master criminal. Probably just some petty wedding guest."

"That's crazy petty," I say, whistling. "I mean you would have to be almost evil to do something like this a day before their wedding."

"Maybe not evil, but we're definitely dealing with a narcissist. There are a few of those here. We just need to figure out which one it is."

"Are you going to tell Seb and Sophie?"

"No," she says, pointing at me, "and I don't want you to tell them. This is just some stupid prank. I don't want to ruin their weekend."

"I won't tell them if you don't want me to," I say as I pull the Jeep back onto the road. "Is that note what's bothering you this morning?"

She pulls her hair into a ponytail as we pick up speed. "Yeah, it bothers me. I don't want anyone hurting Sophie. There are a lot of people here that don't seem to even like her. I'm not sure what's going on with that."

I shrug. "Jealousy. Seb's a good catch."

She spins toward me and crosses her arms. "Sophie's a good catch, too."

"What?" I look at her for a second. She's scowling hard at me. "Raine, I know she is. And more importantly, Seb knows she is. He's not cheating on her. I know Seb. I mean, he was with his share of women before her, but believe me, he stopped thinking about anyone except Sophie the second he met her."

"Yeah," she says, looking away from me. "I guess all ballplayers get around."

"Get around?" I look over at her again and tug on her arm a few times. "Is that what's bothering you? You think I get around?"

"Well, don't you?" She turns toward me—the scowl deepening. "I'm sure you've had your share of women, too. But, you're single. Do what you want."

I press my lips together to stop myself from laughing. "I wasn't celibate before I met you if that's what you're asking."

"I wasn't asking anything—"

"Weren't you?"

She looks away again.

"Raine," I say, grabbing her hand. "Here's what I can tell you. From the moment you closed the door to your room last night to the moment I saw you this morning, I thought of nothing else. I was awake most of the night thinking about when I got to see you again. That hasn't happened in years. And were you celibate before you met me?"

"No, but I'm sure I'm not quite as experienced as you—"

"Believe me, I couldn't tell from your performance last night."

"Stop!" She pulls her hand out of mine and slaps my arm —a smile finally starting to crack through the scowl. "And honestly, I was thinking about you all night, too."

"Look, Raine, I date a lot, but I haven't met a woman—in a very long time—who I've been interested in past one night. Until last night that is. You're different. I mean, you're sexy as hell, but it's more than that. I think we have something in common. We don't have to have sex again, but I'd like to get to know you a little better. Is that okay?"

"I didn't say I didn't want to have sex again," she says, the little line forming above her brows.

"Okay. We can have sex again, but only if you promise me that you're not just adding to your long list of men."

"Shut up," she says, shoving me. "Can we please find a restaurant? I'm starting to get low blood sugar."

"Emergency situation. Let's go." I park the car, grab her hand, and start pulling her down the street. "I hope they get our food out quickly. I don't want to have to pull you off the waiter."

We find a little breakfast place that's right on the beach. Our table is in the sand—only about a hundred feet from the water. The sound of the waves gently lapping up onto shore seems to calm Raine down a little bit. She chugs her orange juice the minute the waiter sets it down. She inhales and closes her eyes.

I motion to the waiter to bring her a refill. "You okay?" I say, stroking her arm. "I don't want you to pass out."

"Better." She opens her eyes. "Hey, do you think your agent left that note for Sophie? He obviously doesn't like her."

"Uh," I say, pouring some milk into my coffee. "That doesn't feel like his move. And I'm not sure that he doesn't like Sophie. He's just a dick."

"He's definitely that," she says with a little growl in her voice, "and anyway, he's probably figured out that they're married by now, so the note wouldn't do him much good unless he's just a revenge freak or something."

"He wouldn't risk losing Seb." I take a long drink of coffee. "He's an asshole, but he's not dumb."

"Why do you have an asshole as your agent?"

"I've been asking myself that a lot lately, especially after the way he treated you last night, but the short answer is that he gets me a lot of money. Does that sound bad?"

"Not really," she says, taking a long drink of the orange juice the waiter just delivered. "I mean you might as well max out while you're playing. What happens if you go to law school? Do you quit playing?"

I look out at the ocean and sigh.

"I'm sorry," she says, touching my arm. "I forgot you don't want to talk about that. We can do small talk."

"No, I don't mind telling you about it. What happens is if I go to law school, I quit baseball. It's a big decision. I haven't been able to make it yet. Everyone's coming at me—my agent, my dad, the team's GM. I have to make a decision, but I can't seem to get there."

"Do you want to quit playing? You know, law school will always be there. You're young."

"Not that young. I'm almost thirty."

"Oh my God," she says, tugging her hand away from me. "I had no idea you were that old. Will you please take me back to the resort right now?"

The waiter sets our plates in front of us.

"Good timing," I say, looking up at him. "She was getting combative again."

She stuffs two pieces of bacon into her mouth before I can even look at my plate. "God, I love bacon so much."

"Are you going to chew that?" I say, watching her face melt into satisfaction. "Or are you just swallowing the strips whole?"

"Don't watch me eat." She sticks the tip of her tongue out at me. "And thirty is still very young. You have plenty of time to do whatever you want."

"So you think I should sign another contract—keep playing?"

She looks up from her omelet. "I have no idea. I barely know you."

"I wouldn't say that exactly. We got to know each other pretty well last night."

She rolls her eyes. "I mean I don't know anything about your professional life. Do you still enjoy playing?"

"Uh," I say, slapping her hand away as she grabs a piece of my bacon. "I don't not enjoy it, but I feel like I'm ready for something else."

"Then quit. Go to law school."

"It's not that easy. You don't understand. I would disappoint a lot of people—including my dad."

"Can you bring us another side of bacon?" She looks up at the waiter as he passes and then back at me. "I understand that. I've been disappointing my parents for a long time now."

"I find that hard to believe. I can't imagine any parent not thinking that you're perfect."

"You've obviously never met my parents," she says as she starts in on her fruit cup.

"Can I ask you something?" I say as I drown my eggs in ketchup.

"No, it's not okay to put ketchup on scrambled eggs, especially that much. There's your answer."

"Not quite what I wanted to ask." She shudders as I drag some eggs through the ketchup. "You haven't told me anything about what you do for a living. I'm interested."

"Is that a question?" She looks out at the ocean as she puts a chunk of mango into her mouth.

"It's just," I say, watching her eyes. I've noticed that when she doesn't want to talk about something, they stop blinking. "I've done a lot of reading about SEALs—fiction and non-fiction."

"Oh yeah," she says, turning back toward me. "If you have any insight into figuring out Butch let me know."

"I don't think there's any book in the world that can explain Butch."

She laughs as she takes another drink of coffee. "I think it would be a best seller if someone could just figure him out."

"I'd much rather figure you out." She looks up at me and then turns back toward the ocean. "In every book I've read, they've never mentioned the SEAL teams working with a State Department envoy. They mention CIA operatives, though. There's always a few embedded with the teams."

"Huh. Yeah, I've met a few agents on the job."

"Is that right?" I polish off the rest of my eggs—my eyes still fixed firmly on the side of her head. "What are the agents like?"

She shrugs. "Couldn't tell you. They kind of keep to themselves. They're not very friendly."

"That's not the impression I get at all," I say, reaching for her hand again as she puts her coffee cup down.

She looks at me and tilts her head. "Oh yeah, do you know a CIA agent?"

"Yeah," I say, nodding as I squeeze her hand. "I think I just met one."

"Huh, well you should probably ask him these questions. He might know a little more than I do." She looks back at the ocean. "It's really pretty down here, isn't it?"

"Okay," I say, squeezing her hand once more before I let it go. "We can do small talk."

Chapter Twenty-Three

RAINE

"Stop it!" I say, trying to break out of the human sandwich Sophie's brothers, Luke and Jake, have formed around me.

Alex and I arrived at Seb and Sophie's villa about five minutes ago. When her brothers saw me walk in with him, they grabbed me, pulled me away, and immediately started teasing me.

"But we've missed you, little Rainey," Luke says, kissing the top of my head. "We haven't seen you for years and now you show up to Sophie's wedding with Alex Molina. Please tell us everything we've missed."

"Everything," Jake echoes as he starts tickling me.

"Get away from me! You're grown-ass men with wives and kids. Why are you still acting like you're ten?"

"Because we love you," Jake says as he looks back at Alex who's standing about ten feet from us, "but obviously not as much as Alex does. He hasn't stopped looking at you once since we took you away from him. Maybe if we keep you over here long enough, he'll come over and rescue you."

"I don't need anyone to rescue me from you anymore." I finally break their hold. "And not that it's any of your business, but I met him yesterday. I barely know him. He just gave me a ride over here."

"Oh he definitely gave you a ride," Luke says, whistling as he turns around to look at Alex again.

"Luke, I swear to God," I say, grabbing his face and turning it back to me, "if you don't shut up, I'll tell both of our mothers that you got Sophie and me high when we were fourteen."

He takes an exaggerated step back.

"And Maisie," Jake laughs. "She was there, too."

"Yes, thank you, Jake," I say, pointing at Luke, "and Maisie. Do you want me to tell Melinda that you let her perfect baby girl smoke pot at fourteen? She still hasn't forgiven you for teepeeing their house. That was twenty years ago. Mel holds grudges better than anyone I know. She'll end you if she finds out you got Maisie high."

"I seriously think she might." Luke nods and narrows his eyes. "Well played, Rainey. You were always smarter than the other two."

"I know you're not talking about me," Sophie says, pushing Luke from behind as she walks up to us. "Come on, Raine. Maisie and I want some alone time with you."

"Alex wants some alone time with her, too."

"Luke!" I mime smoking a joint with my hand and then point at him. "Don't push me."

He holds up his hands and starts backing away. "I surrender. You have me beat."

As I watch them walk away, I link my arm with Sophie's. "God, I still want to punch your brothers so badly."

"Who doesn't?" she says as she starts pulling me toward the beach. "I think I started falling in love with Seb when he told me he would kick their asses for me."

I stop and close my eyes. "Ah, please tell me that happened and that it can happen again—with me watching."

"Unfortunately it hasn't happened yet," she says, sighing as she continues to pull me toward the water, "but it's something to look forward to."

As we get to the bottom of the stairs that lead to the beach, I see Maisie lounging in an enormous inflatable pink flamingo on the edge of the water. Her head's propped up on one side and her feet on the other. She has a plastic cup balanced on her bare stomach with a long straw that connects the cup to her mouth.

"About time," she says as she peers at us from underneath a huge sun hat. "I've been waiting down here forever."

"Yeah, you look really uncomfortable," I say, flipping some water on her.

"God that feels good. It's so hot out here," she says as she sucks hard on the straw.

"Nice ride, sister," I say, flipping the flamingo's beak. "Is it sea-worthy?"

"I guess we'll find out. It's just the right size for three people and a pitcher of mai tais," she says, pushing her hat back as she holds up an oversized thermos. "Get in. We're going floating."

"Oh, uh," I say, looking back to the pool deck. "I should—"

"Tell Alex?" Sophie says, pulling me onto the flamingo. "I don't think you have to tell him where you are. He hasn't taken his eyes off you since you got here."

"I was going to say that I should get my sunscreen and hat."

Maisie dumps her beach bag on the floor of the flamingo. She waves her hand over her supply of sunscreen, ponytail holders, chapstick, and a baseball hat with Seb's number 20 on it. She hands me the hat. "Sit down, Raine. We have some talking to do."

"Fine," I say, pulling the hat low on my head. "Make me a drink. I have a feeling I'm going to need it.

"Hey, Dad," Sophie yells. "Will you pull us out further?"

Her dad wades over and starts pulling us out into the water. "So Raine, I saw you walk in with Alex Molina. What's going on there?"

"Not you, too, Mr. Banks. Seriously?"

He shrugs. "I'm just thinking that maybe I can get another one of my daughters married off—"

"Stop," I say, pointing at him. "It's not like that. And don't mention to my mom that you saw me with a guy. And tell Mrs. Banks not to say anything. You know how Mom gets."

"My lips are sealed, but I can't guarantee Deb won't say anything." He laughs as he walks back to shore. "Don't drift out too far, ladies."

"It's not like that, huh?" Maisie says, smiling at me. "Then please do tell us what it's like."

"Sophie, make her leave me alone."

"No way," Sophie says, pouring herself a drink. "I'm on her side on this one. And take off your cover-up before you sweat to death."

I already know what's coming. I sigh as I pull my cover-up over my head.

"Holy shit, Raine!" Maisie says, sitting up as she stares at my very small, very pink bikini. "Did you wear that for Alex or for me? Because I'm about to pass out just looking at you."

I slap her hands away as she points to my cleavage. "Stop it. I'm wearing it for me. I'm trying to take more risks."

"From the way Alex is looking at you today," Sophie says, "I think you're already at risk of him throwing you down on the sand and taking you, but if not, that suit's going to push him over the edge."

I take a long drink of my mai tai. "That's already happened."

"What?" Their combined screech is so loud that everyone at the party looks out to us.

"We're fine," I say, waving up at them and then turning back to Maisie and Sophie. "Keep your voices down, maniacs."

"You slept with him last night?" Sophie whispers.

"And this morning—"

"Oh my God! Who are you right now?" Maisie says, spilling some of her drink as she tries to sit up. "How was it? Is he any good? He has to be, right? I mean, God, just look at him."

"Mae! Raine might not want to talk about that." Sophie slugs her leg. "But seriously, is he any good? And exactly how good? Be specific."

"Crazy good—like I'm sweating just thinking about it," I mumble as I pull the baseball hat over my face. I shove them both as they start squealing again. "Stop! They're going to know what we're talking about."

"So is it going to happen again?" Maisie whispers. "Or was it like a one-night thing?"

"Uh," I say, taking a long drink as I ease my head back onto the side of the flamingo. "I think that's up to me."

"And?" Sophie says, grabbing my arm.

"No squealing." I point at them. They cover their mouths —eyes wide. "Yeah, I think it's going to happen again. I know I want it to."

They both twist around as they muffle their screams.

"Is it just lust at this point?" Maisie says. "I mean, I get it if it is. He's so beautiful."

"It's definitely lust, but I like him, too. We've gotten to know each other a little bit. He seems sweet and smart. And he has a really cute sense of humor."

"He's all of that," Sophie says, patting my leg. "And really, it sounds like you just described yourself, so a perfect match."

I smile at her as I take her hand. "Don't get too excited, Soph. It's probably just for the weekend. He's in Miami and I'll be in San Diego soon. That doesn't work too well for dating. You know?"

"I know," she says, putting her arm around me. "Just have fun while you're down here and get to know him better. You never know."

"Can we talk about you now?" I say, laying my head on

her shoulder. "Let's start with why you're lying about already being married."

"What?" Sophie says as Maisie sinks down as low into the flamingo as she can. "We're getting married tomorrow."

"Shut up, Sophie. I don't even have to look at you to know you're lying. You're worse at it than I am—and that's saying something."

Maisie starts giggling underneath her hat.

"Mae! Did you tell her?"

Maisie jerks her hat up. "No! You know I'm a vault."

Sophie pushes me off her shoulder. "Who told you?"

"No one told me. Come on, Soph. I know you way better than to think this is the kind of wedding you'd have. It would stress you out. And even if Seb wanted a big wedding, there's no way he'd deny you anything. Did you get married up in Michigan?"

She sighs and lowers herself back onto the side of the raft. "Yeah, over All Star break. Don't tell anyone."

"I already told Seb's agent. He was being a dick and I wanted to fuck with him."

"Yeah, Seb told me he's trying to get me to sign a prenup—"

"What?" Maisie sits up. "Too late for that, asshole. Did Seb ask you to sign one before the wedding?"

"No, but I would have if he wanted me to. I don't need his money. I just want to be with him."

"And he just wants to be with you," Maisie says, holding her hand. "You're going to have a great life together if you can ignore all of the nonsense from some of the people around him. Just concentrate on each other and block out everything else."

"Agree," I say. "I can't imagine why you even invited a lot of these people down here. I'm not even sure some of them want you and Seb together."

"Exactly," Maisie says, pointing at Sophie. "Like Ricky and Savannah and now probably the dick agent."

Sophie sighs. "Yeah, Seb and I talked about that last night. We should have kept this trip a little tighter, but nothing we can do about it now."

"So," I say, trying to sound nonchalant, "is there anyone in particular that you think is trying to cause trouble?"

"Ricky—"

"Mae, I told you to lighten up on him. He's important to Seb."

"He's a pain in the ass, but yeah, I don't think he'd try to do any real harm. He wouldn't risk being cut off from Seb's fame." She sits straight up. "Oh! I forgot to tell you. At the party last night, I overheard that bitch Caroline talking some smack about you to Jack's wife. I forget her name."

"Casey." Sophie rolls her eyes. "Those two are the meanest little women I've ever met. They're crazier than Savannah. Did you say anything to them?"

"Of course I said something," Maisie laughs. "I told them to shut their bitch mouths or I'd shut them for them."

I spit out a little of my drink. "Yeah, that's pretty much what I told Savannah last night, too. Just tell me that the actual wedding had better energy than this shit show."

"It was so perfect." Sophie smiles and takes a deep breath. "Just our families, Maisie and Ryan, and Stone and his wife.

We got married at sunset on the deck of Seb's lake house. It was beautiful."

"So beautiful," Maisie says. "It was quiet and intimate—just perfect. We stayed there for a few hours to celebrate, and then left them alone for the rest of the week—a perfect Sophie wedding."

"It sounds lovely. Do you have pictures?"

Maisie pulls out her phone and hands it to me. The picture's taken from behind Seb and Sophie as they look at the minister—with an orange and pink sunset framing the lake behind him. Sophie's wearing a long, white sundress with her hair flowing in curls down her back. Seb's wearing khaki shorts, flip-flops, and an untucked white shirt with the sleeves rolled up to his elbows. They're holding hands. Her head's resting on his arm and he's kissing the top of her head.

"It's so perfect," I say as tears start falling from my eyes.

Sophie lays her head on my shoulder and looks at the picture. "Yeah, it was. I found my soulmate. Mae found hers. Now, we have to find yours. And I think we might have a good start on that already."

Chapter Twenty-Four

ALEX

"Anything happen after we left last night?"

Seb cranes his neck again to look out at the ocean. We're sitting by the pool. Raine, Maisie, and Sophie are lounging in the ocean on an inflatable flamingo the size of a small island.

"They weren't screaming because they were in trouble," I say, shoving his shoulder. "Settle down. They're just having some fun out there."

"I don't want them to get too far out," he says as he looks again.

"Seb, they're fine. Chill out. You don't have to have your eyes on Sophie every second."

He turns back to me. "Yeah, you're one to talk. You haven't taken your eyes off Raine since you two walked in. Did something happen there?"

"I don't kiss and tell."

"Since when?"

"Since right now." I point at him. "Leave it alone."

"Huh," he says, nodding, "you have a thing for her, don't you?"

"I don't know about that," I say, looking away. "But yeah, she's cool. Much more interesting than anyone I've been around in a long time."

"That's not setting the bar very high, but I agree. She seems like she'd be worth some effort—maybe even a keeper long term."

"Pump the brakes," I say, flipping my beer cap at him. "We've known each other for like a day."

"That's all it took me with Sophie. Seriously, I think I knew the second I laid eyes on her."

"Yeah, it seemed like it. How'd you know so quickly?"

"Oh, man, a lot of different things," he says, leaning back in his chair and closing his eyes, "but the one thing that just slapped me in the face was that when I talked to her, I could see life after baseball. I'd never really thought about it before, but when I met her, not only could I imagine it, but I couldn't wait for it."

"I understand that completely," I say, taking a long drink. "You think you'll keep playing after this contract ends?"

"I don't know. That's a couple of years off, but Sophie's already talking about kids. We both want to start trying soon. And I don't want to be traveling all the time when we have a family. But you're probably closer to retiring than I am. Have you made up your mind about the contract?"

"No," I growl. "I can't see the answer. It's pissing me off."

"I'm not telling you what to do, but law school will always be there. There's no age limit. Maybe play a few more years."

"That's what Raine said this morning."

"Really?" he says, grinning. "You'll barely talk to me about this, but you talk to her? Huh. I think someone else might be seeing life after baseball."

I roll my eyes at him as Stone walks over to us. "Is this a private conversation?"

"Naw, man," I say. "Rescue me from him."

Seb looks back out at the flamingo.

"Don't sit down yet," he says, standing and grabbing the beer cooler. "Let's move down to the sand just in case they drift out too far. We can get to them faster."

"Good Lord, you're a control freak," I say, trying to grab his arm to stop him.

"Bruh," Stone says as he starts to follow Seb. "He's been this way since we were kids. Believe me, it's easier to just go along with it."

"Fine," I say as I follow them, "but you're just enabling him."

When we get down to the beach, we find Sophie's dad sitting on one of the chairs down there—looking out at the flamingo. He looks up and laughs. "I'm keeping an eye on them, Seb. I won't let them drift out to sea."

"Thanks, Bob," Seb says, patting him on the back. "Guys, you remember Sophie's dad, Bob. This is Alex and Stone."

As I shake his hand, he stares at me a little too long. "So, Alex, I saw you walk in with Raine. I've known her since she was a week old. She's like a daughter to me."

"Yes, sir," I say, backing up and sitting in the chair furthest away from him, "she's a very nice person."

"She is at that," he says, nodding, his eyes still fixed on

me. "Her parents are some of our best friends. Seb met them the last time he was in town. Good people, right, Seb?"

"Yep," Seb says. "They seemed like it."

"They are," Bob says. "They look after our kids. We look after theirs. Do I need to go on?"

"No, sir," I say quickly. "I—"

"They said y'all were down here," Butch says as he rounds the corner onto the beach. I'm about to thank God for his arrival when he opens his mouth again. "Where are the ladies? Seb, I don't think I've ever seen you without a good chunk of Sophie's ass in your hands."

Seb groans as he rubs his forehead and nods toward Bob. "Butch, this is Sophie's dad, Bob Banks."

Butch lets out a low whistle. "Well, sir, I think I probably owe you an apology for what I just said."

Bob stands up. "My grandma told me only to apologize if you're wrong. And you're not wrong about where Seb's hands spend most of their time."

Seb covers his face. "Then I probably owe you an apology, Bob," he mutters.

"I doubt that apology comes with any regret or intent to be better in the future, so save it," Bob says, shaking his head. "Now if you'll excuse me, gentlemen, I'll leave you before the boy talk gets too uncomfortable for me. Nice to meet you, Butch."

"My pleasure, sir." Butch steps out of his way and watches him until he clears the corner. He pats Seb on the shoulder. "Damn, I stepped into that one. Sorry, Seb. And no one answered my question. Where are the ladies?"

"Flamingo." I hand him a beer as I nod out to the ocean. "You catch any fish?"

"Butch caught the biggest fucking tuna I've ever seen," Roman says as he makes his way down to us. "Didn't even take him that long to haul it in. I think the damn thing gave up the second he got a good look at Butch's face."

"I do like a good surrender," Butch says, pointing out to the flamingo. "Seb, the tide's coming in. They're not going anywhere."

"What?" Seb turns his head around to look at Butch.

"You haven't taken your eyes off that flamingo since I walked down here," Butch laughs. "I'm telling you, the tide's coming in. Stop worrying about them."

"I don't know," Seb says. "They keep getting further away."

"He's a fucking Navy SEAL," Stone says. "He knows more about tides than you do. And I'm sure Butch has done a few at-sea rescues, so if they're attacked by pirates or something, he can save them."

Seb looks over at Butch. "Why don't we go out and grab them now so I can relax a little?"

Butch squints his eyes. "Seb, do you think pirates are going to hijack that flamingo?"

"Stranger things have happened." Seb looks back at the ocean as we hear a peal of laughter explode again from the flamingo.

"Not many, brother." Butch looks at me for backup. I roll my eyes and shrug. He lets out a long breath. "Good Lord, Seb, you're more of a control freak than I am and I didn't think that was possible. If it'll make you feel better, I'll swim out there and tie them to your boat."

"Oh, that's not my boat," Seb says, pointing to a small yacht that's anchored a couple of hundred feet off the shore.

"Whose is it?" Butch says.

"I don't know," Seb says. "It's been sitting there since we arrived."

"You seen anybody on it?" Butch looks out at the boat.

"No, but I haven't really been looking. Something weird about it?"

"No, not at all," Butch says, turning around and smiling. "I'm sure it's just some tourists enjoying this beautiful bay. And they won't mind me hitching the flamingo to their ride."

"You need me to swim out there with you?" I say, standing up.

"That's about three hundred feet of the calmest water I've ever seen," Butch says. "Sit your ass down. Unless you can't stand to be apart from Raine any longer."

I shake my head as Seb and Stone start laughing.

"Well spotted, Butch," Stone says, giving him a fist bump. "Alex looked like he was about to swallow her whole when they walked in."

"I think that already happened last night—"

"Enough, Butch," I say, glaring at him. "Don't talk about her. I thought you said she was like a little sister to you."

"She is, but I think little sis has grown up a bunch in the last day or so."

"Stop," I say, looking around at them again. "All of you."

Seb laughs. "He won't talk about her. I already tried. I think Alex has got it bad."

"Enough," I say, glaring at him. "I didn't ride you like this when you met Sophie—"

"What the fuck are you talking about? Between you and Manny, I barely got any peace. Not to mention Dane's stupid ass always talking about her."

"Where is Dane, by the way?" I say, trying to change the subject. "I haven't seen him down here."

"You think I invited that asshole? I don't even like him."

"Why'd you invite Manny then?" I say, laughing. "I've never seen you fight with anyone more than him."

"That's professionally. He's one of the most stubborn pitchers I've ever caught, but he's an okay guy. His wife sucks, but he's good."

"Yeah," I say, "seems like Caroline and Casey kind of gang up on Sophie."

"They do," Seb snarls. "And I'm about to shut it down. Sophie told me to leave it alone, but I don't think I can. I swear I feel it deeper than she does."

"Friend, if that's the case," Butch says. "you're doing sex really wrong."

"Oh look," I say, pointing out to the ocean, "pirates just boarded the flamingo. You better get out there, Butch."

"All right, brother, I'll leave y'all alone." He starts running out into the water. "They can have the flamingo, but they will not take my women!"

We watch him as he dives into the water and takes out swimming at a record pace. He's covered half the distance before I can even take a breath.

"Man, they don't get any stupider than him," I say, laughing, "but I'd damn sure trust him with my life."

"I got to know him a little better this morning," Roman says. "He's for real. I'm not scared of many people, but I wouldn't fuck with him for a second."

"Yeah, I don't think we've seen much of his SEAL side yet," Seb says, watching him as he closes in on the flamingo, "but it looks like he can kick it in at a moment's notice."

"Does he ever stop talking, though?" Stone says.

"I tried to get him to talk a little bit more about Raine this morning," Roman says, "but he clammed right up."

"What about Raine?" I try to control the tension in my voice.

"Settle down. I haven't switched teams," Roman says. "I just think there's more to her than meets the eye."

"Meaning?" I sit up straight as I look at him.

"Meaning, I think she does something a little more covert than working for the State Department."

"Naw," I say, lounging back. "She's who she says she is. We've done a lot of talking. She told me all about it. Sounds like a cool job."

When I look over at Roman again, he's nodding with a slight smile coming to his face. I think I just found the only person—besides my mom—who can tell when I'm lying.

Chapter Twenty-Five

RAINE

"Brace yourself!" I yell as I see Butch's eyes pop over the side of the flamingo.

Sophie and Maisie scream as he pushes the side up and acts like he's going to dump us in the water.

"It's just Butch," I say, whacking the top of his head. "Put us down. Now."

The flamingo eases back into the water as Butch drapes his arms over the side. "Ladies," he says, grinning.

"Butch, I don't know you very well," Maisie says, pushing his forehead, "but I swear to God, I'll kill you if you lose our drinks in the ocean."

She holds up the thermos that's holding our mai tai backup stash.

"Yes, ma'am," he says. "Save the liquor at all costs. I respect that energy."

Maisie lets out a long sigh. "Thank God I didn't know you

when I was a teenager because that accent would have made me jump into bed with you in a hot second."

"Never too late, darling," Butch says, winking at her.

"Stop!" I say, swatting his hand. "You're not allowed to deepen your drawl when you're talking to my friends—especially my married friends. And no winking ever—to anyone. I feel like that should go without saying."

He winks and blows me a kiss.

"Behave!" I say, trying to pry him off the side of the flamingo. "And leave. This is a female-only zone. We're deep into girl talk."

"Believe me, I want no part of your girl talk. I just need to borrow you for a second." Butch squeezes my arm. "And I wouldn't be out here at all if Seb weren't such a control freak. He's worried y'all are going to drift out to sea and he's never going to see Sophie again."

"What?" Sophie lifts her head and looks back toward the beach. "We're fine, but he's so cute, right?"

"Just adorable." Butch squeals and shakes his shoulders.

"Stop," I say, laughing. "And you don't need my help to haul us back in."

"I'm not swimming you back in. I'm tying you to that boat, so you stay with its anchor."

"Or maybe we could just chill on the boat," I say. "I'm not sure how much longer this thing's going to stay afloat."

"It's not Seb's boat." Butch squeezes my arm again—harder this time. "He doesn't know who it belongs to and it's been anchored there since they arrived. He hasn't seen anyone on it."

"Huh." I sit up straight. "You probably need my help."

"I do at that," he says, locking his eyes with mine.

"I'll be right back," I say. "Don't drink all of the mai tais."

"No promises," Maisie says as I roll over the side of the flamingo into the water.

Butch grabs my arm. "Can you make it over to the boat by yourself?"

"I think so."

"Here, get on my back," Butch says as he pulls me over to him.

My mind flashes back to last night when Alex had me on his back.

"What? No!" I say, trying to pull away from him.

"You're not a good swimmer, Raine. Get on my back and I'll swim us over there."

I scrunch up my face as I push him away from me.

He shakes his head. "Oh good Lord, you had sex in the ocean last night, didn't you?"

"No!"

"You definitely did something in the ocean." When I start swimming away from him, he grabs my foot and pulls me back. "Why are you still so bad at lying? I thought you were working on that. I don't know how you do your job."

"I'm an analyst. I'm not undercover." I start breathing harder as I continue to dog paddle. "I don't need to be a good liar."

"Would you quit paddling? You're going to drown in about a minute." He grabs me and holds me to his stomach as he starts doing a hybrid backstroke toward the boat. "Relax, Raine. I promise I'm not going to try to have ocean sex with you. I'll leave that to Alex."

"Shut up," I say, relaxing back on his chest as I try to get my breathing back to normal. "Now tell me about the boat. It's been sitting there—unoccupied—the entire time they've been here?"

"That's what Seb said. Suspicious as fuck, right?"

"It is. Is Seb suspicious?"

"I don't think so, but your boy toy and Roman might be."

"Yeah, I showed Alex the note this morning, so he's probably got his antenna up. And I think Roman's freaky perceptive. I've got a feeling he could do my job better than me."

"Yeah, he doesn't miss much." Butch swims us up to the boarding ladder. "Hang on here until I check it out."

After a minute, he signals me from the top. "You're good. We're alone."

As I get to the top of the ladder, he's already broken into the lockbox and is reviewing the captain's log.

"It doesn't look like the boat's moved for almost two weeks. That was well before Seb and Sophie got down here."

"Or maybe they just haven't logged. Check the gas tank."

"Yes, Master Chief," he says, saluting me. "It's not my first day on the job, sister. Uh, yeah, the gas has settled in. I don't think it's been moved for a while. And it doesn't look like anyone's living here. Let me check the toilet."

While he's below deck, I get into the lockbox. There are registration papers, binoculars, and a professional camera.

"The compost container's completely clean," Butch says, coming up the stairs. "There's no one living here. Maybe it's just abandoned."

I hold up the camera and the binoculars. "Surveillance?"

"Or whale watching. Anything on the memory card?"

"A few sunset pictures."

"Yeah," he says, sitting down on one of the benches. "I think this is a dry hole."

"It probably is," I say, sighing. "Why do our minds always go to the worst-case scenario first? Do you think the suspicion from our jobs will ever leave us?"

"Naw, I don't think it ever will. Shit, I've been doing this job for twenty years. That's just the way my mind's programmed now."

"Alex guessed that I worked for the CIA."

"What?" he says, his head jerking back. "You're not that bad of a liar. Did you yell it out when you were having sex or something?"

"I did not. He's just smart and very observant."

"Did you confirm it?"

"No. Of course not. You know I can't do that."

He shrugs. "You know, I lost two decent marriages because we didn't communicate, and a large portion of that was because I couldn't discuss my work with them. I know y'all just met, and I'm not saying you should tell him, but if it progresses with him or someone else, it wouldn't be the worst thing. It's hard to have a relationship worth anything if you're constantly hiding something."

"Yeah, I agree. Maybe I should marry a SEAL after all—at least I'd be able to share everything with him."

"I would be pleased and proud to make you my third wife."

"Hard pass."

I jump as Alex's head pops over the side of the boat.

"Am I interrupting something again?" he says.

"Not a thing," Butch says. "We were just catching up. You swim all this way by yourself?"

Alex laughs as he climbs over the ladder. "I mean, I'm not a SEAL or anything, but I can stay afloat. You've been out here for a while. Everything okay?"

"Yeah," I say. "We thought it was weird that this boat was parked out here, but it seems like it's been abandoned. Or maybe the villa's owners just let it anchor out here. Nothing suspicious."

"Not even that camera you're holding," Alex says, pointing to my lap.

"He is observant," Butch laughs.

"Is there anything on it?" Alex's face gets very serious. "Do you want me to disable it?"

"Settle down, Macgyver," Butch says. "We looked at the memory card. Nothing there. No need to destroy a five thousand dollar camera."

"What are you going to do with the boat?" Alex says.

"I just hooked up the explosives," Butch says. "We better get off pretty quickly."

"Stop playing, Butch," I say, shoving him. "I'll call it in as abandoned when we get back to the resort. The Coast Guard can come and get it."

"All right," Butch says. "I've had way too much physical activity for the day. I'm going to tie the flamingo up and get myself a beer—or three. Alex, can I count on you to make sure Raine gets back safely? She's a horrible swimmer."

"I remember," Alex says, sliding his hand around my waist. "I'll take care of her."

"I know you will," Butch says as he launches his body into the water—landing with a gigantic cannonball.

After we watch him take off toward the flamingo, Alex takes me to the swim deck on the back of the boat. He pulls me down on his lap—facing him.

"I missed you," he says, kissing me. "And before you say people are going to see us, I don't care. I'm having bad withdrawal symptoms."

He pushes my head into his and almost inhales my face.

"Alex," I whisper. "I missed you, too, but really, people are going to see us."

"Don't care." He slides his hands under my butt and pushes me closer into him. "First, I look out here and see you wearing Seb's number on your hat and then I overhear Butch trying to make you his third wife. I'm jealous."

"I wouldn't marry Butch if he were the last guy on earth—which seriously, I think he might be one day." I push back and look at him. "And Seb's hat was the only one that was offered to me."

"Well we're going to have to do something about that right away," he growls. "I want you wearing my number."

"Which is?"

"Six," he says, smiling. "It was my grandpa's favorite number."

"Then I'm only wearing the number six from this day forward. Do you feel better now?"

"Marginally," he says, hugging me to his chest. "I don't know what's happening. I'm not a very jealous person. This is a new feeling for me. Any suggestions?"

"Maybe stop eavesdropping on conversations—"

"Yeah, you're one to talk," he says, resting his head on my shoulder.

"How much did you hear?"

"Probably too much," he says, taking a deep breath. "I don't care what you do for a living. I really don't. As long as you're happy and safe, I'm good. We don't have to talk about anything you don't want to talk about. I just want to be with you."

"I can't talk about my job and you can't tell other people." I pause for a second. "It's a safety thing."

"I won't say a word to anyone," he says, taking my face in his hands. "The last thing I want is to put you in danger. Just the opposite, I want to protect you from everyone and everything."

"Can you handle me not sharing work stuff with you? Most people can't and I get it."

"Seriously, I don't care about your work. That's not who you are any more than baseball is who I am."

"I don't know," I say, laying my head back on his shoulder. "Sometimes I think my work is all I am."

"That's not at all true. What we do for a living, where we live—that's all demographic bullshit. It doesn't have a thing to do with who we are."

"You don't know me very well—"

"Says who?" he says, kissing the top of my head. "I know a lot about you. For instance, I know that you get combative when you have low blood sugar. I know that you love bacon more than you love most people. I know that you're scared of sharks, but only at night. I know that you're adorably shy sometimes and other times you're the boldest person I've ever met. And I know that you're ticklish inside your left thigh, but not your right."

"Stop," I say as he starts stroking the inside of my left thigh. "Stop! You're going to get me all horny again."

"Yeah, well, welcome to the party. I've pretty much been here all morning."

Chapter Twenty-Six

ALEX

"Wait here," I say as I lift her off of me. I grab two lifejackets from under a bench and toss one to her. "Put this on."

"What?" she says, looking up at me. "We don't need life jackets to swim back, do we?"

"We're not going back yet. I want some alone time with you and out here is the only place I'm going to get it. Put it on."

When she hesitates, I slide it on her and pull the straps tight.

"Everyone knows we're out here together," she says, looking back at the beach.

"Good," I whisper as I start to kiss her neck.

"Alex! Control yourself."

"You're going to wear that bikini and tell me to control myself?"

"Stop. Everyone can see us," she says, as I run my hand down to her waist and tug on her bikini bottoms.

"That's why we're getting in the water," I say, sweeping her up into my arms. "Hold your breath."

"Alex!" she screams as I jump.

As we surface, I grab her and pull her behind the boat. "No one can see us in the water. Come here."

She wraps her body around mine. "I already told you I can't do this in the water."

"We don't have to do anything. I just wanted to feel you against me again."

She breaths in quickly as I reach under her life jacket and start stroking her breasts.

"God, I missed them, too. Do you think we can sneak out of here and go back to the resort?"

"I think we have to stay to eat at least," she says, wiggling as I start playing with her nipples. "I think this is like their rehearsal dinner or something, but we can leave right after—"

"I don't think I can wait that long," I say as I reach into her bikini bottoms. "Hmm. I can't tell if that's you-wet or ocean-wet?"

"I think that's mainly me at this point," she says, kneading her hands into my back. "You know what feeling your back muscles does to me."

I laugh as I flex a few times under her hands. "Oh, believe me, I remember."

"Alex, let's wait until we get back to the resort," she says, wiggling more as I start stroking her. "People will hear us."

"Then don't be as loud as you were last night," I say as I stick a few fingers into her.

She moans as she closes her eyes. "I think that's up to you—"

"Then people are going to fucking hear you," I say as I start pumping my fingers in and out.

As she starts bobbing up and down in the water, she lets out another little moan. My mouth dives into her neck and starts sucking as I push her butt harder into my fingers. I let her ride for a minute before I start stroking my thumb on her throbbing clit.

"Alex," she says, shuddering. "God, stop. I think I'm going to cum already. I can't control it."

"Bury your face in my neck," I say, rubbing harder. "It'll muffle the sound."

Her head collapses down between my neck and shoulder as she starts moaning louder. I let my thumb rub over her a few times until her body shakes violently. She screams into my neck and then lets out a few more soft sounds before she looks up at me.

"Fuck," she says between pants. "Why are you so good at that?"

"Do you want me not to be good at it?"

She looks behind her like someone's about to surface out of the water. "Do you think everyone heard me?"

"I think only Samuel heard you," I say, nodding behind her. "We might have disturbed his nap."

"Well he can get over it," she says as she reaches down to see if I'm hard. "Really? Even in this cold water?"

"The water's not that cold," I say, sucking on her neck again, "and the sex sounds you make are ridiculous."

"Get me back to the boat," she says, stroking me once before she tries to break away.

"Wait, are you done already?" I say, pulling her back. "Come back here."

"I'm far from done. I just can't hold my breath long enough for what I need to do to you right now. Get me back on the boat—right now."

"Yes, ma'am," I say, hauling her the ten feet back to the boat. I push her up onto the swim deck and follow.

I try to pull her down on top of me, but she climbs over the wall into the main area of the boat.

"Get in here," she says. "Sit right there."

"See," I say, sitting down, "I do know you—shy one minute and bossy as hell the next."

She kneels and wrestles my swim trunks down.

"Stop talking," she says as she closes her mouth over me.

"Fuck," I say, leaning back on the side of the boat.

She plunges me deep into her mouth once and then starts licking up and down. I close my eyes as I weave my fingers through her hair. She works me until I'm about ready to cum. I pull her off and sit down on the floor of the boat with her.

She moans as I slide deep inside her. As she grabs at my back again, I start pushing her up and down on me. I'm so stimulated right now that it only takes about a minute to get there.

"Baby, I'm going to cum," I whisper. "Are you almost there?"

"Yeah," she says, burying her face in my neck again. "Give me a second."

"Take your time," I say, reaching down to rub her with my thumb. "I can hold it."

She starts vibrating hard on top of me and lets out a loud moan that she doesn't even try to muffle. I let myself go as she collapses on top of me.

She takes a shaky breath and groans. "What are the chances they didn't hear that?"

"About zero," I say, rubbing her back. "Sorry."

"It might be the dopamine that's raging through my body right now," she says, hugging me. "But I'm kind of not sorry at all."

"Yeah, me either," I laugh, "but we're definitely in for it when we go back to the party. You think we should jumpstart this boat and try to get away?"

"You know what? I think we should own it," she says, stretching up so she can look back to the party. "Let them talk."

"Yeah, the hormones have definitely taken control of your body," I say, kissing her stomach, "but I'm good with that. I want to own every bit of this."

"It looks like they're starting to eat. We should probably head back. Do you think you have enough energy to get us to the beach?"

"Yeah, but seriously," I say, lifting her off of me. "I'm going to need a nap when we get back. Or a lot of vitamins or something. You wear me out."

She pulls her bikini bottoms back on and stands up. "Well if I'm too much for you—"

"I didn't say that," I say, grabbing her hand and leading her over to the ladder. "You go second so I can watch your butt while you climb down."

She smiles and tilts her head. "Don't you think you've

looked at it enough?"

"Trust me," I say, squeezing it, "that day will never come."

As she gets to the bottom of the ladder, I pull her onto my back and start swimming toward the beach. I swim as slowly as I can partially because I'm worn out, but mainly because I don't want to share her with anyone else at this point. When we get closer in, I see Butch lounging on the beach.

"Y'all have a good *talk* out on the boat," Butch says as we walk out of the water.

"Leave it alone, Butch," Raine says. "Why aren't you up on the patio eating with everyone else?"

"Because I wanted to make sure lover boy had enough stamina left to get you back here."

"So you heard us, huh?" I say, rubbing my face.

"People on the next island over heard you."

"The rest of this party is going to be torture, isn't it?" Raine says.

"Naw," he says. "Everybody else was up on the patio. I turned the music up when I heard—"

"Stop," she says, pointing at him. "We're done talking about this. Come on, Alex. Let's get this over with."

She pulls me behind her up to the patio. Everyone's sitting around—eating, drinking, talking. The music's cranked. No one even looks at us.

"You think we dodged a bullet?" I whisper to her.

"Or maybe they're just being polite," she says, her hand closing around mine tightly.

I lace my fingers through hers. "You don't mind if everyone sees us holding hands?"

"I guess that's the least of our privacy concerns now, right?"

"Yeah. I guess." I pull her over to the buffet table. "We burned a lot of calories. Let's get you fed before you change your mind."

"Raine!" Sophie yells from across the patio. "We saved you guys seats over here."

After we load up our plates, we head over to their group—steeling ourselves for the teasing we think is about to explode.

"Hey," Seb says, looking up at us, "take a seat. You need a beer, Alex?"

"Yeah," I say slowly as he tosses me one. "What do you want to drink, Raine?"

"Here, I made you a mai tai," Maisie says, passing it across the table. "I'm glad you two finally made it over here. Alex, Seb's trying to convince us that Miami could win the World Series next year. What do you think?"

I take a deep breath and squeeze Raine's hand under the table. Amazingly, it looks like they might not have heard us.

"Uh," I say, "yeah, I mean we have to get to the playoffs first, but our division's so competitive if we get past the first round, I don't think the rest of the league's much competition. You never know."

Stone nods. "That's what Paul and I always say. You have a better record than half the league, but you're in the most competitive group. They need to stop doing it by division and just invite the teams with the best records."

"And, of course," Paul says, "there's no way Miami makes it without you, Alex. Have you signed your contract yet?"

"Not yet," I say as Raine puts her hand on my leg. "I'm still thinking about it."

"Yeah," Seb says, "and he doesn't need any help to make the decision, so next topic."

As the table melts into a conversation about Ricky's wipeout on a jet ski this morning, I turn to Seb.

"Thanks for the save, man. That's the last thing I want to talk about right now."

"The last thing? Really?" He shakes his head. "I thought I'd save you from that topic because later—when it's just the guys around this table—you're going to get destroyed for how loud you are during sex."

I jerk my head back. "What?"

"Do you think we didn't hear that? Unfortunately for everyone, sound travels better on the water."

I start rubbing my face. "Oh God, this is horrible news. Did everyone hear?"

"Everyone in the world heard. Like people in China are talking about how loud you are. I'm never going to un-hear that, asshole."

"Well, now we're even. I heard you and Sophie on that road trip in Atlanta and I still have nightmares about it."

Raine pulls on my hand and stretches up to whisper in my ear. "Sophie said everyone heard us."

"Yep," I say, squeezing her hand. "That's what Seb said. Do you want to run? Or should we own it?"

She pauses for a second and then says, "Own it."

"Then own it, we will," I say as I kiss her forehead.

As I slide my arm around her shoulders, Sophie tugs on

my arm from the other side of Raine. When I look over, her face is scrunched up with tears starting to form in her eyes. I push her shoulder and roll my eyes then quickly bury my face in Raine's hair to prevent her from seeing the smile that's exploding all over my face.

Chapter Twenty-Seven

RAINE

When Alex and I get back to the resort, the porter that gave me the note this morning jumps in front of our Jeep.

"Jesus!" Alex says, slamming on the brakes. "Bruh, wait until cars stop before you try to get the keys. I don't feel like I should have to tell you that."

He ignores Alex and jogs over to me on the passenger's side.

"Another note," he says, panting. "The woman gave me another note, but not for Sophie Banks. This one's for that baseball player."

"What baseball player?" Alex growls.

"Seb Miller." The porter spins his head around to see if anyone's watching us. "She said to give it to Seb Miller. Have you seen him?"

"Thank you for bringing this to me," I say, smiling at him. "I'll get it to Seb."

"Are you sure? She asked me if I gave the last one to

Sophie." He looks over his shoulder again. "I told her I did. She gave me another twenty. What if she talks to them and finds out that I didn't deliver the notes?"

"She won't," I say, patting his arm to try to calm him down. "Believe me, she won't talk to them. Did you get a better look at her this time? Was the man in the sports car here again?"

"He picked her up right after she gave me the note at like noon—same guy, same car. She was still wearing that big floppy hat and glasses. I think her hair might be blonde, though. She had it in a braid. It looked a lot lighter than yours, at least."

"Okay, good job," I say as I get out of the Jeep. "If you get another note, it comes to me."

"I'm off in like ten minutes. Should I tell someone else to look for her?"

"No, you're good," I say. "Just go home."

Alex hands him the keys to the Jeep and a hundred from his wallet. "What's your name?"

"Jimmy," the porter says, shoving the bill into his shirt pocket.

"You did good, Jimmy. Go home and get some rest." Alex puts his arm around my shoulders. "What's the note say?"

SOPHIE TOLD ME SHE'S ONLY
MARRYING YOU FOR YOUR MONEY.

"I'm about to kill someone," I say, letting out a long breath. "You think this could be your agent?"

"No way," Alex says, grabbing the note. "This is the most immature bullshit I've ever seen. Jeff's an asshole, but this is not his thing at all."

"He wanted her to sign a prenup, though," I say, leaning against the wall. "I heard him."

"Hold up," Alex says, dialing his phone. "Where are you? Yeah, stay there. I'm coming down. Jeff's at the restaurant. Let's just ask him."

"Yeah, we might as well," I say as he grabs my hand and starts pulling me across the lobby.

As we enter the restaurant, I see Butch sitting at a table with his arm around Ava. He looks up as I walk in. His face tightens when he sees my angry expression. He starts to stand up until I shake my head. He lowers back down slowly as Alex pulls me across the room.

"Well I was hoping you were here to tell me you wanted to sign your contract," Jeff says, looking from Alex to me. "But from the company you're keeping, I'm guessing that's not it."

"Hey Carli," Alex says, nodding to the woman sitting next to Jeff. "Do you mind if we have a second alone with Jeff?"

She stands up and looks at me. "I'm Carli Akers—Jeff's wife."

"Oh, hey," I say, extending my hand to her. She doesn't take it. "I'm Raine Laghari."

"Yes," she says, glaring at me as she walks away. "My husband told me all about you."

"Does she have to be here?" Jeff says, flipping his hand dismissively at me.

"Yes, she does." Alex grabs the note out of my hand. "Did you leave this note for Seb?"

Jeff reads it and drops it on the table like it burned his fingers. He jerks his head up and looks back and forth between us. "I did not! I did not leave this note for Seb. What the hell is this? It's not from me!"

I sit down across from him and grab the note. "Did you find their marriage license?"

He looks up at Alex once more and then locks his eyes with mine. "I did. They were married July 16 in Michigan—over All Star break—just like you said. I told Seb I knew. I'm not happy that he didn't make Sophie sign a prenup, but that's done. Seb and I are solid."

I look up at Alex. "He didn't send the note. Let's get out of here."

"Alex, may I have a second alone with you?" Jeff says, still glaring at me.

"No."

"It's fine." I touch Alex's arm. "I need to talk to Butch for a second anyway."

Alex squeezes my hand before I walk over to Butch's table. Butch has his eyes fixed on me. Ava has disappeared.

"Everything okay?" Butch says as I slide into the chair next to him and hand him the note.

"The mystery woman left it for Seb."

He laughs as he reads it. "This is getting downright stupid. Seriously. Not only aren't we dealing with a master criminal, I'm not sure we're even dealing with an adult. I'm guessing the agent didn't leave it."

"No," I say, sighing. "We had to check, but he already

knows they're married. And he's stupid, but not this kind of stupid."

"Who do you think it is?" Butch says, handing the note back to me. "Savannah? Ricky?"

"I don't know. Honestly, I don't really care." I grab his beer and take a long drink. "I just want Seb and Sophie to get through the weekend without knowing about it."

"You want me to round up all the wedding guests and question them?"

"So much," I say, smiling. "And please do it exactly like you do for a group of enemy combatants. Feel free to punish anyone and everyone who doesn't obey you."

"Punish, huh?" Ava says as she sits on the other side of Butch and grabs his arm. "I'm not sure that I'm totally into that, but I guess we can try."

"Wow," I say, looking at Butch. "Look at that. I think you've found your perfect woman."

"Ava, this is Raine."

"I remember," she says. "We met last night. You're the one who's hanging out with Alex, right?"

"Uh," I say, looking over to him. He's still talking to Jeff. "Yeah. I guess."

"No need to be embarrassed," she says, smiling. "Alex is great. Just don't get in too deep there. He's not known for commitment."

"Noted," I say, standing up. "I'll leave you two alone."

Butch grabs my arm as I start to walk away. "You good?"

"I'm fine," I say, trying to pull my arm away.

"Raine," he says, tugging me back over to him. "I asked

you a question. Give me a real answer or we're going to talk privately."

I kiss the top of his head. "I'm fine. Really. All good. I'll tell you if that changes. Okay?"

"Okay," he says as he looks over my shoulder. "Hey, Alex. You recover from your strenuous workout this afternoon."

"Butch," I say, slapping his shoulder. "That's plenty. I'll see you tomorrow."

I grab Alex's hand and pull him away from their table. He pulls back and stops me. "What's wrong? Your voice sounds all tense."

"I'm just tired—a full day in the sun and now this bull-shit," I say, waving the note at him. "Can we take a nap maybe?"

"Yeah, baby," he says, wrapping his arm around me. "Your room or mine?"

"Yours. I don't want to risk running into Allie." I notice Jeff glaring at me as we walk by his table. "What did the dick agent want? Everything okay?"

"Yeah, it's fine. He was just trying to nail me down on my contract again."

"And?"

"And, I still haven't decided. I asked him to get an offer for a one-year deal and see what that looks like."

"Is that the way you're leaning?" I try to act casually unin-terested, but as crazy as it sounds, I've been hoping he won't sign, and that he'll move to San Diego. I've only known him a day and I'm already having these thoughts. I'm doing every-thing I can to suppress them, but they keep popping up.

"I'm not signing more than a one-year deal," he says,

pulling me closer to him. "I know that much, but that's it. Can we not talk about it?"

"Yeah, that's fine," I say, yawning. "I seriously can't concentrate anyway. I'm so tired. I feel like I'm about to fall over."

"Here, get on my back," he says, leaning down. "I'll carry you."

"I'd like to say that I can make it to your room on my own," I say, climbing on his back and laying my head on his shoulder, "but I don't know if I can. If I'm asleep by the time we get to your room just throw me into bed. These last twenty four hours have been exhausting."

"And that's more than half your fault," he says, laughing as he starts trudging toward his room. "Close your eyes, baby. I've got you."

When we turn the corner to his hallway, he stops suddenly. I peek over his shoulder and see Allie leaning against his door. I try to get down, but Alex won't let me.

"Allie, what are you doing here?" he says, pushing past her and swiping his key card with me still on his back.

"I'm waiting for you," she hisses as she looks up at me. "We need to talk."

"Let me down," I whisper to Alex. "I can take a nap in my room."

"You're not going anywhere," Alex says, wrapping his arms tighter around my legs. "Allie, we don't need to talk. I've said everything I'm going to say."

"You broke up with me and moved to her in like two seconds," Allie whines. "I understand a rebound, but that's ridiculous."

"Alex," I say sternly. "Let me down. I don't want to be a part of this."

"Neither do I," he says, backing into his room and putting me down. "Leave me alone, Allie, or I'll get team security involved."

She tries to push her way in as he slams the door. He turns around and sees my wide-eyed expression.

"Raine," he says. "I'm sorry. I know that was awkward. Can we just forget about her and take a nap?"

Allie starts pounding on the door. "Alex!"

"It doesn't look that way," I say, pulling my hand away from his. "I should leave. This is really weird."

"You're not leaving. Hold up," he says, pulling out his phone. "Hey. I'm room 407. Allie's stalking me again. She's outside pounding on the door. Yeah. Thanks, man."

"Who was that?"

"Joe, our team security guy," he says, pulling me away from the door and into the gigantic bathroom suite. He grabs a T-shirt out of his suitcase. "Here, you can wear this after you take a shower. I'll take care of Allie."

"This is making me uncomfortable, Alex. Maybe you should talk to her. Did you guys date long?"

He sits on the side of the tub. "We didn't date at all. I took her to dinner once. Then we went to a friend's party together. We had sex a few times. That was it. Seriously, it took place over two weeks. I told her then that I didn't want to see her anymore and I told her again last night. She's a stalker. Unfortunately, that happens a little in my profession."

I sit down next to him and pat his leg. "Well, if it makes

you feel any better, we've only known each other for a day, so I promise I won't stalk you after this weekend."

"What if I want you to?" he says, smiling. "Or maybe I'll stalk you."

"Are you forgetting I work with Navy SEALs?"

"Yeah, that could be a problem." He looks down at his phone. "It's Joe. I need to talk to him. Take a shower. I'll be back in a minute."

"Do you mind if I take a bubble bath instead? This tub is ridiculous."

"I don't mind at all. Just don't drown before I get back. It's way too big for one person, especially a you-sized person."

I smile as I start running the water. "No promises. You know what a bad swimmer I am."

Chapter Twenty-Eight

ALEX

When I wake up for the fourth time this morning, her head's still on my chest, and now one of her legs is slung over my body. My arms are wrapped around her with my head resting on top of hers. I'm checking to see if she's breathing again when I finally feel her head moving.

I smile at her as she peeks up at me. "Good morning. Did you sleep better last night?"

"So much," she says, yawning. "I seriously think I might have passed out. What time is it?"

"About nine." I pull her completely on top of my chest so our stomachs are pressed together. "I've been awake for a couple of hours, but I didn't want to wake you."

"A couple of hours?" She yawns again and lays her head back on my chest. "Why didn't you move me?"

"I've been in and out of this bed three times," I laugh. "Every time I get back in, you wind yourself around me like an octopus—somehow without waking up. I'm not even sure how that's possible. You're a deep sleeper."

"I'm not normally." She stops when her stomach growls loudly again. It's been doing that for the last half hour. "I'm starving."

"I figured that's why you finally woke up. Do you want to order room service?"

She rolls off me and stands up. "I don't think I can wait that long. Let's go down to the restaurant. I can grab a banana on the way."

"The restaurant? In public? Are you going to sit at the same table with me?"

"Will you let me have your bacon?"

She starts pulling on her swimsuit underneath my T-shirt. She looks so cute in it. It almost comes down to her knees.

"I promise I'll order plenty of bacon for both of us."

She crawls back over and straddles me. "Okay, then I'll sit with you."

"So you don't mind being seen with me anymore?" I say as I run my hands up and down her arms.

"I never minded being seen with you," she says, collapsing back down on my chest. "I'm just a private person."

"And why has that changed?"

"Because today is our last full day here," she whispers, "and I don't want to be away from you for any of it. I know I sound like a clingy mess, but you told me to be honest with you and that's what I'm feeling right now."

I hug her and kiss the top of her head. "That's what I'm feeling, too, baby. I don't know if I'm going to be able to leave you tomorrow. Why don't you come to Puerto Rico with me for a little bit? My family would love you."

She sits back up as her stomach growls again. "I'd love that, but I can't. I have to get back to Virginia and pack. I'm moving right after the holidays. I have so much to do. What are you doing when you get back from Puerto Rico? Maybe come and see me."

"I'm going to be with my family through the holidays. Are you going back to Chicago?"

"Not for Thanksgiving, but probably Christmas." She takes a deep breath. "So I guess after tomorrow, we're not going to see each other for a long time—or maybe ever."

"We're going to see each other again. I'll make sure of that. I promise."

"Okay," she says, looking away from me. "Can we get breakfast? I'm starting to get combative again."

"We'll see each other again," I say, taking her chin and making her look at me. "There's no question about that. We just have to figure out how. Okay?"

She nods as she stands up again and pulls me up with her.

I pull on my swim trunks and a fresh T-shirt. "Let's get you fed before your body and mind start breaking down."

"I guess this is what I'm wearing since I don't want to go back to my room," she says as she slides into her flip-flops. "And somehow you let my cover-up get washed away in the tide last night."

"It was your idea to go for a midnight skinny dip."

She rolls her eyes. "Yeah, you really put up a fight. Seriously, though, you're a baseball player. How can you not make a twenty-foot throw to the beach?"

"Well first I was preoccupied," I say, smacking her butt, "and second, your cover-up thing didn't have the same zip as a baseball. Come and see me play next year. You'll see how I throw."

She takes a step back. "Come and see you play? That sounds like you made up your mind."

"I think I have," I say, grabbing her hand and pulling her out the door. "When we were talking about the World Series yesterday, it got me thinking. I haven't won a title yet. I think I want one more year to try, but then that's it."

As I close the door, Manny's walking toward us. He tries unsuccessfully to control the broad grin that breaks out over his face.

"Well, good morning, campers," he says, grabbing my shoulder. "I was wondering why you weren't golfing with us again today. And now I'm wondering no more."

I put my arm around Raine's shoulders. "Manny, you remember Raine, don't you?"

"I do. Nice to see you again. Are you the reason I haven't seen much of my friend this weekend?"

"She is," I say before she can answer.

"Well, at least you have a good excuse," Manny says. "I need to get to the lobby before they leave without me. I'll see you at the wedding tonight. Maybe you two can sit with Caroline and me."

"Yeah, we'll see," I say. When Manny gets out of earshot, I whisper, "That's not going to happen. I'm not ruining our night by subjecting you to her."

"Maisie said something about her yesterday," Raine says. "Like she was talking smack about Sophie or something."

"Probably. She's jealous of Sophie for some reason. Caroline has the maturity level of a ten-year-old."

As we get to the lobby, the porter from yesterday runs full speed at Raine. I grab him before he crashes into her.

"The man," he says, panting as he gets up to us, "the man who left with the woman who gave me those notes. He's here. He just arrived and gave me his keys. I didn't see where he went because I had to park his car, but he has to still be here because I have his keys."

As he holds up the keys, Butch walks over to us. "What's going on?"

"Take the keys," Raine says, nodding at Butch. He grabs them from the porter. "Did the man give you another note?"

"No," the porter says, taking a deep breath. He looks at Butch. "I swear he didn't. And he didn't give one to anyone else that I saw. He just drove up and left his car with us."

"Was the woman with him?" Raine says.

"No, but I think I saw her earlier at breakfast. She was with a different guy. He's a lot taller and bigger than this guy. I'm not positive it was her, but she had the same—um—the same—"

He sweeps his hands over his chest in a wide curve.

"Chest?" Raine says. "She had the same chest? Is she large?"

"Enormous," he says, nodding. "Like they have to be fake."

"Okay," she says. "Good work. We're keeping his keys for a minute. We'll bring them back to you. Thanks for the information."

"And what information has Jimmy given you?" Roman

says as he closes in on us. He looks at Raine. "Are you using my valet as a spy?"

"Not exactly—"

"Then what exactly are you doing, Raine?" he says, staring at her. "I know the three of you are up to something. The stuff with the boat yesterday and now this. What aren't you telling me?"

Raine reaches in her bag and hands him the notes. "Someone gave him—Jimmy—these notes yesterday to give to Sophie and Seb. We intercepted them."

Roman reads them and spins his head to me. "Is this true? Is he cheating on her?"

"Not at all," I say, holding up my hands. "Come on, Roman. You know how much he loves her."

Roman's face relaxes a little bit as he looks at Jimmy. "Thank you, Jimmy. Any more notes come directly to me. You can go back to work now. The rest of you, follow me. We need to talk about this in private."

"I seriously need food first," Raine says, looking at the restaurant. "I'm about to pass out."

Roman grabs a front-desk clerk. "Bring three full break-fasts from the buffet to my office as soon as possible. It's a rush."

I grab a banana from the drink table and push Raine behind Roman as he leads us into his office. Two waiters follow quickly with three heaping plates of food and a pot of coffee.

Roman looks at Raine—his face frozen in a scowl. "Who left the notes?"

"We don't know," she says, inhaling a few pieces of bacon

from her plate. "Some woman who's been in and out of your resort with a guy. Apparently the guy's here now. Can we look at your security cameras from the valet area?"

"They're not functional yet," Roman growls. "This damn island only has one decent electrician and that's being generous."

"Okay, then we need to put a plant at the valet stand for when the guy comes back for his car," she says, pointing to the keys that Butch is holding.

"I'll do it." I grab the keys from Butch. "Just give me a uniform or whatever."

Butch snatches them back. "You're too famous. Someone will recognize you. And I'm not going to pass for a porter."

"No, you will not," Roman says, doing a quick scan of Butch's tattoo-filled arms. He nods at Raine. "And Mighty Mouse here couldn't see over most dashboards, so let's just have Jimmy do it."

"Rude," Raine says, pointing at Roman as she takes a long drink of her coffee. "And Jimmy can't do it. He's too hyper."

"I've got the right person," I say, dialing Ant on my phone. "Hey. Where are you? Well, get your ass out of bed. I need you. Meet me in the office right behind the check-in desk in the lobby. There's a Cuban flag on the door. Get down here fast or I'm sending you back a day early."

"Who'd you call?" Raine says, looking up at me.

"My wedding guest. He's a buddy of mine from Miami. He's barely twenty-one and he's as chill as they come. He'll be perfect."

There's a knock on the door. Butch opens it to reveal a

very hungover-looking Antonio—wearing only boxer shorts and a T-shirt.

"Good Lord, Ant," I say, pulling him in the door. "You had time to put on pants and maybe run a brush through your hair."

"You said you would send me back early if I didn't get down here quick," he says. "I don't want to go back. I love it here so much."

"Antonio?" Roman says, standing up.

"Oh, hey," Antonio says, running his hand through his hair. "Mr. Garcia. What are you doing here?"

"This is my resort. I own it," Roman laughs. "What are you doing here?"

"I came with him," he says, pointing at me.

"How do you two know each other?" I ask, looking at Ant.

"I work for Mr. Garcia in Miami," he says. "I landscape his hotel and his house. Sophie introduced me to him."

"Speaking of Sophie," Roman says, "someone left her an unkind note with one of our porters. We're trying to figure out who it was. We might need you to go undercover as a valet for a few hours. Do you think you could do that?"

"Sure, I'll do anything for you, but if it was a hate note, it probably came from Caroline Roa—"

"What?" I look over at him. "Why would Caroline leave Sophie a note?"

"Man, she hates Sophie—like rage hate. She's always talking smack about her back in Miami."

"Really?" I say, my face tightening. "Like serious stuff?"

"Not like physical threats or anything," he says, "but she's obsessed with Sophie. She's jealous as hell of Sophie and

Seb's relationship. She talks about how annoying they are all the time to her sister."

"I believe that," I say, nodding, "but she's a lot of talk. I can't imagine her actually trying to break up their relationship."

"I can," Ant says. "She's always trying to create some drama. And leaving a note is just her style. She's a big coward underneath all that mouth."

"Yeah, but the woman who left the note has been seen leaving the resort with a man," I say, "and it's not Manny."

Ant accepts the pancakes that Raine pushes across the table to him. "Maybe it's the guy she's having an affair with. I thought I saw him here yesterday."

Chapter Twenty-Nine

RAINE

"What?" Alex says, grabbing Antonio's shoulder. "Don't exaggerate about stuff like that. Caroline's not cheating on Manny."

"Well, she's having sex with another guy, so I guess call it what you want."

"Are you sure?" Alex slumps down in his chair.

"One hundred percent," Antonio says. "He started showing up to their house when the team was on road trips. He even stays overnight."

"And she doesn't try to hide it from you?" Alex starts rubbing his temples. "Are you sure they're not just friends or something?"

"I told you that she barely acknowledges my presence. Most of the time, I don't think she knows I'm there. And if they're friends, it's definitely with benefits. She was sucking on him pretty hard by the pool—"

"Stop!" Alex says. "That's plenty. Why haven't you told anyone about this?"

"You're the one who told me to keep quiet about what goes on in my clients' homes. Seriously, man, I thought Manny knew. They have a strange relationship. I thought they might be open or something."

"They're not open," Alex growls. "At least he's not."

"What does this guy look like?" I say to Antonio.

"Short, white, young, dark hair, wears it slicked back a lot—"

"Does he drive a Bentley?" Roman says.

Antonio jerks his head up and smiles. "Yeah, sweet car. Continental GT V8 Convertible. White. Black interior."

Roman stands up and leads Antonio toward the door. "Enjoy the rest of your vacation. We'll see you back in Miami."

Antonio stands up slowly. "You don't need me to do the spy shit or whatever?"

"We're good," Roman says, opening the door and motioning to the man standing outside. "Curtis, will you make sure Mr. Reyes has everything he needs for the rest of his stay?"

Roman turns back toward us as he closes the door. "Your mystery man is Gentry Randall."

"What?" I say, jumping up. "The guy who harassed Sophie?"

"That's the one and I'm assuming he's followed us all down here, like the complete dumbass he is."

"Remind me who he is again," Butch says.

"He's the son of the former owner of the baseball team in

Miami. Sophie exposed him to the media for a long list of sexual harassment complaints. After the story hit, the PA's office filed a few criminal charges against him. He's out on bail right now—waiting to go to trial or plead out of it somehow."

"He's on bail?" I say. "Under what restrictions?"

"They took his passport away and I don't think he's supposed to leave Florida without the judge's permission." Roman grabs his phone. "Yeah, check to see if Gentry Randall is still on travel restriction with his bail and if he got the judge's permission to leave Florida. Call me back. It's urgent."

"I need to use your computer." I shoo Roman away from it as I take a seat behind his desk. "Do you have Gentry's cell phone number?"

He flips through a few screens then holds his phone up to me. I put it into a locator app and point at the screen. "His cell phone is at this resort right now—or at least close to here. I can't log into my work account from this computer to pinpoint the exact location, but his phone is definitely around here somewhere."

Alex takes a deep breath and blows it out through his teeth. "I don't think we have to guess about where he is. Manny just left for golf, so I'm assuming Gentry's in their room with Caroline."

Roman answers his phone. "Still? Good. Thanks," he says, hanging up. "We have a bail jumper at my resort and I'm about to make him regret that decision."

"Stop," I say. "No violence from you or anyone. Let's make sure he's here and then we can call the local authorities. If he jumped bail, they'll get him back to Miami."

"Let's go," Roman says, heading to the door. His face looks like he's about to kill someone.

"Hold up, chief," Butch says, blocking the door. "Does Gentry carry any weapons?"

"Not that I'm aware of," Roman says, walking back to a closet. He opens it to reveal a safe. "But just in case."

He opens the safe and waves his hand over a pile of cash and weapons.

"Holy crap," Butch says. He pulls out a gun and discharges the clip. "Is this even legal?"

"Do you want me to answer that?"

"No, he doesn't," I say, jumping between them. "Butch is the only one who carries a gun."

Roman looks down at me. "These are my guns."

"And Butch is the only one with extensive firearms training—including being trained on gun discipline—unless there's something I don't know about you," I say, stretching my body up as tall as it will go. I stare at Roman. "You're too emotional. Butch is the only one who carries. Period. No more discussion."

Roman tries to stare me down, but when I don't back up, a smile starts to form on his face. "Raine, you're a very interesting person. I want to get to know you better when this is over."

"That depends entirely on how well you follow my instructions for the next few minutes," I say, downing the rest of my coffee. "Come on. Let's get this over with."

Alex grabs my shoulder. "I'm coming with you."

I look up at him. "You don't have to come. I'll be fine."

"I promised you we wouldn't be apart today," he says, putting his arm around me. "I'm keeping that promise."

Butch slips a gun into the back of his waistband and pulls his T-shirt over it. We all follow him up the stairs toward Manny's room. When we turn the corner to the hallway, Manny's walking toward his room.

"Manny!" Alex says, running to position himself between Manny and the room. "I thought you were golfing."

Manny laughs. "Settle down, man. I forgot my wallet."

"I'll grab it for you and bring it down to the lobby."

"What?" Manny tries to get around Alex to the room.

Alex pushes him back. "Don't go in there, man."

"What the fuck is going on?" Manny takes a step back and looks around at all of us.

"Alex, we need to do this now," I say, grabbing his arm. "I'm sorry. Roman open the door."

Manny tries to stop him, but Butch holds him back. Roman swipes the card and Butch walks in—gun drawn.

"Who the fuck are you?" A man who must be Gentry rolls off Caroline and looks up at us—his face drained of all color. "Get out of our room."

"Hands," Butch says, walking toward them. "Now. Let me see your hands."

Caroline screams as Butch pulls the sheets down. They're both naked. Butch snarls, "Let me see your hands. I won't ask again."

They both jerk their hands over their heads. Butch nods and throws the sheet back over them. He pulls open the night-stand drawer and does a quick sweep of the room. "We're clear. No weapons."

"What the fuck is going on here?" Manny says, walking in slowly. He looks over at Alex. "Did you know about this?"

"As of five minutes ago," Alex says. "I'm sorry, man."

Caroline sits up—pulling the sheet up to her chest. "Manny, I can explain."

"Shut up," Manny says, pointing at her. He grabs Gentry by the arm, pulls him out of the bed, and slams him against the wall. "I'm going to fucking kill you."

Roman grabs Gentry's clothes from the chair and throws them at him. "Get dressed, Gentry. You're out of the Florida jurisdiction. I believe that's a no-no for you, so you get to go directly to jail. Manny, let him go. Jail's going to be worse for him than anything you could dish out."

Manny shoves him one more time and then walks across the room and collapses down on a chair.

Gentry pushes Roman away from him. "Man, get away from me. St. John is part of the U.S. I'm not going anywhere near a jail."

"It's not part of Florida, dumbass," I say, walking up to him. "Do you know the difference between a state and a country? I'm trying to gauge your level of ignorance, so I know where to go from here."

Gentry tries to shove me, but Alex pulls me behind him and punches Gentry so hard that he crumbles to the ground. Butch grabs Alex by the shoulder and pulls him back.

"All right, champ, that's plenty," Butch says as he picks Gentry up. "Get up, asshole. You're interrupting my beach vacation and that pisses me off. Let's go, Roman. I'll come with you to take him to the local authorities."

As they walk out, I turn to Caroline. "Did you leave the notes for Sophie and Seb?"

"What notes?" Manny says from the corner of the room.

I look back at Caroline. She's doing a very bad job of hiding her surprise. "Your wife left anonymous notes for Seb and Sophie trying to break up their relationship or ruin their wedding or something. I'm still not sure what she was trying to accomplish."

"I don't know what you're talking about," Caroline squeaks as she looks over at Manny.

"Yeah, you do." I walk over to the side of the bed. "Guess what? They never got the notes because I intercepted them. Nice try, though."

"Raine," Alex says, pulling on my hand. "Come on. Let's leave them alone."

I lean down and get right in Caroline's face. "If you ever come at Sophie again, I'm coming after you, and believe me, I'm going to be the last woman standing. And some free advice from me to you, grow the fuck up."

"Raine, let's go." Alex grabs me around the shoulders and pushes me toward the door. He looks back at Manny. "You good, man? Do you want me to stay?"

"No, you can leave," he says, looking at Alex briefly and then walking over to Caroline. "And you can leave, too. Get dressed, pack your bags, and get out of my room. You have two minutes."

"Manny—"

"Shut the fuck up," Manny says, holding his hand up to stop her. "Gentry Randall? Fucking Gentry Randall? If you're not dressed and out of here in two minutes, I'll throw you out wearing that sheet."

"Where am I supposed to stay tonight?" She pulls the sheet up higher. "Our plane doesn't leave until tomorrow."

"*Our* plane? Ah, no honey, that's a team plane—reserved for players and their guests. Which one are you?"

Caroline stands up and edges around the room to get her clothes. "You can't leave me on the island, Manny. We're married—"

"And that's the first thing I'm going to change when I get back to Florida."

As Alex pulls the door closed, I grab him and hug him. "I'm sorry that just happened to your friend."

"So am I, but honestly, it's probably for the best long term," he says, burying his face in my hair. "Are you okay? I didn't think we'd start the morning with criminal apprehension."

I smile up at him. "That's pretty much how I start most of my mornings when I'm not on vacation."

"Hmm," he says. "I'm not ready to get back to reality just yet. Can we fight against it for the day?"

"Yes, please," I say, grabbing his hand and pulling him down the hall. "What do you have in mind?"

"How about we find a private beach? We can read, nap, swim, makeout—"

"Umm, let me see," I say, tapping my lips. "Yes, yes, yes, and definitely yes."

Chapter Thirty

ALEX

"Have you been to St. John before?" Raine says as she crawls on top of me in the hammock. "How did you even know this place was here?"

After the drama of the morning, I drove us to a beach on the north shore. We found a hammock strung between two palm trees that's only about ten feet from the water. We've been here for about ten minutes. There's not another person in sight.

"I told you that I explored the island before you got here. I found a lot of cool places," I say, pulling her closer. "I was just waiting for you to get down here so I could use them."

"You didn't even know who I was when you were exploring," she says, laughing. "I think what you meant to say is that you were waiting for *any* woman to get down here, so you could take her to all the romantic beach spots you found."

"That's not at all true," I say, kissing her forehead. "If I hadn't met you, I'd just be hanging out with my buddies.

Believe me, there's not another woman down here who interests me."

"It's fine. You don't have to lie. We've already established that you were a whore before we met."

I lift her head so I can look her into her eyes. "We didn't establish anything—you did."

"Okay," she says, kissing my cheek before snuggling her head into my shoulder again. "But I've had two people confirm that information for me—without me even asking. They just walk up to me and tell me you're a player."

"Yeah, well don't believe everything you hear. I'm not a player."

"Alex," she says as she sits up and straddles me. "I'm not mad about it. We're both adults and we're having a fun weekend. There's nothing wrong with that."

"A fun weekend? This is more than that to me," I say, taking her hands. "I want to keep talking to you after we leave."

"We've only known each other for two days," she says, smiling. "Can't it just be what it is?"

"And what is it for you?" I say, raising my eyebrows. "Frankly, you seem more like the player here than I do."

She laughs and shakes her head. "I'm not a player, but I am a realist. After tomorrow, we're probably not going to see each other again."

"Says who?" I try to keep the edge out of my voice, but I'm starting to get a little pissed.

"Alex, you'll be in Miami and I'm going to be in San Diego. When are we going to see each other?"

I take her face in my hands. "We can visit each other. I'll

pay for you to come to Miami whenever you want. I'll even charter a plane so it works with your schedule."

"That's very sweet," she says, kissing my hand, "but I'm going to be busy with my new assignment. And if you're signing a contract, you'll start training in like February, right?"

"Yeah, but you get vacation."

"This is the first real vacation I've had in five years. I'm not exaggerating. My job is all-consuming."

"So you're okay with this being it?" I say, frowning. "We leave tomorrow and never see each other again?"

She lays her head back down on my shoulder and whispers, "No, I'm not okay with it. I'm just trying to come to terms with it so I won't have a breakdown when I have to leave you tomorrow."

"Don't leave me then. Come to Puerto Rico," I whisper. "Even just for a week."

"I can't. I want to, but I really can't. Let's just enjoy the next twenty-ish hours and whatever happens, happens."

"Hmm," I growl. "I'm not willing to give up on this that easily. I like you. We have a lot in common. I haven't had anything in common with a woman in so long—like probably back to college."

"We definitely have stuff in common. I haven't clicked this quickly with a guy in—well, ever. I don't think this has ever happened to me before."

"Exactly. Same," I say, holding her tightly to me. "If we were in the same city, I'd be trying to get a date with you every night at this point."

"And I'd be saying yes to every night, but we're not going to be in the same city."

"Not every day, but we can be sometimes. After Puerto Rico, I'll come out to San Diego and visit you. We can still get to know each other better and see what happens."

She sits up again. "Alex, I suck at long-distance communication. Like I really suck at it. Ask Sophie. If someone isn't right in front of me—"

"What? You forget about them?"

"No," she says, the little line forming over her eyebrows again. "Of course not. I just maybe don't prioritize that as much as what's right in front of me."

"Okay, well that's a pattern for you, but you can change it. I think we have a good start here. That's something to fight for. Will you do that for me? At least agree to try after tomorrow?"

"I don't know," she says slowly. "I mean I want to say yes, but what's the best we can hope for long term?"

I take a deep breath and exhale slowly. "You're thinking too much about the big picture. Let's handle it in smaller chunks."

"Meaning?"

"My mom has always told me when you can't figure out the big decision, start by making small decisions that will eventually lead you to solve the big question. Like for law school versus baseball, I'm still not a hundred percent, but I've decided that if I sign another contract, it will only be for one year. Then I have options, you know?"

"Yeah, that's smart," she says, "but what small decisions can we make about us—if any?"

"Well, I know I'm not done with this," I say, stroking her hair, "so for me, a small decision is that I'm going to call you and text you every day until you tell me to leave you alone."

"I'm not going to tell you to leave me alone."

"Good, because I'm not going to," I say, smiling, "and I'll see you in San Diego in January if you have the time."

"I'll make time, but that's almost three months from now."

"Small decisions, Raine. It's all we can do until we're both settled. Make a small decision right now."

She sighs. "I promise I'll make an effort to be better at communicating, but I'm still not sure what our goal is here."

"Uh, I think it's the same goal as any romantic relation-ship," I say. "My dating goal is to find someone to marry eventually."

She pushes me back and stares at me. "Marry? Talk about looking at the big picture. That's taking like a hundred steps forward. Marriage is not even on my mind. My job makes that kind of difficult."

"Quit using your job as an excuse to not be happy."

"What?" she says, frowning again. "Who says I'm not happy?"

"I didn't mean it like that," I say, rubbing my face. "It's just that's what would make me happy eventually—marriage, kids, the whole thing. Do you want to get married?"

"Okay. Fine. Yes, I accept your proposal," she says, taking my hands. "Maybe we can have a double wedding with Sophie and Seb tonight."

"Stop trying to make a joke. I meant eventually. Is that one of your goals?"

"Stop trying to get out of marrying me. You officially asked and I said yes. We're getting married tonight. But I didn't bring a white dress, so we're going to have to stop and buy one on the way back to the resort."

"With what we've done over the last few days, I'm not sure you should wear white."

"Wowww. Okay," she says, rolling out of the hammock and standing up. "I'm calling off our engagement right now."

I grab at her hand, but she dodges me, throws off her cover-up, and starts running into the ocean. I leap up and catch her just as she reaches the water's edge.

"No way, woman," I say, throwing her over my shoulder. "You've already said you would marry me. No take backs."

"Put me down!" she says, laughing as she pounds on my back. "You can't force me to marry you."

"Yes, I can," I say, running out into the water with her still on my shoulder. "Samuel's going to marry us right now."

"Samuel's a minister, too? Damn, he's a real renaissance man."

"Shark," I say, lowering her into the water. "He's a renaissance shark."

"You know, you're kind of full of nonsense," she says, kissing my nose. "It's one of the reasons I like you so much. Everything around me is so serious all the time—my job, my family. It's nice to be around someone kind of silly. It brings out that side in me."

"I was just about to say that about you. I'm rarely comfortable enough with anyone to act this way. You bring it out in me. And believe me, you're the first person to ever call me silly. Everyone thinks I'm too serious all the time."

"I like silly you," she says, snaking her arms and legs around me.

"Fuck," I say, taking a deep breath. "I'm really going to miss the feeling of you wrapping yourself around my body like this. You're like a little koala bear."

"Not quite," she says, laughing. "I read somewhere that koalas cling to trees because it cools their bodies down. Clinging to you has the exact opposite effect on me."

"Hmm. Same," I say, rubbing my face on hers. "I'm sorry I got all serious about marriage and stuff. I just really like you."

"It doesn't bother me," she says. "I'm glad you're being honest with me, but I'm being honest, too. I just want you to know who I am."

"I appreciate that because I want to know everything about you. And I'm not going to stop learning about you after this weekend. This is just the beginning for me."

Chapter Thirty-One

RAINE

When Alex walks me back to my room after our perfect beach day, Butch is waiting by my door.

"I've been texting you," he says, holding up his phone.

"Oh, my phone's in my room. I didn't even take it with me."

"Since when do you go anywhere without your phone?" Butch says, shaking his head. "I'm headed to the airport. My grandma died this morning. I need to get to Georgia."

"Oh, Butch," I say, throwing myself into him. "I'm so sorry."

"It's fine, Raine." He lets me hug him for a second and then pushes me back. "I've known it was coming. I'm fine."

"Sorry for your loss, man." Alex steps forward and pats his shoulder. "Anything I can do?"

"Appreciate it," Butch says. "Yeah. Look after Mighty Mouse and make sure she gets on her flight safely tomorrow."

"I've got you." Alex kisses the top of my head. "I'm going to run back to my room and get a shower before the wedding. I'll pick you up in about an hour."

I nod as he reaches out and shakes Butch's hand. "I've enjoyed getting to know you, man. Hope we run in the same circle again."

Butch looks down at me and smiles. "Somehow I'm guessing we will."

I watch Alex turn the corner and then swipe my card. "Do you have to leave right now? Come into my room."

"My car's leaving in thirty minutes," he says, plopping down on a chair.

"Where did y'all disappear to today? I looked for you when Roman and I got back from the police station."

"A little beach on the north shore. We pretty much read and slept all day. This morning was a lot."

"Yeah, it was," he says. "The cops said Gentry's going to jail when they take him back to Miami. The judge revoked his bail for leaving the jurisdiction."

"Good. At least we know he won't bother Sophie."

"Does she even know this little subplot is happening? Or does Seb know?"

"I don't think so," I say. "And I want to keep it that way."

"Do you think Roman will tell her?"

"No way. He loves her. He would never subject her to any pain. And I'll make sure Alex doesn't tell them."

He smiles. "From his puppy-dog love eyes, I'm guessing Alex will do about anything you want him to do at this point. Are y'all going to keep up after tomorrow?"

I collapse down on the bed. "Don't make me think about that right now. This weekend has been so perfect. I'm not sure how I'm going to be able to get on the plane tomorrow."

"If you like him that much, keep it going. It's not like you're going to live in different countries or something."

"Almost," I say, grabbing a pillow and hugging it to my chest. "San Diego to Miami is a trek. And it's really not even that. I mean, when are we going to have time to see each other? I'm starting the new assignment. You know how busy we're going to be. And if he signs his contract, he'll be tied down for at least nine months of the year. It's just not going to work."

"You sound like you want it to work though."

"He's amazing, Butch. He's sweet and funny and smart and—"

"And apparently decent in the sack from those sounds you were making yesterday."

"Shut up," I say, throwing the pillow at him. "Remember —what happens in Vegas, stays in Vegas. No talking about this when we get back."

"I'm not going to tell anyone."

"I won't tell anyone about your stuff, either. How many did you bag?"

"How many did I bag?" he says, rolling his eyes. "Don't ever use that phrase again. And only one."

"What? How is that possible?"

He shrugs. "I kind of dug Ava. She's interesting."

"Like how interesting? Like keep-in-touch-with-her interesting?"

"Naw, that's not going to happen, but we had a nice weekend," he says, rubbing his beard. "It's got me thinking."

"About?"

"About what you said on the way down here. About me hooking up with forgettable women so I won't have to put myself out there. I might be ready for you to set me up with someone—a woman who might be a real possibility."

I jump out of the bed and throw myself into him for a hug. "This is maybe the greatest news I've ever heard."

"Settle down," he says, hugging me tightly. "We can talk about it when we get to San Diego. I have to leave now."

"Okay," I say, kissing his cheek. "I love you, Butch."

"I love you, too, little buddy. Text me when you're safely back in Virginia. You know I'll worry."

I nod as he opens the door. "Travel safely. Give your family my love."

After Butch left, I had to hustle to get ready. I'm just putting on the finishing touches as I hear a knock on the door.

"Damn," Alex says as I open the door. "Is there any color that doesn't look good on you? I thought yellow was the best, but that red is almost too much for me. You're breathtaking."

I do a little spin for him. "I wasn't sure if this was right for a wedding, but I thought you would like it."

"I like it a lot, especially how it clings to all the right places." He grabs me and pushes me against the wall. "Do we have to go to the wedding?"

"Well since they're already married, it's kind of a sham. Let's just stay here," I say, running my hands over his closely tailored chinos. "Why does your butt look this good right now?"

"Right back at you," he says, turning me around. "Seriously, we need to leave this room in the next five seconds or we're not leaving until the morning."

"Fine," I say, taking one more look in the mirror, "but I'm leaving under protest."

As we're walking down to the wedding area, we pass Allie, Savannah, and Serena. They're staring at us, but it doesn't make me feel at all uncomfortable anymore. I wrap my arms around Alex's waist as he pulls me closer. This is starting to feel so right. I can't imagine not being next to him.

When we walk into the pool area, I inhale quickly and hug him even more tightly. I feel like I've just walked into a dream. White flowers and deep green palm plants surround the round tables that are placed around the deck. Strands of white lights criss-cross the area—highlighting the hundreds of candles floating beneath them in the pool. Sophie and Seb are already sitting at a private table—almost completely hidden behind sheer white panels that are moving gently with the ocean breezes. It's the most gorgeous setting I've ever seen.

"Do you mind if we sit with my teammates?" Alex whispers. "I've been ignoring them all weekend."

"Of course. I'd like to get to know them better." I look up at him as he leans down to give me a gentle kiss. He takes my hand and leads me over to their table.

"Has everyone met Raine?" He squeezes my hand tightly

as he pulls out my chair. "Introduce yourselves if you haven't. Where's Manny?"

"Hey, Raine. I'm Jack. Manny left on the afternoon flight to head back to Miami."

"I'm Cole. Nice to meet you, Raine." He smiles at me. "Alex, Manny said you'd tell us why he left early."

"He must have gotten into a fight with Caroline," Jack says, "because she and Casey have been huddled in my room all day. They refused to come to the wedding. What's going on?"

Alex grabs my hand under the table. "Caroline's having an affair with Gentry Randall. We caught them in the act this afternoon in Manny's room."

"You can't be serious," Jack says, his face scrunching up like he's about to throw up.

"I am," Alex says, nodding across the pool. "I don't want to talk about it for the rest of the night. Let's concentrate on Seb and Sophie. In fact, it looks like the wedding's about to start."

Seb and Sophie have left their love den and made it to the microphone that's set up across the pool from us.

Seb picks it up and taps it a few times. "Can I have your attention? I just wanted to let you know that there's not going to be a wedding tonight."

A few people gasp in the crowd. Seb takes a long pause.

"I had no idea he was such a drama queen," I whisper to Alex.

"Oh, he is," Alex laughs. "Believe me."

"There's not going to be a wedding because Sophie and I

got married over All Star break in Michigan. We've been married for almost three months."

Sophie buries her head into his chest as guests start clapping and whistling.

Seb waves them quiet and then continues, "I met Sophie a little more than a year ago. After talking to her for only a couple of minutes, I already knew I wanted to marry her. I could barely wait until July much less until today. We had a small, private wedding at my family's lake house. It was perfect, but we did want to celebrate it with all of you tonight. Thank you for being with us this weekend. Now, let's get back to the party."

He leans over and kisses Sophie softly to more cheers from the crowd, and then leads her by the hand back to their private table. Seriously, I couldn't have imagined a more perfect fake wedding for her.

Alex's teammates try not to talk about Manny and Caroline during dinner, but by dessert time, the beer and whiskey have fully kicked in and they can't resist any longer.

"Come on," Alex says, pulling me up. "We're not spending our last night talking about this bullshit. Grab your cake."

He picks up our drinks and guides me down to the beach chairs we sat on the first night.

"Do you remember the first night we got here?" he says, smiling. "We were sitting right here when you told me that you got awkward when hot guys started showing you attention. We've come so far in a couple of days."

"That seems like so long ago, doesn't it?" I say, feeding him a bite of my cake.

"Yeah, like ages ago. Maybe we can hide down here from the world for the rest of the night—or for weeks, days, years—"

"Done," I say, laying my head on his shoulder. "Let's stay here forever."

Chapter Thirty-Two

ALEX

Raine and I were awake most of the night—trying to get in every bit of together time we could before we left the island today. I think I finally drifted off to sleep about four.

Although my flight back to Miami doesn't leave until this afternoon, I'm awake at seven to make sure she gets on her morning flight. She's been protesting from the moment she opened her eyes.

"Alex." She looks up as she continues to stuff her belongings into her suitcase. "You don't have to go to the airport with me this early. Your plane doesn't leave until three. Go back to bed."

"I'm coming with you," I say, handing her a few pieces of clothing that are hanging in the closet. "I'll sleep on the plane later."

"But what are you going to do all day in St. Thomas? It wouldn't make sense to come back here on the ferry just in time to catch your ride to the airport." She tries to zip her suitcase, but it's too stuffed. "Why don't you stay here and enjoy the resort for another few hours?"

"I'm going with you. I'll find something to do over there until my flight leaves." I pull her away from the suitcase as I try to reposition a few things.

"Wait, is this my T-shirt?" I say, holding it up.

She grabs it and buries it in her suitcase. "Yes, and you're not getting it back. It smells like you."

"I smell like me, too," I say as I hug her. "You'll get to smell me in January when I visit you."

"That's almost three months away," she says, breaking away from me. She checks in her parrot bag to make sure she has everything. "And that's if we make it that long."

"Raine," I say, pulling her over to me. "You promised. We're going to talk every day until I get back from Puerto Rico. Then I'll come out to San Diego to see you."

"Okay," she says, looking down.

"Raine." I pull her chin up. "You promised."

She nods and tries to zip her suitcase again with no luck. She lets out a huge sigh and leans against the wall.

"Here. I'll do it. Just make sure you have everything. Our car leaves in ten minutes."

"My car," she says, sitting on the bed. "You don't have to come with me."

"Really? I had no idea. It's not like you've said that before."

"I'm too tired for sarcasm, Alex."

I lift her newly zipped suitcase off the bed. "I promised Butch that I'd get you to the airport. I'm going to keep that promise. I don't want him coming after me."

"I won't tell him."

"He'll know. In fact, he's probably watching us right now," I say, looking around the room. "I wouldn't be surprised if he installed cameras before he left."

"Yeah, he probably did," she says, finally smiling. "For protective and perverted reasons."

"Then he's seen more than enough already," I say, grabbing her suitcase in one hand and her in the other. "Let's get out of here before we miss the car."

"But I don't want to go," she whines as I pull her out of her room. "Please don't make me."

"If you behave right now, I promise I'll bring you back down here when you get time off from work." I keep pushing her reluctant body toward the lobby. "And it will just be us— no more of the spring break vibe."

As we round the corner into the lobby, Roman makes a beeline over to us. "Raine! Your car's here. And I didn't want to let you get away without saying goodbye. I enjoyed working with you on our little mission."

"Our very little mission," she says, laughing. "The Case of the Immature Note Writer."

"You know I'm always available if you need extra, uh, spy help," Roman says, lowering his voice.

"What exactly is 'spy help,' Roman?" She rolls her eyes. "I'm going to pass, but thanks for the offer."

"Well, at least I hope we'll see you again," Roman says, hugging her. "When you come to Miami, make sure we get to see you. Alex can't take all of your time."

"Wanna bet?" I say, shaking his hand. "Thanks for your

hospitality down here. It's an amazing resort. I can't wait to get back."

"Maybe you two will get married down here—"

"Roman," I say, holding my hand up. "Stop. I'm having a hard enough time getting her to agree to keep in touch with me. Let's not freak her out completely."

"Alex." I turn around to see Jack walking toward us. "Are you leaving early? I thought we had a van taking us to the airport at one."

"Yeah," I say, loading our bags into the trunk of the car. "I'm taking Raine to catch her flight—"

"You don't have to—"

"Stop. When are you going to learn that I don't give up?" I say, smiling at her. "I'm going with you. Jack, I'll see you on the plane. Will you make sure my buddy Antonio gets to the airport?"

"Yeah, I've got you," he says. "Just FYI, Caroline's still in my room. She's going to try to get on our flight. Any suggestions?"

"Yeah, stay out of it," I say. "I'm sure Manny had her name removed from the flight list. There's nothing we can do about it."

"How's she going to get back to Miami? Casey wants me to buy her a ticket on a commercial flight."

"That's up to you," I say. "Or maybe Gentry will pay for it."

"Uh, that's going to be difficult," Roman says. "He's already back in a Miami jail. I think he's going to be there until his court date. And just so we're all on the same page, Caroline's not staying here after you leave. She can sleep on the streets for all I care. No one comes after Sophie on my watch. Actions have consequences."

"They do," I say, shrugging. "She'll have to figure it out. Come on, Raine. We have to get you to the airport."

Roman pats me on the back. "All right, you two, travel safely. Alex, I'll see you back in Miami."

Raine smiles and waves at him as she slides into the back of the car. When I get in, she puts her head on my shoulder as I wrap my arm around her.

"I'm glad you're coming with me," she whispers. "I'm not ready to leave you yet."

"I'm never going to be ready to leave you, baby. Never."

After she checks in for her flight, I walk her to security. I have my arm around her so tightly that I'm a little surprised our bodies aren't starting to physically merge.

"Okay. Do you have everything?" I say, handing her the parrot bag from my shoulder. "Phone, wallet, charger, ID."

She takes the bag and collapses back onto my chest. "Why do I feel like a teenager leaving for summer camp?"

"I'm just making sure you're set," I say, inhaling the intoxicating smell of her hair one last time. "Although if you left something, I'm willing to meet you back down here to find it."

"Then I'm leaving something," she says, hugging me tighter. "I should go or I'm going to miss the plane."

"Okay." I lean down and give her one last, slow kiss. "Call me when you get to Virginia."

She nods and starts walking toward security. When she's

about to disappear into the airport, she turns around again and smiles at me. Despite her smile, I know by the look on her face that I'm going to have to stay on her constantly if I want her to be in my life long term. And from the sharp pains that are shooting through my body right now, I can tell that's definitely what I want.

"Bye, Trouble," I say under my breath as she disappears.

Epilogue

Three Months Later

It's been three months since that glorious weekend in St. John. Alex and I talked every day until the holidays hit. Then it became every couple of days, then once a week, and now it's been almost two weeks since we've talked.

To Alex's credit, he's trying a lot harder than I am. I still miss him like crazy, but I know the things I'm capable of and a long-distance relationship is not one of them. It became more and more apparent as the hours stretched into days and the days stretched into months.

Alex signed a new contract with his team on New Year's Eve—a one-year deal worth almost twenty million dollars. He said he wasn't quite ready to move on yet. I'm happy for him, but that means he's going to be in Miami for at least another year. And I'm going to be in San Diego. In fact, that's where I'm headed today. My plane touches down in fifteen minutes. I have a week to get settled in and then my new assignment begins. I'm going to be really busy. At least, that will help take my mind off of Alex—maybe just a little bit.

Sophie hasn't left me alone for a day since we left the island. And actually, I'm happy she hasn't. I didn't realize how much I missed her until I spent some time with her at the wedding. And then we reunited for Christmas in Chicago and it felt like we'd never spent any time apart. We text each other almost every day. I thought it would eventually annoy me, but I'm addicted to it now.

When I turn on my phone after we land, there's a text from her.

Call me. Now!

"Hey, Soph," I say, glancing out of the window as the plane pulls up to the gate. "What's wrong?"

"You tell me." Her voice has the little snarl it gets when she's about to lecture me.

"I don't have time for guessing games," I say as I start wrangling my bag from the overhead. "I just landed in San Diego. Can I call you back?"

"No, you can't," she says. "Alex told Seb this morning that he's been calling and texting you for a week and you haven't responded. I was worried about you."

"I'm fine. You know that. I talked to you yesterday. I've just been busy with moving stuff."

"You left out the part about ghosting Alex. And if you have time to talk to me, you have time to talk to him." Her voice is getting more snarly. "Come on, Raine. You have to try if this is going to work."

"Soph, I already told him that I don't want to do a long-distance thing. I like him—really like him—but it would be hard enough to keep something going with someone in the same city. I can't do San Diego to Miami. It's too much."

She sighs loudly. "Can't you at least keep talking to him? He really likes you."

"I told you, I really like him, too, but what's the point? It'll just make me more frustrated and sad. Do you want me to be sad?"

"Of course, I don't want you to be sad," she says, pausing for a second. "But I think you're going to be sadder if you eliminate him from your life."

"I'm already without him and yeah, I'm sad, but it's going to get worse if I keep talking to him. I can't take talking to him and not being able to touch him."

The guy in front of me in line turns around and looks down at me—his eyebrows raised.

"Quit eavesdropping," I say, glaring at him. "Eyes forward."

"Who are you talking to?"

"Some asshole," I say. "Soph, come on. Could you have a long-distance relationship with Seb? You two can barely go an hour without touching each other."

"I know, but—"

"But nothing. You're holding me to a different standard. Think about what you'd do if you couldn't see Seb for three months."

"Die," she whispers. "There's no way I could do that."

"Exactly." My phone's starts blowing up. "Hold on. I'm getting a bunch of texts. They're from Millie. She and Mason are picking me up."

We're running late. Be there in about 20.

Mason said I had to tell you it was my fault.

He doesn't want you to think that he would ever be late to anything.

Scratch that. He says to tell you if it were just him picking you up he would have been at least an hour early.

I had low blood sugar. Really needed a taco.

———

No worries. My plane just landed. Meet me by baggage. Did you bring me tacos?

———

Of course. And Dad and Chase are back at our place BBQing.

We'll have plenty of food for our catch-up session.

I'm so happy you're finally here. See you in a few!

"I'm back," I say to Sophie.

"Everything okay?"

"Yeah, they're just running late."

"Good. That gives us more time to talk. What does Millie tell you to do about Alex?"

"I haven't told her about him," I say, plopping down in one of the chairs in the airport.

"I thought you said you two were close."

I let out a deep breath. "We are, Soph. But what's the point of bringing her into this? I knew a day after Alex and I left the island that it wasn't going to work. I don't want to get her all hopeful like you."

"I am hopeful and I'll remain hopeful," she says. "I think you two belong together."

"Soph, can we leave it alone for now?" I close my eyes and take a cleansing breath. "I have to grab my luggage. I'll call you in a few days, okay?"

"Raine," she says, her voice getting edgy again. "If you try to shake me this time, I'll come to San Diego and hunt you down. I don't want to go another two years without talking to you. Do I make myself clear?"

"I'm not going to try to shake you," I say, smiling. "I don't want to shake you. I missed you."

"I missed you, too, honey. I'll see you when Miami plays in San Diego in May. Maisie and Ryan are coming out, too. Maybe we can do a triple date with you and Alex after a game—"

"Stop."

She sighs again. "I will—for now. Be careful. Call me after you get settled."

As I get to the luggage area, I look around for Millie and

Mason, but don't see them yet. I head to my assigned baggage carousel. When I get there my bags are already on the belt. I snatch the small one off and then tug on the big one until another hand grabs it.

"You're going to have to learn to pack lighter."

My head spins around to see Alex standing behind me. I jump on him with such force that it makes him drop my bag back onto the carousel.

"Raine," he says, laughing as he tries to steady me on his chest while he grabs for the bag. "Your bag is going in the back area again."

I wrap my arms and legs around him tightly and start kissing all over his face. "Let it. The airport can have it. Why are you here? Wait, I don't care. Just kiss me."

He finally gives up on my bag and kisses me a few times before he hugs me to him.

"I'm here," he whispers, "because you stopped returning my calls. I already told you that I don't give up—ever."

"Wait," I say, looking up at him. "How did you know I was arriving today?"

"I have an inside source," he says, nuzzling his face into my hair.

"Butch is supposed to be on my side."

He pushes me back a little. "Your side? Are we on different sides?"

"Alex, I'm so happy to see you. And I don't want to get off of you ever, but nothing's changed. I told you I can't do the long-distance thing."

"Actually, something has changed—"

"Well, well, well." I hear Millie's voice behind me. "And

what do we have here?"

"Put me down," I whisper to Alex.

"I thought you didn't want to get off of me ever, but fine," he says, laughing as he reluctantly lifts me to the ground.

"Millie, Mason, this is my friend Alex."

"Your friend, huh?" Millie says, her eyebrows raised. "Yes, it seems like you're very good friends."

Alex puts his arm around me and extends his hand to Millie. "Hey, it's nice to meet you. Raine's told me a lot about both of you."

"And yet," Millie says, looking at me as she shakes his hand, "she's told me absolutely nothing about you."

"Well I can't say that bodes very well for me," Alex says, squeezing me to him a little tighter. "Hey, I'm Alex Molina."

"Yeah, I know who you are. I'm a big baseball fan," Mason says, shaking Alex's hand. "And Butch told me he met you in St. John."

"God, please don't believe a word Butch said about me," Alex says. "I'm not sure I made the best impression on him."

"Naw, he said good things," Mason says. "Well, mainly. He said you sucked at beer pong."

"Wait," Millie says, looking up at Mason. "Butch told you that Raine was hanging out with a guy in St. John and you didn't tell me?"

"Butch told me that *he* hung out with Alex and a bunch of other baseball players in St. John," Mason says, kissing the top of her head. "He didn't tell me anything about Raine. You know I would have told you that."

"Maybe Raine can tell us about it now?" Millie says.

"Where's Mo? I can't believe my little nephew isn't here to greet me."

"Don't try to change the subject, Raine." Millie crosses her arms, her eyes narrowing.

"Who's Mo?" Alex says.

"Our son," Millie says, not taking her eyes off of me. "And when we left, he was hanging out with his grandpa and his Godfather on our back porch. Are you done trying to distract me, Raine? Start talking."

Alex grabs my bag as it cycles back around and sets it down next to us.

"Umm, I don't want to get in the middle of this," he says, looking from me to Millie, "but do you mind if I get a minute alone with Raine?"

"That's Raine's decision," Mason says, looking at me.

"I'm good, Mase."

"Okay," he says, starting to push Millie away. "We'll be over here if you need us."

"Wait, no." Millie spins away from him. "If we go over there, we can't hear what they're saying to each other."

"Mason," I say, pointing at Millie. "Remove the threat."

"Roger that," he says, sweeping her up into his arms and starting to walk away. "Threat neutralized."

"Stop," she says, laughing as he squeezes her butt. "You're going to embarrass the new guy."

"I don't embarrass easily," Alex says. "Carry on."

Mason looks back at me and nods. "I like the new guy."

Alex turns to me, shaking his head. "You know who they remind me of?"

"Sophie and Seb. It's uncanny, right?"

"Like weirdly so," he says, still looking at them. "I mean, have you ever seen them all in the same place?"

"Sophie and Millie, yes, but we were drinking that weekend. I could have been seeing double." I grab his arm. "Wait, did you say something had changed? What?"

"While I'm out here visiting you," he says, pulling me over to a row of chairs. "I have to do something in L.A. I was hoping you would come with me. I'm kind of nervous."

"What?" I reach out to hold his hand as we sit down. "What are you nervous about?"

"I have an interview with Pepperdine to get into law school."

"What? You told me you signed another year with the team."

"I did," he says, stroking my arm, "but I told them it's my last year. I'm starting law school next January—less than a year from now."

"Alex," I say, hugging him. "That's amazing. I'm so proud of you."

"It's not a hundred percent yet, but I'm hoping to get registered this week."

"At Pepperdine?"

"I hope," he says, taking a deep breath. "They've already accepted me conditionally. One of my old UCLA coaches is the head coach at Pepperdine now. He put in a good word for me and my college grades were good enough to get me this far, but I have to go through a bunch of interviews. That's why I'm nervous."

"Why?" I stroke his cheek. "You're amazing. They'll love you."

"I hope because I'd like to be living closer to you this time next year," he says. "If you're willing to wait that long."

"Alex, a lot can happen in a year."

"Yep, and I already have that planned out," he says, leaning back against the wall. "I figure if we can see each other at least once a month this year, we can make it to next January when we'll only be two hours away from each other."

"Two hours is a lot better, but you're going to be so busy with law school—"

He puts his hand up to stop me. "Raine, do you want to be with me? Because I want to be with you and I'm willing to work at it to see where it takes us."

"I want to be with you." I nod slowly. "I missed you so much. I've never felt this way about someone, but it worries me because if we keep getting closer, and then it doesn't work out, it's going to kill me. I don't think I can take that."

"I know," he whispers, "but nothing good comes without putting yourself out there a little bit—being vulnerable. We have to do that if we want this to work. I think we'd be really happy. Do you want to be happy?"

"I want to be happy," I say, hugging him. "But you have to be patient with me. I get frustrated easily."

"I'll be patient," he says, kissing my forehead. "And I'll make sure you're properly fed at all times. That will give us a fighting chance at least."

"Speaking of," I say, looking back over to Mason and Millie. "I'm starving. Millie said there's barbecue at her house. Can we go there?"

"Yep," he says, pulling a banana out of his backpack. "Will this hold you until we get there?"

DONNA SCHWARTZE

Epilogue

ALEX

The Same Day

"Well look who made it all the way to California," Butch says, grinning as he walks out to greet us when we arrive at Mason and Millie's house. "You couldn't stay away from me, could you?"

Raine runs ahead of me and shoves Butch in the chest. "Why didn't you tell me he was coming out here?"

"What fun would that be?" Butch says, grabbing her hands and balling up her fists. "For a genius, you're a slow learner. Fists, remember?"

She jerks her hands away from him. "I don't like surprises. You know that."

"I don't like them either, except when they're happening to other people. Then they're hilarious," Butch says. "But if you don't want him here, just say the word and I'll make him leave."

"I didn't say that," she says, reaching back and grabbing my hand. "Of course, I want him here. Just tell me next time so I won't attack him at the airport."

"I kind of liked the attacking part, to be honest," I say, laughing. I stop abruptly when I see three guys—who look disturbingly like Butch—approaching us.

"Hey Raine," the biggest, scariest one says. He pulls her away from me and hugs her. "Welcome to San Diego. We missed you."

"Hey Hawk," she says. "I missed you, too."

"God, you really are multiplying," I whisper to Butch as I pull him to the side. "These guys look exactly like you."

"Naw," he says. "They aren't even close to being as good looking as I am."

"No, but seriously, man, I thought you were frightening alone, but each one's scarier than the next."

"That's our goal," he says, patting me on the back. "In fact, I think I'm going to suggest that to the Navy as the new creed—Navy SEALs: Each one's scarier than the next."

I look around as Raine continues to hug the Butch looka-likes. "What are the chances I'm going to leave here without getting killed?"

"Low odds, man," Butch laughs. "But I said you had low odds with Raine, too, and look at you now—even making cross-country house calls."

"Honestly, the Raine odds are still kind of low," I say, "but I'm putting in the work. She's worth the effort."

"She definitely is," Butch says. "Gentlemen, this is Alex. He's got a thing for Raine. This is Hawk, Mouse, and Bryce."

"What kind of thing would that be?" Another guy joins our

group. He's older than the rest of them, but somehow even more terrifying.

"Hey Mack," Raine says as she hugs him. "I missed you."

"I missed you, too." He hugs her tightly, but doesn't take his eyes off me. "I don't think you answered my question. What kind of thing do you have for my daughter?"

"Wait, you're her dad?" I take a step back and look at Raine. "I thought your parents lived in Chicago."

"They do," Raine says, grabbing my hand again. "This is Millie's dad, Mack Marsh. He's kind of my adopted dad."

"No 'kind of' about it," Mack growls. He gives me one more deadly look and then looks down at Raine. "I thought I told you to leave the baseball players alone."

"Mack, stop," she says, wrapping her arms around my waist. "Alex is a great guy."

"We'll see," Mack says, extending his hand to me. "You're a great shortstop anyway, but don't think that gives you a pass if you fuck with her."

"I won't do that. Ever," I say, trying to hold his stare as I shake his hand. His eyes are so intense that I think they might be burning a hole in my forehead.

Mason walks up and pulls our hands apart. "I see you've met my father-in-law. If you're wondering, I can confirm he's every bit as scary as he seems."

"You two," Millie says, grabbing Mack and Mason, "quit terrorizing our guest. Alex, why don't you come with me into the house so we can talk a little bit?"

"Oh, hell no," Raine says, positioning herself between Millie and me. "When she says 'talk,' she means interrogate and she's stupid good at it."

"What?" I say. "No, I want to talk to Millie. You've told me so many good things about her."

"Huh," Butch says. "You really are dumber than you look. Millie's way more terrifying than all of the rest of us combined."

Mack turns his stern look from me to Butch. Butch takes an extended step away from him.

"Dad," Millie says, kissing his cheek, "Carol's trying to get your grandson down for a nap and he's resisting again. Maybe you can go help with that. You know Mo sleeps better for you than for anyone else."

Mack nods as he lets Millie push him away. He turns around and gives me one more look before they disappear into the house.

"You let him touch your kid?" I say, looking at Mason. "I've never been more scared of anyone in my life."

"Naw, he's a big teddy bear underneath all that show," Mason says, laughing.

"So he's all talk?"

"No, man. That's not what I said. His bite is even worse than his bark when someone gets on his bad side, but he has a soft side, too, especially with my wife and son. He transforms into a different person when he's with them—gentle, soft spoken. But God, don't tell him I said that because I'd like to go on living past today."

"I'm not going to tell him anything. I'd like to avoid him for the rest of the day if possible." I shake my head and whistle. "He must be a bitch to have as a father-in-law. How long have you been married?"

"A little over a year."

"Is he used to you yet?"

He laughs. "No, that's not going to happen. He tolerates me, but I know he'd murder me in a second if I ever hurt Millie. And honestly, I would want him to."

"Yeah," I say quickly. "I'd never do anything bad to Raine."

"You better not, brother," he says, patting my back. "Every guy here would kill for her. You hungry? We've got barbecue and beer in the backyard."

Raine comes up behind me as Mason walks away. I hug her to me tightly. "You should have warned me that I was walking into the *Fight Club*."

"I could have if you would have told me you were coming out here. And they're not as scary as they act."

"Maybe not to you," I whisper. "Do they all carry weapons?"

"Pretty much." She looks up and smiles. "You hung out with Butch. You're not scared of him. The rest of them are no different once you get to know them."

"First of all, just because I hung out with Butch doesn't mean I'm not scared of him. And second, if I have to get to know them to hang out with you, I'll do it. I'm willing to risk my life for you."

She rolls her eyes as she starts pulling me toward the backyard. "Don't be so dramatic."

"I don't think I'm being a bit dramatic when I say that Mack guy would kill me if I even looked at him wrong."

"Yeah, Mack might," she says, smiling, "but the rest probably wouldn't."

"Oh, well that makes me feel so much better. Thank you."

As we walk through the back gate, several more guys start hugging Raine. Millie comes up behind me and pulls me over to where Mason and Butch are sitting.

"This is probably the friendliest place for you right now," she says, smiling and sweeping her arm toward the other guys. "You get used to them, but if anyone gives you trouble, tell me. I'll shut them down."

"They listen to you?" I say, sitting next to Butch.

"They damn well better," Mason says, pulling Millie onto his lap. "So what brings you out to San Diego? Just visiting Raine?"

"Yeah, that's my main reason," I say as Raine sits down beside me. "But I'm also out here to interview for law school. I'm hopefully starting a year from now."

"Oh yeah?" Mason says. "I saw you signed a one-year deal. Are you done after this season?"

"Definitely."

"That's awesome," Millie says, smiling at me. "What law school?"

"Pepperdine up in L.A."

"Huh," Mason says. "That's cool. My buddy's new girl-friend is at Pepperdine law school. I can hook you up if you have questions or anything. She just started, though. I'm not sure she could be much help."

"Who's this?" Millie says as she cuddles into him.

"Nash Young. I told you about him. He's the one who lives in that little town up by Big Bear—like Blitzen Bay or something."

"Why does his name sound familiar?" Hawk asks as he joins the group.

"You know him," Mason says. "He was Delta. He worked with our team in Afghanistan a couple of times. He's the one who went out with a knee injury after his buddy tripped that wire—"

"Yeah," Hawk says, nodding, "now I remember. He lives out here?"

"Two hours from here—up in the San Bernardino Mountains." Mason pulls a blanket from the back of the chair and covers Millie with it. "He invited us to visit this summer. We're thinking about going up there in July."

"Oh right," Millie says, "to celebrate your birthday. Maybe we should all go up there—including you Alex."

"Alex is going to be playing baseball in July, babe," Mason says, wrapping the blanket around her tighter.

"Well, I have the All Star break in July if it lines up with your plans."

"I'm guessing you're going to be playing in the game," Hawk says. "Like every other year since you entered the league."

"I would gladly forgo the game if it meant spending some extended time with Raine," I say, taking her hand, "but that depends on her work schedule, too."

"Let me know when the All Star break is," Millie says. "And I'll make sure we have the week off. That could be fun —all of us up in the mountains. We don't want to overwhelm them, though."

"I'll talk to Nash to see if there's a big place we could rent," Mason says, "but he said there's a little inn up there, too."

As everyone melts into conversation, I pull Raine to me

and whisper, "What do you say? Do you want to spend a week with me at some bay up in the mountains?"

"Yes. So much," she says, burying her face in my neck. "It will be the perfect follow-up to our beach vacation. Water's kind of our thing, right?"

"That lake's going to be cold as hell even in the summer," I say, laughing. "We're going to have to find another place for that weekend. That little inn sounds cozy, though."

"Yes, it does," she says, looking up at me. "I wonder if the rooms are sound-proofed."

"I can't wait to find out, baby."

Seb, Sophie, Alex, and Raine are back in the third book of The Grand Slam Series—*Leave It On The Field*. Butch's love story is in *No One Wants That*. Both are available on Amazon. Read free on Kindle Unlimited. **Keep flipping pages to read the first chapter of each book.**

What's Next?

Thank you for reading this book. I hope you enjoyed it. If you did, will you please leave a review on Amazon? You don't have to write anything if you don't want to—a star rating is plenty. I really appreciate your time.

This is a chapter from *No One Wants That*. It takes place seven months after the *Raine Out* epilogue. The entire crew is gathering in Blitzen Bay for summer vacation. It's from Butch's perspective.

(Keep flipping pages to get to the first chapter of *Leave It On The Field*.)

Butch

"What do you mean you want me to go with you?" Millie and Raine are sitting across from me on the patio sipping dirty martinis. They're about three drinks in which is usually when they start getting stupid. I should have known when they started whispering that I was in for it again.

"Just what we said," Millie coos at me. She only uses that tone as a last resort when she's trying to get me to do something. "We want you to come with us tomorrow. You have to go."

I raise my head off the lounge chair and glare at them over my sunglasses. In my twenty years as a Navy SEAL, this look alone made grown men put down their weapons and drop to their knees. It's highly effective, but unfortunately Millie and Raine have never been scared of it. They know I wouldn't hurt a hair on their heads and that I'd kill anyone who tried.

"I'm not going on your stupid love fest in the mountains," I say, snarling. "That's been settled for months."

They're leaving tomorrow with Millie's husband, Mason, and Raine's boyfriend, Alex, to head up to some little resort town in the San Bernardino mountains. They've been talking about it for six months. I've made it clear at least twenty times that I have no interest in going.

"Nothing's settled," Millie says, tilting her head and pursing her lips into a pout. "It won't be as much fun if you don't go."

"That's stating the obvious. And don't give me that sexy look. That bullshit doesn't work on a guy unless you're sleeping with him."

Raine tilts her head against Millie's and gives me the same look. "Ple-e-e-ease," she whines.

"You're not sleeping with me either, Raine," I say, pointing at her. "Save that look for Alex."

"Speaking of Alex," Raine says, taking a slow sip of her martini, "he'll be sad if you're not there. You know how much he likes to hang out with you."

"Seriously? That's your strongest argument?" I lay my head back down and close my eyes. "I told you I'm not going to be a third wheel. I get too much of the happy-couple bull-shit down here. I don't need to drive two hours up into the mountains to get more of it."

"Well technically," Millie says, "you'd be the fifth wheel."

"That's not making your argument any stronger, Millicent."

I hear more loud whispering and then the quick clapping of their flip flops coming toward me. I open my eyes as I feel them sit down on either side of me. They each take one of my hands.

"Maybe take the Patti woman from Starbucks," Millie says, pulling off my sunglasses and putting them on herself. "Did you ever go out with her again?"

"One time was plenty."

"She's still hurt that you didn't call her," Raine says, squeezing my hand. "She talks about you every time I go in there. She had a good time."

"Everyone has a good time with me, but it doesn't always work both ways." I pause for a second. "I mean, she's okay, but she's way too nice. I'd run all over her in a relationship. It would be boring as hell for me, and it wouldn't be at all fair to her."

"What's going on here?" I look over to see Mason walking out of the house, holding his and Millie's son, Mo.

"They're trying one more full-court press to get me to go on your trip tomorrow," I say, holding up my hands that are still firmly in their grasps, "complete with hand holding, pouting, and whining."

"Buh," Mo says, his chubby, little face smiling as he points at me. That's the best he can do with my name right now.

I jerk my hands free as Mason hands Mo down to me.

"Get him to sleep and I'll take care of them." Mason lifts Millie and Raine around their waists—one in each arm—and carries them back to the couch. He points at them. "Stay. And quit bothering him. He'd be a bachelor on a couples' trip. No one wants that."

As I polish off my beer, Mo tries to grab it.

"Dink," he says. I pull it away from him. "Dink!"

"Yes, Mo-Mo, that's right. Beer is delicious to drink." I kiss the top of his head as I put the beer can on the table out of his reach.

"Dink!" He stretches his little arms out as far as he can.

"Damn. He's likes beer almost as much as I do." I turn the can over to show him it's dry. "Sorry, brother. Uncle Butch finished this one."

Mason turns around and laughs when he sees Mo trying to climb on the table to get to the beer. "Charlie gave him a sip of beer at that Memorial Day barbecue. He's been obsessed ever since."

"Well, he's definitely your kid," I say, trying to distract Mo by putting my baseball cap on him. He starts grabbing at it as it falls over his eyes.

"I'll get you another beer," Mason says, turning back toward the house. "Just get him to sleep. It's way past his bedtime."

As soon as the door clicks shut behind Mason, Millie starts back in. "Butch, we're not done talking about the trip."

"Mo Man, tell your mom to quit nagging me." Mo finally gets the cap off his head. I bow down and help him put it back on my head. "Thank you, little buddy. That's my favorite hat. Maybe we'll get you one so we can be twins."

"Wins," he says, tugging on my beard as I start massaging the back of his neck. It's my go-to move to get babies to nod off.

"He's become quite the little parrot since the last time I saw him," I say as I extend the massage up to his head. His forehead finally drops onto my chest.

"Yeah," Mason says, walking back out and handing me another beer. "He repeats everything we say, especially the cussing."

"Well, he has to learn how to cuss at some point," I say. "Might as well be now."

Mo's head starts nodding back and forth on my chest.

"I still don't understand how he likes you more than me," Raine says, scrunching up her face as she watches Mo's body collapse into mine. "You scare the crap out of grown men but a one-year-old loves you. It doesn't make any sense. I'm much nicer than you."

"Kids love me," I say, shrugging. "It's always been that way. Probably because I have six little brothers and sisters. I practically raised the youngest ones. I think kids can sense if you're comfortable with them."

"I'm comfortable with him," Raine says, crossing her arms over her chest.

"Please," I say, kissing Mo's head again as he lets out a long sigh—his last stand against the approaching sleep. "You hold him like you're handling a grenade."

"I do not."

"You do kind of hold him like that," Millie says, patting Raine's arm. "Or like he's poisonous or something."

"I'm an only child," Raine says, huffing. "I wasn't around babies growing up."

"Neither was I," Millie says, circling her arm around Raine's shoulders. "But you learn quickly when you have one. Believe me, when you and Alex have a baby, you'll be a pro overnight."

"Stop!" Raine pushes herself to the other side of the couch. "We haven't even been together a year. No one's having babies."

"You never know," Mason says. "Mo wasn't planned. Maybe you and Alex will have a surprise baby, too."

"Shut up," Raine says, flipping her head around to him. "And don't talk like that around Alex. He already has baby fever and when he's around Mo, it gets ridiculous."

"How can you not want one of these?" I say as Mo's breathing becomes slow and rhythmic.

"Do you want one?" Millie says, looking back at me. "I mean, you're amazing with him, but I didn't think you wanted a baby of your own. You've been married twice with no kids."

"Married twice—both times to the wrong women. Yeah, I want kids. I want them right now, but I might be getting too old. I'll have to make do with helping to raise my little nephew here."

"I can't believe he's already down." Mason walks over and carefully lifts the sleeping Mo off my chest. "You've got some voodoo magic going on or something."

"I told you, man, babies love me," I say, cracking open my fresh beer. "I've got that good energy."

Mason shakes his head as he carries Mo into the house. I watch them and then look back at Millie and Raine. They're in a huddle again—whispering and staring at me.

"Do you think I should use it?" Raine says.

"Use what?" I say, taking a long drink.

"I'm not talking to you," she says, not taking her eyes off me. "Mills, yes or no?"

"Yeah, I think you have to," Millie says, her eyes fixed on me, too. "It's the only way to make him go."

"Oh, good Lord," I say, throwing my head back. "When can we be done with this?"

"When you agree to go," Raine says. "Which will be right now because I'm cashing in on our bet from St. John."

I sit up slowly. I'm starting to get a little nervous. Raine hasn't tried to collect on our bet in the almost eight months since she won. I was hoping she'd forgotten about it. "The bet was that you get to set me up with someone. Not that I have to go on vacation with you."

"I am setting you up with someone," she says. "Someone in Blitzen Bay."

"What the hell is a Blitzen Bay?"

"The name of the town where we're staying for the next week. All of us—Mason, Millie, Alex, me, *and* you."

"I'm not going to a town that has that stupid of a name."

"So you're welching on your bet?" Millie says, tapping her fingers on her lips. "I thought that was against our code."

"I don't welch," I say, growling at her, "but you both know that wasn't our bet."

"I know nothing of the sort, Gabriel," Millie says, tilting her head and smiling.

"Don't try to use my real name on me. That only works for my mom."

"Welcher," Millie says.

"You don't know anyone in Blitzen-whatever," I say, glaring at them. "You have to have a real person in mind or I'm not going. I need a name."

"No, you don't," Raine says. "All you need to know is that the person I'm setting you up with is in Blitzen Bay. We'll figure out the rest when we get there."

"That's not going to work."

"Wel-l-l-lcher," Millie says. "Big, old welcher."

I jump up and take two enormous strides until I'm hulking over her. I lock my eyes into hers with my best alpha-dominant stare. She stands on the couch—so we're the same height—and leans toward me until she's about an inch from my face.

"And don't give me that sexy look," she says, kissing my nose. "That bullshit doesn't work on a woman unless you're sleeping with her."

I press my lips together and growl to try to stop a laugh from escaping. It doesn't work. "You're a piece of work, Millie," I say, shaking my head.

Raine grabs my hand and tugs me down onto the couch. "Let's talk about what you should pack."

Millie plops down and takes my other hand. "Swim trunks and hiking boots to start with and probably something casual-cute in case we want to go out one night. Right, Raine?"

"Definitely, but more mountain-cute, than city-cute."

"I hate both of you so much," I say, looking up as Mason walks back out. I close my eyes and tilt my head back on the couch.

"Did you finally cave?" he says, laughing. "It was inevitable, man. Nice effort, though. You lasted a lot longer than I would have. Millie's bad enough. Add Raine to the mix and I'd be done before they even started in on me."

Buy or download No One Wants That on Amazon.

This is a chapter from *Leave It On The Field*. It's from Sophie's perspective. It happens one year after *Raine Out* —two years since Seb and Sophie first met.

Sophie

"Seb! Stop. Joe will be here in fifteen minutes."

"Thirty," Seb says as he backs me up against the kitchen island. "We have plenty of time."

I grab his hands as they start pulling up my dress. "You know he's always at least fifteen minutes early."

"Okay, he'll be here in fifteen," he says as his face plunges into my neck. "Like I said—plenty of time."

"Stop." My body arches into him like it always does when

he gets anywhere near my neck. "You know the neck thing makes me crazy."

"Really?" He starts nibbling. "I had no idea."

"You did too," I say, running my hands down his back. They land on his butt. "And stop flexing. You know how I feel about your butt muscles."

"They like you too," he whispers as he continues to flex underneath my hands. He knows exactly what to do to put me in the mood. Honestly, it doesn't take that much. Just looking at him does it for me most of the time.

I unzip his jeans and pull him out. Hard again. "We already had sex last night *and* this morning."

His hands dart under my dress. "Not even close to our record for a twenty four hour period."

"I swear you have more than two hands." I sigh as I feel my body pass the point of no return. "And you're way hornier than usual."

"Incorrect. I'm always this exact same amount of horny." He lifts me onto the island.

"Not here," I say, trying to get down. "I'm entertaining later."

"We've had sex on every surface of this house including this one. We can clean it."

He continues the neck work as he pulls my legs around his waist. He fingers me a little before he slides inside. I let out an extended moan as he fills me up.

"That's better," he whispers. "I knew you would come around to my way of thinking, eventually."

I wrap my arms around his neck as he starts pumping. I know it will happen like it always does. The tingling starts in my toes and shoots up my legs. Then my entire body starts shaking. It's such an intense sensation that sometimes it's all I can do not to pass out.

The intercom beeps to announce that security has cleared someone through the gate. "Joe Porter," the voice announces.

"Seb." I groan as he starts panting against my neck. "He's here."

"Take your time." He slides his hands under my butt and picks me up. "He's not getting in until I let him in."

He pushes me against the wall. The shelves to the left of my head start shaking. I think something falls off. My head drops to his shoulder as he whispers something to me. I can't hear him. The roar has started in my brain like it does just before I'm about to lose control.

I hear a knock on the door just as my body releases. I bury my mouth against Seb's neck to try to deaden the long series of sounds pouring out of my mouth. He pumps hard a few more times before he erupts inside of me with a loud grunt that rattles around inside my head as I collapse against him.

He pants into my hair for a few seconds, then whispers, "You had perfect timing, as usual."

"I'm not sure I should get much credit for the timing." I shiver as the sensations continue to tingle through my body. "You know I pretty much lose control once you're inside."

"Really?" He wraps me up tighter. "I had no idea."

"You're such a liar. I really horny liar," I say, laughing as I rub my head against his chest to try to get it to stop spinning. "Joe's waiting."

"He can wait." He kisses the top of my head as he starts rubbing my back. "You need your recovery time."

"Since it usually takes me about an hour to recover from all that, you might as well let him in now."

He presses me more firmly against the wall as his tongue parts my lips. My head starts spinning again as he takes a slow, deep kiss.

"Stop," I say when he finally pulls back. "That doesn't help my recovery."

He brushes his cheek against mine. "I'm going to miss you so much."

"It's only a couple days," I say, running my fingers through his hair.

"It shouldn't be any days. I've played for this team for nine seasons. They've never made us stay in a hotel before home games."

"This is your first World Series. I guess they think it's different."

Another knock at the door. Well, really more like a pounding.

He carries me over to the intercom. "Be there in a minute, Joe."

"Yep," Joe gets out before Seb clicks it off.

He sets me back down on the island and nuzzles his face into my hair as I start to unwind myself from his body. "You're everything to me. I'd quit baseball today if you wanted me to. You know that, right? If this all gets to be too much for you, just tell me and I'm done that second."

"It's not too much. I don't want you to quit." I nod toward the front door. "You need to let him in before he breaks down the door. Go."

He brushes his lips over mine, sighs, and then heads toward the front door.

"What took you so long?" Joe's gruff tone vibrates through the house. "We're already running late."

"Do we really have to do this?" Seb asks as he walks back into the kitchen. "It's bullshit."

"Hey, Soph." Joe follows Seb around the corner. "You ready for this week?"

"Hey, Joe." I glance up at him as I'm picking up the book that fell off the shelf. "Yeah, I think. It's going to be crazy."

Seb pulls me back against him. "It would be less crazy if the team would let us stay with our wives like we're grown-ass men."

"I'll be fine," I say as he circles his arms around me. "Really. Just worry about baseball for the next few weeks."

Joe points toward the front door. "Seb, we need to leave. Drew said everyone had to be in the hotel by two. It's 1:28. With traffic, we'll be lucky to even make it on time at this point."

Seb doesn't move. "I play better when I spend the night before a game with my wife."

"Why are you arguing with me?" Joe throws up his hands. "You know it's not my decision. I'm paid to get you where you need to go safely. And right now, where you need to go is that fucking hotel."

"Babe, you have to go." I take Seb's hand and pull him toward the foyer. He follows me, dragging his feet. "I'll see you at the party tonight."

"For what? Like twenty minutes?" He picks up his suitcase as Joe opens the front door.

"Babe," I say, squeezing his hand, "it's not like we'd be alone here anyway. Our parents are arriving in the next few hours. And your sister and my brothers come in tomorrow. Our house will be packed."

"I'm here!" Maisie bursts through the front door. Joe grabs her and pushes her against a wall. She screeches. "Jesus, Joe! It's me. Lighten up."

"Have you ever heard of knocking?" Joe releases her slowly. "Don't surprise me. You know I hate that. How did you even get in here? Security didn't call to clear you."

"The door was open. And I'm on the no-ring list. You know how much Sophie hates that intercom going off." Maisie pats his back. "You really need to settle down. I mean, you're hyper most of the time but the World Series is going to kill you."

"Sophie," Joe says, narrowing his eyes, "what did I tell you about the no-ring list? The more people you put on it, the more confusing it gets for the guards. They make more mistakes as the list grows longer. I don't want anyone surprising you—not even your best friend."

"Maisie's the only person I've added," I say, pulling her away from Joe and hugging her to my chest. "But yes, this is a surprise. What are you doing here?"

"What do you mean?" She looks at Seb who's trying to subtly shake his head at her. "Seb asked me to come over and hang with you until his parents get here."

"Seb." I look back at him—my eyebrows raised. "Really? I don't need a babysitter."

"I'm your husband. I get to be worried." He puts his suitcase back down. "Too many people are talking about you right now. The social media stuff has gotten out of hand. That one bitch said she would kill you—"

"It's a figure of speech," I say. "She didn't mean it literally."

"Joe," Seb says, "has she posted anything since this morning?"

"No. And I agree with Sophie. It's just smack talk. You should be used to it by now."

"I'm used to it for me, not for Sophie." Seb pulls me back over to him. "I'm going to lose it if people don't stop talking about her."

"Babe," I say, rubbing my forehead against his chest. For some reason that usually calms him down. "It's gotten so much better since I deleted my accounts. I don't even look at it unless you show me."

"Seb." Joe points toward the door again. "Now. Let's go."

"Okay." Seb's voice is as tense as his body.

"I'll be fine," I say, looking up at him. "I'll see you tonight."

"I wish you would let me hire a bodyguard—"

"Seb, no. We talked about that. I don't want a stranger following me around." I nod back at Maisie. "She can be my bodyguard."

He grunts. "Well it's better than you being alone. Mae, will you stay until my parents get here?"

"I'm not leaving her side. And who's going to get to her in this house? It's on an island with only one way in."

"No one monitors the bay," Seb says. "They could come off the water."

"Your security system—including on the bay side—is

almost better than what they have at the White House," Joe says. "All we're missing is Secret Service agents."

"Okay." Seb takes a deep breath and slowly exhales. "Soph, remember to text me when you leave for the hotel."

"I will. Go. You're playing in your first World Series. I'm so proud of you, baby. Promise me you'll enjoy every minute of it."

He nods and finally smiles. "I promise, but just for you. Come on, Joe. Hurry up. We're late."

"Unbelievable," Joe says as he watches Seb walk out of the door. He turns to me. "I'm going to kill him by the end of this."

"You're a saint, Joe." I pat his shoulder. "Not many people could deal with him when he gets this way."

I close the door and turn back to Maisie. "Good Lord. I didn't think Seb would leave. He's been pacing around all morning."

"He's worried about you." She takes my hand and pulls me into the kitchen. "I didn't think he would recover after that guy grabbed your ass at the game in June."

"The only reason he recovered is because I agreed to sit in the owner's suite for games now. There's no way he could concentrate if I was still sitting in the stands." I take a bottle of wine out of the refrigerator. "Too early?"

"Never. What time are you leaving for the sponsor party tonight?"

"I need to get there around six to help Dottie prep her speech."

"I'm still confused." Her forehead crinkles up. "Are you officially working for the team again?"

"No, but this is Dottie's first year owning a team and she's already hosting a World Series." I give the island an extra wipe down before I place a charcuterie plate between us. "She's freaked out. I told her I would help her through the postseason."

"Dot seems like a tough old broad. I can't believe she's letting this rattle her."

"She is tough, but I think since her husband died, she feels more exposed. You know? She doesn't have that backup."

Maisie grabs a piece of cheese. "Well, I hope she doesn't die for a while. Seb seems to like her."

"*Loves* her. The entire team does. She's so sweet. She's like a grandma to them. I was going to tell her no when she asked me to help out in the postseason. Seb talked me into it just so Dottie would feel more secure."

She sticks out her tongue as she takes a bite of the Limburger. "This tastes like butt."

"It's Seb's dad's favorite," I say, handing her a napkin. "It smells awful."

She spits out the cheese and rinses the bad taste out with a swig of wine. "We're sitting in a suite for the games, right?"

"Yeah, it's so much easier than buying individual tickets for everyone. With our family and friends, we have twenty-seven people, and that's after cutting the list several times."

She drains her wine glass. "Don't players get free tickets?"

"Only six for postseason games. Seb's are right behind the dugout. He's giving them to his parents, his high school coach, and his Michigan friends. They've been with him from day one. He said they deserve those seats more than anyone."

She smiles. "That Seb is just a good guy."

"Yes, he is. He's the best guy."

Maisie jumps when the security booth intercom beeps. "God, I don't know how you've gotten used to that thing. It's so loud."

I shrug as I answer it. "Hey, this is Sophie."

"Hey, Mrs. Miller. It's Steve. Seb's parents are at the gate. They're on the permanent clear list, but they wanted me to call you before they came in."

"Thanks, Steve. Send them up."

"Done. They're headed your way."

"You drink way too slowly," Maisie says as she grabs my wine, drains it, and then puts our empty wine glasses into the dishwasher. "Hide the evidence. I don't want your in-laws to think you're a drunk."

"They both drink way more than I do. His mom always thinks I'm pregnant when I turn down alcohol. She can't accept that I'm just a lightweight."

"She hopes you're pregnant," Maisie says, rolling her eyes. "I've been married longer than you, but I don't have near the amount of pressure you have to reproduce."

"Right? And it's from all sides. Everyone wants the heir to the great Seb Miller to be born."

"Except for the great Seb Miller," she says as we head toward the front door. "Does he still want to wait?"

"Yeah, and I get it. He wants to spend as much time as possible with our kids. He can't do that while he's playing. I'm ready now, but we're waiting. We're trying to time it with his retirement in a few years."

I open the door just in time to see the Millers turning into our driveway. Seb's mom, Adie, has her arm out the window —waving at us.

"I'm leaving," Maisie says, hugging me. "I can't take too much of Adie's enthusiasm until I've had more to drink. I'll see you at the game tomorrow night."

Buy or download Leave it on the Field on Amazon.

About the Author

Donna Schwartze is a graduate of the University of Missouri School of Journalism. She also holds a Master of Arts from Webster University. With the exception of walking on a beach, Donna would almost always rather be snuggling on her couch with a fluffy blanket and an even fluffier dog. She is an avid yogi and plans to still be able to do the splits on her 100th birthday. Her favorite character from her books is Mack (all the alpha, all the tender) from The Trident Trilogy.

Made in the USA
Middletown, DE
16 April 2023

28939503R00187